Irtania Adrien

HIS MATE AND HIS MISTRESS

By

Irtania Adrien

Copyright © 2017 by Irtania Adrien. All Rights Reserved. No part of this book may be reproduced in any manner without written permission except in the case of brief quotations included in critical articles and reviews. For information, please contact the author.

Published and bound in US Florida.

All characters appearing in this work are fictitious. Any resemblance to real persons, living or dead, is purely coincidental.

Contents
His mate and his mistress

By

Irtania Adrien

Chapter 1- "Married..."

Chapter 2- "Rules...?"

Chapter 3- "Fate...? Part 1"

Chapter 4- "Say what?"

Chapter 5- "Changing his mind"

Chapter 6- "Attraction"

Chapter 7- "Denial"

Chapter 8- "New Friend"

Chapter 9- "Stubborn"

Chapter 10- "Moving on..."

Chapter 11- "...Or so I thought"

Chapter 12- "Anger"

Chapter 13- "Heated Jealousy"

Chapter 14- "Not a Date"

Chapter 15- "Road trip"

Chapter 16- "A kind of Deja Vu"

Chapter 17- "Happy ending"

Chapter 18- "Marked"

Chapter 19- "Motives & Reasons"

Chapter 20- "Dance of confusion"

Chapter 21- "Mystery Letters"

Chapter 22- "Explanations, and Ambush"

Chapter 23- "Secret plan" - Part 1

Chapter 24- "Secret Plan" -Part 2

Chapter 25- " Secret Plan" -Part 3

Chapter 26- "Secret Plan" -Part 4

Chapter 27- "Secret Plan" -Part 5

Chapter 28- "Secret Plan" -Part 6

Chapter 29- "Acceptance"

Chapter 30- "Inner Voice"

Chapter 31- "Let the Games Begin"

Chapter 32- "Game time"

Chapter 33- "Cozy Picture"

Chapter 34- "Cat Fight! The She-Wolf Way"

Chapter 35- "The Expected Unexpected"

Chapter 36- "The beginning"

Chapter 37- "Dirty secrets" Part- 1

Chapter 38- "Dirty Secrets" Part- 2

Chapter 39- "Winner & Loser"

Chapter 40- "The Alpha"

Chapter 41- "The Luna"

Chapter 42- "The Moon Goddess" -Part 1

Chapter 43- "Talk of the past" Part- 1

Chapter 44- "Talk of the past" Part- 2

Chapter 45- "Heat" Part- 1

Chapter 46 "Heat" Part- 2

Chapter 47- "Good Morning!"

Chapter 48- "Date ? -Demitrey"

Chapter 49- "Date? -Adelina"

Chapter 50- "Plan: DESTROY ADELINA!"

Chapter 51- "The Moon Goddess" -Part 2

Chapter 52- "The Moon Goddess" -Part 3

Chapter 53- "Tease and please challenge"

Chapter 54- "Buffet Surprise"

Author's note

Chapter 1- "Married..."

Third person's pnt. Of view

Adelina stood frozen, staring in fear as the event unfolded before her eyes.

One second her father's pack was fighting off rogues, the next she was being handed over to the Alpha of the Red Moon pack in marriage.

Her parents explained that it was for the best, and that she would be safe, but she wasn't sure why she had to be the one to be wed to this man.

She had older sisters who had yet to be mated and would jump at the opportunity, so why her?

She wanted to have a word in the matter, she wanted to voice her opinion, but most importantly she didn't want to get married to someone that wasn't her mate.

Ever since she was little, she learned that a mate was the other half that completed you.

Mates were made to fulfill your happiness in so many ways, they made you whole mentally, spiritually, emotionally, and physically.

So, it just wasn't fair for her to be married off to an Alpha just because her parents wanted to assure the safety of their pack.

But then again it made sense that her parents wanted to do away with her since they never wanted her, and she was claimed to be a mistake.

Her parents originally wanted 4 children, but when her mother fell pregnant with her after becoming Luna of the Silent Moon pack, her parents had no other choice but to keep her, because their image to the pack was important.

This did not mean that her parents didn't try to get rid of her secretly, but their plans usually had a mishap, but this time it seems as though their plan would finally work.

At her thoughts Adelina was snapped back to reality when her father's booming laughter shook her mind as he said "it was a pleasure settling this treaty with you Alpha Demitrey. I'm sure Adelina will own up to her position and fulfill your needs as you see fit." At his words, her father's eyes glared her way, sending a secret warning.

"Of course, I hope she does." Spoke Alpha Demitrey in a very domineering and intimidating tone, which caused fearful tremors to ravage Adelina's entire being.

"I will send for her after I've made a few arrangements, tell her to be ready by tomorrow afternoon. My driver will be here exactly at 4:00 PM." Added the Alpha, speaking as though Adelina wasn't in the room.

"Understood. Until next time Demitrey." Her father spoke

up.

"Likewise." Demitrey responded curtly, then he turned and headed for the door not even sparing Adelina a glance.

Adelina's pnt. Of view

I stared at the closed doors in which Demitrey just departed from.

I still couldn't believe what just took place, my father just gave me up so that he could protect his pathetic pack.

By the sudden goosebumps that rose on my skin, I was able to determine that my father was suddenly close behind me.

He was always too close for my comfort.

I felt his hand on my shoulder as he whispered in my ear "you my dear are going to make me a lot of money and you are going to assure my security. So, you better be a good little slut like I know you are, and you better be a good girl, follow all the rules, and do everything that Demitrey says." With that he turned and left.

I wasn't sure how to react to his words, I mean they no longer hurt my feelings because I'm used to his degrading tone towards me, however what he said about following the rules and doing everything that Demitrey said did strike fear deep within me.

Alpha Demitrey was already intimidating. The mere mention of him caused everyone to be on alert, not to mention his presence.

He had the looks as though he was sculpted by the Gods.

He had a dark smoldering gaze that said, "Don't fuck with me." Yet the girls drooled over him.

He had a fit, strong build that was determined by the

bulging muscles that showed through the shirt that he wore today, and his height only added to my fear.

His voice was deep, yet there was this seductive tone that resonated in every one of the syllables that escaped his delectable lips. There was also a slight accent that followed his words and if you listened to him long enough it would feel as though he was caressing you without even touching you.

If that made sense...

Anyways, what I'm trying to say is that I didn't want to get married to him, because I'd lose my chance at finding my real mate.

I would lose the chance at feeling true happiness, I would no longer experience true love, and the special gift I saved for the man of my dreams would be taken away by that ruthless Alpha.

Oh, did I forget to mention that Demitrey ran one of the largest wolf Packs in North America? That he fights like a warrior, punishes restlessly, and even kills you without needing a reason?

I didn't?

Well now you know.

It wasn't until I felt something wet fall on my chest that I realized that I was crying. So, before I started bawling, I ran.

I ran out my parent's mansion and headed straight to Peter's house.

Peter has been my best friend ever since I can remember. I thought he and I would be mates, but not everything worked the way we want it to.

When we turned 18 two years ago, Peter met his mate Clarissa, and they instantly fell in love.

I guess the mate bond does that to you.

Anyways I was happy for him, as much as I was feeling sad for myself. I mean Peter was sweet, charming, handsome and just everything a girl could wish for, but he wasn't mine, and eventually I began to realize that Clarissa takes care of him in ways I possibly couldn't.

At first Clarissa was bit jealous of the relationship between Peter and I, but now 2 years later, we are all 20 years old, she has warmed up to me until Peter started becoming jealous at our relationship.

When I reached their house, as if on cue Clarissa opened the door and I crashed in her arms bawling my eyes out.

She held me for hours, petting my hair, kissing my cheeks, and murmuring sweet nothings, until my sobs were gone and all I had left were tears.

"H-h-he did it Car, he married me to Alpha Demitrey, and I didn't even have a say in it. H-he signed the papers, and n-now I'm getting p-p-picked up t-to-t-tom-morrow at 4:00." I stuttered out as another river or tears cascaded from my eyes.

"Tomorrow?! Why so quick?" Clarissa questioned, her eyes puffed up from her own tears.

"I don't know." I sobbed again, feeling another tantrum building up.

"I'm so sorry baby." Cried Clarissa.

"What's going on here?" Came Peter's voice from behind us.

"Baby? Why are you crying? Aden? The fuck happened to

you?" Asked Peter as he suddenly became lethally overprotective to both of us.

He never wanted to see us upset, especially Clarissa, if he had to buy her tons of ice cream to make her happy, he would do it, and if he had to murder someone for me or Clarissa, he would do that too.

After a moment of silence, I managed to explain everything that happened to Peter, his reaction wasn't exactly what I expected, for a second, he seemed calm, then he punched the nearest wall, and headed to his room and locked himself in, not uttering a word.

Clarissa and I stayed in complete silence for a bit until it was time for me to go. Before I exit, I headed up to Peter's room, I knocked on his door but there was no answer, so I leaned my head against the door and I said "Pete look, I know you're angry, but I can't do anything about it. It's already settled I can't change this, but I don't want my last memory of you to be a door between us. Please open up and hold me one last time Peter Pan." I begged, using my nickname for him.

I stood there for a few, and when I realized that he wasn't going to open I turned to leave, except as soon as I took my first step Peter opened the door and engulfed me in a hug.

As he held me, he said "trust me Aden, this is not the last time." Then he kissed my forehead and said "I will see you off tomorrow. Okay? And I'll try to find a way to come visit you, no matter how far you are. Promise."

"Okay." I said with a smile.

And just like that I left. When I made it downstairs, I kissed Clarissa goodbye, then I headed back to my parent's mansion. A place I would never call home.

Chapter 2- "Rules...?"

Adelina's pnt. Of view

I found myself standing outside the gates of my parent's mansion, they had locked me out since three o'clock, although Demitrey said that his driver would be here at four o'clock.

They just couldn't wait to get rid of me. And my so-called sisters wanted to sneer at me, saying that I don't deserve to be with Demitrey, if only they knew that I didn't want to be with him.

I mean my "dad" is quick to call me a slut, yet whenever he gets my mom drunk just to sneak to my sisters' room to have sex with them, they're the perfect angels.

I wouldn't give a flying fuck in the world if one of my sisters got chosen, but since my dad needs his little fuck buddies around, he would rather get rid of me.

See another reason why "dad" hates me is because I don't just open my legs and say welcome. Instead I fight him off. I've stabbed him, burned him, and cut him, just to get him to stay away from me.

So, since I'm not an easy fuck, hey why not get rid of me?

Well for that matter I don't mind going with Demitrey, for I'll always have more integrity than my entire family put together.

"Hey Aden." Suddenly came Peter's voice from behind me. Pulling me out of my thoughts.
"Peter pan!" I squealed excitedly, jumping into his open arms.

"Hey baby girl, how are you doing?" He asked softly, yet his tone indicated his worry.

"I'm alright. Just ready to get this over with." I said trying to smile, except we both knew that my smile wasn't that convincing.

"It's going to be okay. I have a present for you." He said with a mischievous smile.

"Really?! What is it? Gimme! Gimme! Gimme!" I jumped up and down, my current situation suddenly forgotten.

"Uh uh, not before saying the magic word." He scolded.

"Please may I get my gift now..." I said sounding annoyed.

"And...?" He pursued.

"You devilishly handsome human sculpted by the Gods." I said cringing at my words towards him.

"Of course you may!" He said pulling something out from his pocket.

You see, a few months ago Peter and I made a bet, and we decided that whoever won the bet would have a certain name we'd make the loser call us whenever we want to.

As you can tell, I lost the bet, and Peter being so full of himself, chose that nickname, and I was tortured and penalized to call him that until God knows how long.

Anyway, he pulled out the object from his pocket and said "ta-da!"

My eyes widened as the object glimmered in the sunlight, and I drew in a gasp as I said, "no way!"

"Yes way. Here take it!" He said placing the object in my hand.

"You got me a phone!" I exclaimed, my excitement resonating in my sentence, as I looked over the brand-new Samsung that sat comfortably in my palm.

"Yep! My number is already saved on there, and so is Clarissa's. We also took some pictures so you could remember us by, and I downloaded your favorite songs." He explained.

I couldn't hold back the tears that escaped me, and I soon engulfed him in a bear hug as I said, "thank you Peter pan." Although it was muffled, since my face could only reach his chest even though I was on my toes.

Yes people, I'm short, at 5"2 tip toeing can only get you so high.

"No problem Aden." He chuckled then kissed my head.

As soon as we pulled away, a car approached us, and when I checked the time on my brand-new phone, it was exactly 4:00.

At first, I couldn't see who was driving, but when he stepped out of the car my breath got caught in my throat.

It's him! But what is he doing here?

I thought he said his driver would pick me up.

He walked up to us, his eyes drifting between Peter and me, then he picked up the luggage that was sitting in front of me without saying a word and threw it in the trunk.

He then came back and took the duffel bag that was hanging on my shoulder, but suddenly froze, just as I did the same.

His fingers were touching the skin on my shoulder, and I could feel it.

The tingles, the fluttery feeling in your stomach.

I couldn't help it when my eyes connected with his own, and I felt it! Our bond!

"Mate!" Came Aden's voice in my head, my wolf.

"I know." I replied to her in my mind.

"Say something!" She urged.

"Like what?" I asked.

"I don't know." She replied, then refrained to the back of my mind.

Before I could say anything however, he quickly ripped the bag from my shoulders, and repeated his actions as before, then he headed to the driver's side as he said, "let's go."

What?

I looked up at Peter and hugged him again, and he once again kissed my head, and I whispered, "I'll talk to you later Peter pan."

"See you later Aden."

"I would like to get home today if you don't mind." Came Demitrey' scold answer.

And as if on cue, I pulled away from Peter, and headed to the car.

I mean jeez mate, would it kill you to open the door for me?

"We need to talk. I have a few rules on how I run my pack, and everyone has a role. For your role I've chosen specific rules that you must abide to. If you follow them, I'm sure your stay with my pack will be comfortable enough." He finally spoke up, after what felt like hours of silence. But his voice, so deep, so smooth, I could listen to it all day, although it sounded cold, mean even. I guess that's the way he talks.

"Okay." I said. Slightly turning my body giving him all my attention, although I felt like giving him so much more.

"1. Only speak when spoken to.

2. You must always address me as sir.

3. You are to stay in your room unless called out of your room by me.

4. You are not allowed in my office unless given

permission.

5. You are not allowed in my room. Ever.

6. You must show respect to your superiors which are Serena, my beta, and I.

7. You must not have contact with any males from my pack.

9. You must do what you are told.

10. Stay out of my way.

Failure to follow and obey these rules will earn you punishments." He said with a dangerous tone, not for once sparing me a glance.

"What?" I asked breathless.

But he ignored me.

What did he just say? Stay out of his way? Wait! But aren't we mates! I know we are! I felt our connection! And I know he felt it too! So why is he speaking such nonsense?

"Demitrey what are you talking about? Aren't we mates? This is a joke, right?" I asked exasperated, hoping just hoping that he was joking.

"That's sir to you!" He said his voice suddenly darker, his accent a bit thicker, "and I don't have a mate." He said, and my heart stopped.

Chapter 3- "Fate...? Part 1"

Adelina's pnt. Of view

After Alpha Demitrey announced his rules, the drive to his pack became unbearable.

I was confused, and I had so many questions, but no matter what I said seem to receive the deaf ear.

The drive was long and boring, and when I turned on the radio for some type of entertainment, he turned it off without uttering a word.

Throughout the ride I became thirsty and hungry, and my bladder felt as though it would explode, yet I had to keep quiet, afraid of the man that was sitting next to me.

Demitrey seemed to be deep in thought as he drove on and on. He seemed to be thinking of something disturbing for his eyes were very dark, his knuckles where white as he gripped the steering wheel in a death grip, and he never spared me not one glance.

So, I figured the best thing for me to do is to go to sleep, so that's what I did.

But it didn't last very long for soon I was being shaken awake by a girl that I have never seen before.

"Excuse me? Miss, please you must wake up now." Came her quiet voice as she gently shook my arm.
"I'm awake, I'm awake." I said slightly annoyed that someone would disturb my sleep, but then I suddenly became aware of my unknown surroundings, and I didn't waste a second before demanding "wait, where am I? Who are you?"
"You've arrived at the Red Moon Pack. My name is Cilia, I am your assigned maid and or helper. If you need anything you call me." The girl, I mean Cilia smiled kindly.

"Um thank you...?" I said although it sounded like a question.

Cilia giggled as she said "you're welc-"

"I would love to enter my home today Cilia." Came Demitrey' scold and dominating voice, as he interrupted Cilia.

"Uh y-yes s-sir!" Came Cilia's instant yet nervous stutter of a reply, then she turned to me still wide-eyed from the Alpha's demand as she says "Come now, we must go. The master doesn't like to be kept waiting."

At her words, her gentle touch became urgent, as she practically hauled me out of the car.

She then with rushed footsteps, hurried me to fall behind Demitrey's sauntering form, as we made our way to his home.

Wait! No not home, I meant a FREAKING CASTLE.

The estate was huge. With a grand yard that seem to be created to perfection. The grass was a healthy green, the various colors of flowers blending perfectly with it.

The sun shone perfectly as graceful butterflies flew around the roses, and buzzing bees danced from flower to flower. The walkways were made of beige gravel that gave a satisfying crunch with every step you took, and multiple fountains that were randomly spread out throughout the yard, spewed water out into the air.

The entire scenery was enticing, and it was perfectly created to match the off-white color of the exterior of the castle.

When we finally reached the building, we climbed up a few stairs until we made it to a grand double door.

There Demitrey stopped, and Cilia instantly pulled me to a halt, a few feet away from Demitrey, he turned and faced me, and for the first time in hours he finally made eye contact with me.

His glare was so strong, it oozed power and domination, and it was hard for me to keep it, so I shifted my gaze and looked anywhere but him.
"Look at me when I am addressing you." He commanded as my eyes absent-mindedly abide to his rule.

Once my eyes were on him, he seemed to pause for a few, as he observed me, and that was something I couldn't handle.

Having his eyes on me made my body do and feel funny things, I could feel my cheeks reddening, and when his eyes started traveling all over my body, the skin that his eyes glanced over became heated, as if a fire suddenly became alive.

My stomach started doing summersaults, as my heartbeat and breathing started coming out irregularly. My palms became sweaty, and at that moment I wanted to kiss him, love him, but I wasn't sure I could do that, so instead, I clasped my hands behind my back, and bit my bottom lip in order to keep myself from saying something that I would regret.

His glare was intimidating, anyone would want to scurry from him, but with me, it made me do funny things, it made me feel funny things.

What was happening to me?

When he noticed my actions, his eyes seem to dilate, but he shook it off as his voice came out in its domineering tone saying "As I mentioned before, you must always address me as sir. And you must respect those who are superior to you, such as Serena, and my beta. Once we go in, you will meet Serena, and Kade, my Beta, and don't forget only speak when spoken to."

Without waiting for my reply, he turned around and opened the door, and my earlier moment was instantly forgotten, as a sudden pain settled within me.

It wasn't physical, but it was emotional. It was as though he was rejecting me, yet he was still holding on to me, making me suffer in a way.

Anyway, I shook it off as he made his way inside, and Cilia and I followed suite.

The inside of the castle was mesmerizing. I couldn't help it when my jaw went loose and hit the ground in amazement. My eyes were wide as if I was trying to memorize every uniquely spectacular detail of the castle.

The walls were also an off-white color just like the outside, on my right was a doorway that led to a dining room fit for a royal court, and all its subjects, that's how large it was.

To my right was a living room with a white and royal blue theme.

Right in front of me was a double grand staircase that led to the second floor. The sunlight shone through the wide windows, and it radiated off the walls, and the rays that shone through the chandeliers that dangled from the tall ceiling created rainbow like lights that's transparently settled upon the walls, making the sight absolutely pristine.

Being lost in my observation, I didn't notice that a few people approached us until I heard a woman speak up saying "What's wrong with her?"

"Oh miss, please close your mouth, and pay attention."

Then came Cilia's whispering tone.

"Huh?" I asked, reviving from my revenue.

"She acts like she's never seen something like this." Came the woman's voice again, but this time it sounded teasing.

Was she talking about me?

"Trust me baby, she hasn't been to a place like this." Came Demitrey's voice, but instead of the cold tone be has been using all this time, it was replaced with a warm tone, almost as if he was smiling. But I couldn't tell, because his back was to me.

But did he just call that woman baby?

I didn't have to wait long for an answer, because soon Demitrey turned around as he laced his hands around a woman's waist and stood behind her as he looked at me and said, "baby I would like you to meet Adelina Veraso, she's the matter I spoke to you about."

"Mmph!" Came her snotty reply.

"Adelina this is Serena, she is my mistress."

"Uh..." whaaaaat?! Did he just say mistress? Is he holding her like that in front of me? HIS MATE!

"What are you stupid or something?" She spoke again, the bitchiness in her tone couldn't be any easier to decipher.

Wait a minute!

"EXCUSE ME?!" My voice came out booming "did you just call me stupid? Who are YOU to call ME stupid?"

Slap

"Watch your tone with me you slut." She sneered, after her palm made harsh contact with my cheek.

Oh hell no!

SLAP

"And you keep your hands to yourself bitch!" I exclaimed back, striking her back even harder.

"Oh! Babe! You're going to let her get away with that?!"

She gasped over-dramatically, turning towards Demitrey holding her cheek, as he glanced over at me with a dark and dangerous gaze and promised "Don't worry babe, she will be taken care of."

Chapter 3- "Fate...?" part 2

Adelina's pnt. Of view

"Cilia, please take her up to her room, I'll deal with her shortly."

Was how Demitrey dismissed me.

"Of course sir," came Cilia's weak reply, then she placed her hand in the small of my back as she said, "come now miss, we must get going."

And she tugged my arm, as I kept a deadly glare on Demitrey and his "mistress."

When I was finally escorted to my room, Cilia closed the door in a hurry as she said "oh miss, what did you do? Didn't our Alpha give you the rules before your arrival?"

"He did. So, Serena is his mistress huh?" I asked ignoring

the rules.

"Well, yes, yes she is." Answered Cilia.

"Until he finds his mate?" I asked, a little hope fluttering in my heart.

"No miss, he doesn't want one, he-"

"Cilia." Came Demitrey's domineering voice as he opened the door "You may go."

Cilia gave me an apologetic frown, as she slightly bowed, and scurried out the door, and closed it on her way out, leaving me and the handsome asshole alone.

"So, it seems as though you forgot the rules." Was how Demitrey greeted me.

"No, I didn't forget, however it seems as though your dear Serena seemed to have forgotten to keep her hands to herself. So, all I had to do was remind her." I replied smugly, although I was hurting deep inside, like his glare, his voice and his words were like multiple daggers that continuously stabbed my heart, placing me on the verge of tears.

In a split second, however, I found myself slammed against the nearest wall, with Demitrey's hand tightly secured around my neck, as he spoke in a deadly manner "watch how you speak of Serena, I won't hesitate to break your flimsy neck the next time you disrespect her, or me. Now I'm going to let you off easy this once, but don't think for a second I'll let you get away next time. Tonight, you were supposed to have a formal dinner with Serena, my beta and I along with a few other members of my pack, but since you thought to break the rules, you will be left in isolation for the rest of the day. Your dinner will be brought up by Cilia. Don't think to get any ideas, because like I said before, I let you off easy."

Then in a split second, his iron grip was removed from my neck, and I found myself in a haze. Although I feel as though I should be afraid due to his threats, I didn't, because I was distracted. While we were against the wall, wherever our skin connected, it was like multiple fires erupted. His deep threatening voice only made him more attractive, however, there was something else there eating me alive besides the pleasure of being close to my mate, it was his silent rejection.

I mean he obviously didn't care, in fact he only seemed to care about Serena, or should I say his mistress.

But with a final glare, he sauntered out of the room, and just as the door closed, I broke down.

I couldn't believe what was taking place, it's as though all my dreams, fantasies, and wishes are just spiraling into nothingness, like human waste being flushed down the toilet.

Funny that I use that imagery, but nothing made sense at the moment.

I mean, for one my mate doesn't want me, and even worse he has a mistress. A FREAKING MISTRESS! I just can't get over it, but then again, I've been through so much, I shouldn't allow this to take toll on me.

So, I took a second, dried my tears, and that's when I remembered, the phone that Peter gave me.

I quickly ran over to my bag, and I picked it up, then I dialed his number, and I secretly begged that he wasn't training, or getting involved with his mate... if you know what I mean.

And my prayers were answered when I heard the familiar voice on the other end.

"Aden? You okay? Are you safe? Are they treating you alright?" Was how he answered me.

"Geez, hi to you too Peter. And well, I'm safe, but um I'm not okay." I succumbed to telling him.

"Why? What happened?" He asked, a growl suddenly evident in his tone, proving his aggravation.

"Well, for one, the ruthless Alpha is my mate, and guess what? The asshole has a mistress. Even worse that no good for nothing bastard wants me to respect the spoilt bitch he claims as his mistress." My anger was blazing, I should know because I hardly used profanity, yet all I received from Pete was a drawled "wow." And the only thing I could do was reply with a small "yep."

We soon shook off the sad air, and we changed the topic of our conversation to something more lightweight, to the point where I was crying my eyes out laughing at the current story that Peter was telling me, but that moment was cut short, when my door burst open, and for the second time that day, a seething Demitrey made his way towards me.

With a quick "got to go!" I ended the call and placed the phone behind me as my feet carried me backwards, away from the approaching predator.

This pattern continued, until my back was firmly pressed against a wall, and Demitrey became too close for comfort, not that I mind, I mean he's my mate, however the close proximity wasn't helping my situation.

My body started doing funny things, but before my mind became hazy with any vile thoughts, Demitrey held out his palm as he said "hand it over." my eyes tried to focus on anything but him as I said "Hand what over?"
 "Don't play dumb with me, I'm not in the fucking mood, so give It."

"No." I said, refusing to give up my phone.

"Excuse me?" he said taking another step forward, his domineering height and stance making it very hard for me to breathe.

"You're excused" I managed to spell out, while I lifted my head in defiance to meet his gaze, although my heart was palpitating.

He suddenly smiled, like he just smiled, then he leaned down as he said "I know how you feel about me. Your heart is racing." And just as he said it, his warm palm landed firmly against my chest, and the sparks didn't waste a second before becoming alive and spreading throughout my body.

His glare caused my lungs to lose rhythm, and my breathing started coming out in uneven puffs. He slowly started leaning down, his lips feathering above mine, and I absentmindedly opened my lips in sign of welcome, my heartbeat skyrocketing.

His eyes suddenly darkened at my actions and then just like that he was off.

He took his hand off my chest, as if I burned him, then with one last menacing glare he walked away, and slammed the door shut behind him, and I found myself slipping down the wall, with tears streaming down my face, and for another time that day, I found myself crying.

I couldn't believe it, my mate made me cry more than once in one day. He hated me, yet he teased me, just to leave me in tears.

Was this truly my fate? Crying because of a mate? Rejection? Hurt and pain?

Was this truly my fate?

Chapter 4- "Say what?"

Adelina's pnt. Of view

That afternoon, I laid in bed until Cilia came to serve my dinner.

At first it was quiet but soon enough Cilia and I started chatting, and we quickly formed a friendship.

I found out that Cilia is also 20 years old, and she has yet to find her mate. She was taken in by Demitrey after her pack was attacked by rogues, and the only way she can repay her gratitude is by serving in his household.

I also found out that she is very shy, well when she's not familiar with you, but once you get to know her, she's a bundle of surprise.

To be honest, I'm surprised that she doesn't have a mate, I mean the girl is gorgeous.

She has wild bouncy blonde curls that stop at the base of her neck, and bright baby blue eyes to match it. She's a few inches taller than me, and she is a sight to see.

Anyway, after spending a good amount time speaking with Cilia, unfortunately she had to go, so I once again found myself alone, and it didn't take long for my thoughts to drift towards the handsome asshole who seem to occupy a good amount of my brain cells.

Like he is just so... hotitating, hot yet irritating. Yes people, I made up a new word for the beautiful bastard that is my destined mate yet doesn't want me as his.

Soon enough though, I found myself drifting off to sleep, however in the middle of the night, I could've sworn I felt something wrap around my waist, were tingles instantly came alive. But I blame it on my dreams, for the next morning when I woke up, my body was the only thing occupying the bed.

It didn't take long for me to get accommodated with the pack. Cilia was ordered to show me around, and over the days I've spent here, I've already made so many friends.

Everyone seemed to have warmed up to me except for two people, Serena and Demitrey.

With Serena, I believe her jealousy is the main thing that causes her to hate me. I mean I've only been here's for about a week, and I've already made so much more friends than her. Not only so, no one speaks to her, they avoid her like the plague, and I know why.

She's a total bitch.

Simple explanation.

As far as Demitrey goes, I haven't seen him since the day I've arrived, and I couldn't help but feel sad. I mean yeah, he silently rejected me, but shoot, he's my mate, and I cannot not miss him.

I had a feeling he was avoiding me, because during breakfast, he's not present, during dinner he's not present. Whenever I ask Cilia, she says he's either in his office, or training with the pack's army.

I wanted to see him so bad, and call me an idiot but shoot, I still missed him, it just bothered me to be so far away from him, and it just felt wrong, so I made up an excuse to see him.

Cilia led me to his office, and there I knocked on the door, and patiently waited, as my heart beat sped up, by the seconds.

After a few seconds with no reply, I knocked again, and this time my ears registered a gruff "come in." From the other side of the door.

I placed my hand on the door knob, and breathed out a shaky breath, then I made my entrance.

When I walked in, I quickly turned to close the door in order to avoid eye contact with him, which spared me a second to get my wits together.

When I managed to turn around, our eyes instantly connected, and I quickly found myself double guessing my decision to come here.

"May I help you?" Came his deep voice, and I would've instantly been turned on, if it wasn't for the irritating tone that was laced in his voice.

"Um, well yes, you see here's the thing, um I- I was th- th-thinking th- that maybe, I could um, I could-"

"Okay, first and foremost, when you are addressing me, you will look at me, second, stop with the stuttering and speak clearly." He cut off my rambling, as he reprimanded my actions.

   I took a deep breath then, wriggled thumbs with one another, as my palms became sweaty, then I released it as I said " okay, so I have been here for the past few days, and I was wondering if it was okay for me to train with the females in the army, since I have nothing to do."

"No." Was his curt reply.

"What? Why not?" I asked actually surprised, not that I wanted to be with the female warriors though, since I was just using it as an excuse to see him, but his refusal caught me off guard.

"Because I said so. Now if that was the matter you wanted to address, it's been taken care of. Please see yourself out." He dismissed me with a cold glare.

"Okay, can I at least get a job?" I asked, hurt that he wanted to get rid of me so quick.

"Where?" He asked, suddenly interested.

"Um, the pack clinic, I have experience as a nurse from my old pack... So, I could take care of paperwork, and tend to the patients and stuff."

"Patients huh? Does this mean taking care of my men if they get hurt during a battle or even training?" He asked me, his eyes suddenly becoming dark as night.

"Uh, sure. I can also help take care of the women and children." I added, not sure why he questioned me in the first place.

" oh so, you're willing to get close and personal with the patients, to tend to their needs right? Including my men?" He questioned again, a sudden anger taking toll on his voice.

"I mean yes, I could, if it's necessary. I-"

In the next split second, using his super speed, I found Demitrey slamming me against the door, as his hand clasped around my throat, cutting me off.

He soft lips brushed against my cheeks as he gruffly whispered "you think I'm going to allow you to be around my men? Especially as a care taker?"

"I- I D- don't I- "

"You nothing! You want a job? Fine, you're going to have a job, a job as my personal maid." He declared, his grip tightening around my throat as he added "understood?"

"Yes..." I whispered, although my mind was screaming out say whaaaaat?

"Yes what?"

"Yes sir." I submitted, and I could've sworn I felt something poke my thigh at that exact moment.

But I didn't have time to ponder on what it could be, for Demitrey in a flash removed his hand, just for him to hold my hands captive above my head with one of his own.

And I couldn't lie, it was getting hot, or maybe it was just me.

Then he leaned his face down, until his lips were at the crook of my neck, and I became aware of the billions of tingles that traveled my entire being.

He puckered his lips into a soft kiss, and my breath got caught in my throat. My heart started running, ready to leap out of my chest, and he landed another soft kiss on the same spot, causing me to shiver under his powerful form, and like Deja vu, he moved back, then with one deadly glare he said, "get out."

And I couldn't agree with him more, as my feet quickly escorted me out of the office, yet my heart didn't calm down until I was safely stowed in my room.

Chapter 5- "Changing his mind"

Adelina's pnt. Of view

I stood with my back glued to the door as I tried to calm my breathing, my nerves, and my racing heart.

I couldn't be his personal maid, there was no way I wanted to be that. I don't even know what a personal maid does, but I sure don't want to find out either.

I had to change his mind. I couldn't handle the whole "being close to him" thing.

So, I once again found myself walking to his office.

Once I stood at the door, I took in a deep breath and told myself that I could do this.

So, I did, I knocked on the door, and I waited.

Soon enough came his dominant "come in." And I instantly found my extremities obeying as I made my entrance once again.

He looked up at me, smirked then said, "need something else?" Although his eyes had the teasing glint dancing in his pupils.

"No, I just came back to ask you once again if I can work at the clinic, instead of as your personal maid." I explained, and the teasing fire in his eyes died, and was instantly replaced with a raging anger.

"And why is that? Mate?" He addressed me for the first time as his mate, yet his tone seem disgusted, as though he was ashamed that I was his mate.

"Because, well yes I'm your mate, and I can obviously see that you don't want anything do with me, so why not get me out of your way?" I explained, although my heart broke with every word that spilled from my mouth.

"Oh trust me, there are many things I want to do with you, but you're right I don't want a mate, I don't want you, so what're you suggesting?" He demanded.

And my heart shattered, he was just so blunt about it.

He didn't want me.

"Well..." I took a moment to swallow back the lump in my throat, as I silently prayed that my tears stayed at bay, at least until I got to my room, "I can work any shift you want, I can nurse any patient, kids, women, men, seniors, whichever. And I don't mind working over time, however I do want to get paid." I bargained out my choices.

He looked over at me, as he pondered over my words, and soon his eyes started traveling down my body, and I suddenly became aware of my outfit.

Off shoulder blue top, with high waisted shorts that ended a few inches above my knees.

He rubbed his hands on his lips, then he looked me up once again, causing my cheeks to warm up as he said "okay, fine. But I have a few rules. I get to drop in any time, and whenever I come in, if I need you or call you, you drop what you're doing, and you come straight away. Whatever I say goes. Understood?"

"Yes sir." I replied absentmindedly.

And with that, I didn't even wait to be dismissed, I just led myself out.

A part of me still couldn't believe that he agreed, but I was fretting more on what he said.

He wanted to do things with me yet didn't want me.

I couldn't possibly live like that, at least not with my mate.

Was it always going to be like that?

Me making up excuses to see him?

Him dictating what I do around here?

Him teasing me, just to tear me apart?

I couldn't believe what was going on. I don't think I can do this, not like thi-

"Watch where you are going slut!" Came Serena's voice as she shoved me.

I was so caught up in my thoughts I didn't realize where I was going, and I accidentally bumped into her, but she still had no right to speak to me like that or put her hands on me.

So, I shoved her back as I said, "and you keep your dirty claws to yourself!"

"Why you little b-"

"ADELINA! Your room right now!" Ordered Demitrey as he opened his office door.

"WHAT?! ME?! HOW ABOUT YOUR LITTLE BIMBO OF A SLUT YOU CALL A MISTRESS?! She's the one who touched me." I retorted, my anger flaring.

Demitrey breathed in slowly as he said, "you have exactly 1 minute to get to your room, because if you let me catch you, you will regret it."

I was bewildered. Fuming, yet bewildered.

I looked over at a smug smirking Serena, then I stomped my way to my room, locking myself in until dinner time, which Cilia came to serve it for me.

"Hey, haven't seen you since this morning, is everything okay?" Asked Cilia, as we ate dinner together.

"Yep, got a new job at the clinic." I explained, trying not to let the events of earlier to get to me... again.

"Awesome, now you can have money, and soon we can hang out in the city. There's so much I want to show you." Cilia explained happily.

"Sure, whenever you want." I managed to smile.

I made a friend.

We spent some time chatting away, until it was time for Cilia to go, and I quickly found myself tucking in bed, ready to get this day behind me, but I guess the night was still young, for my door opened, and a shirtless Demitrey made his way inside my room, closing and locking the door behind him.

He sauntered towards my bed, holding a captivating eye contact with me, keeping me frozen in spot.

When he towered above me, he said in a deep voice "get up."

At first, I was confused, well no, distracted.

I mean my mate, a man that seem to be sculpted by the gods, stood in front of me shirtless, giving me a knee shaking, heart racing, nerve wracking smoldering gaze, and his deep tone is like icing on the cake, I had to focus on his lips this time as he repeated "get up."

And I found myself blinking a few times before I caught what he said, and I slowly moved out the bed, and stood right in front of him, and without warning, the back of his hand came in harsh impact with my cheek, and I landed face first on the bed.

Did he...? Did he just strike me?

"Get up!" He ordered again, his tone angry.

I was shaking, tears quickly pouring from my eyes.

"I said get up." He declared, as he fisted my hair and pulled me up, as a cry of pain escaped from my lips.

He looked me in the eyes, as his own shone with anger, as he seem ready to strike me again, but then something flashed in his eyes, and his palm came softly against my cheek, as he caressed the spot where he struck me, soothing the burn, then with no warning he pushed me on the bed harshly, turned, and left me.

And just like Deja vu, sobs ransacked my body, as tears flooded my vision.

My mate... My very own mate hit me.

He hurt me.

Chapter 6- "Attraction"

Adelina's pnt. Of view

I stared at my body in the mirror, while my hands nervously patted down my scrubs, trying to smooth out the creases that were too stubborn to flee by the hot iron.

I looked at my phone to see that my shift starts at 8:00 AM, which means I had 30 mins to get there.

So, without wasting anymore time, I shot myself another look in the mirror, and with one last breath, I walked out of my room, and started making my way to work carefully.

See ever since my encounter with my mate, I've tried to avoid him under any and every circumstance, and so far, I've managed to succeed.

On my way to the clinic, I found myself pondering over my current situation, something that I found myself doing often since the past few days.

My mate hurt me, technically rejected me, yet he didn't. For a rejection to officiate he must quote "I, Alpha Demitrey Jackson reject you, Adelina Veraso, as my mate." And on the other hand, I'm supposed to say, "I Adelina Veraso accept your rejection, Alpha."

Or vice versa.

Either way, him not officially rejecting me is taking a toll, I am afraid of him, yet I find my wolf, Aden, becoming restless from being away from her mate.

She wines in my head, and sometimes even manipulates my mind and dreams, and I find myself constantly thinking up erotic fantasies between me and the ruthless Alpha.

But I was quick to find my salvation this time, because I made it to the clinic.

As soon as I walked in, I was hit by the strong scent of cleaning products, mixed with medicine, and coffee. Not that it bothered me, I mean I was used to the environment, but I couldn't help the jitters that seem evident in my stomach.

"Good morning." Came a kind soft voice behind me, and when I turned around, there stood an elderly woman in a lab coat, holding a clipboard, with a stethoscope hanging around her neck, and a kind smile lingering on her lips. "You must be Adelina, the Alpha told me about you." She continued, her smile never fading.

"He did?" I asked surprised.

"Yes, and I am ever so grateful. I've been asking for assistance since the clinic opened, and finally here you are." She chuckled shaking her head, and all I could do was stand there and smile, although very awkwardly.

"Alright, well today is not too much of a busy day, however I do need you to update some files for my patients on the clinic's database. Each of the folders belong to a member of the pack, and we need to update their physical and medical status, so everything you need is in your office, and I'll come around lunch to see how you are doing." Declared the lady, which I still don't know what her name is.

"Right, thank you um..."

"Oh my! Where are my manners, my name is Diana, but you can call me aunty D, since that's what everyone calls me around here." She laughed, as she extended her hand for a handshake.

"Right, thank you Diana." I smiled shaking her hand, then she directed me to the office as she informed "so since the pack is a bit enormous, I suggest you begin by first sorting out the folders in Alphabetical order, based on the last names, and then work on updating the database."

"Got it. Thank you." I said smiling kindly at the elderly woman, then I made my way into the office.

My office.

When I walked in and turned on the lights, my breath was taken away, not that I was mesmerized, but instead overwhelmed.

Folders, books, papers were scattered everywhere, and dust didn't fail to make itself noticeable.

I glanced around, my eyes as wide as saucers, my jaw unhinged. I couldn't believe it, I had my work cut out for me.

After taking a moment to gather myself, I placed my bag in a corner, and first thing first, I opened the curtains that blocked the window and sunlight across the room, but I wished I didn't.

There, right outside my window were the warriors training, and right in between was the Alpha, my Alpha, my mate. Shirtless.

And my jaw hit the floor.

I can't lie...

HE. IS. GORGEOUS!

I couldn't help the way my eyes traveled down his toned body, admiring his sculpted chest and abs. His dark hair glazed in the sun, while sweat beads teasingly rolled off his skin.

His movements were fluent, flexible, and very agile.

And his muscles contrast with every movement, making me fantasize about how it would feel to be wrapped in them in a possessive manner.

He took down each warrior who attacked him with ease, and well, I couldn't help but feel turned on by just the sight of him.

My wolf didn't mind purring *"mmh he could take me down anytime."*

And I couldn't help but agree with her for once.

My vile thoughts cause my body to start tingling in a very unusual way.

My breath started picking up, my vision dilating. I could feel a sudden shudder travel in my chest, and I felt something pool in my treasured placed.

I was turned on.

Too bad it was cut short when his eyes connected with mine, and I got caught staring, causing flames to ignite in my cheeks from the embarrassment.

Without wasting a second, I hid behind the wall to calm my breathing.

I was screwed.

I can't deny, I'm attracted to him... But it can't work.

It's all in vain.

He doesn't want me.

He never will.

And that's okay... I'm strong, I'll survive... I think.

I took a minute to come to terms with my resolution, then after a moment I started organizing and tidying up my work area.

First, I started by picking up and sorting out the papers then I placed them on my desk, then I sorted out the shelves, and soon the floor was clear of materials.

I looked around the room and spotted three doors. The first one revealed an adjoining bathroom, with a shower and everything, the second looked like a closet, and the third was a broom closet. Which was just what I needed.

I fished my headphones out of my bag, and plugged it into my phone, turning on my favorite's playlist, then I placed it in my scrubs' pocket, as I jammed and cleaned at the same time, my earlier thoughts forgotten.

Third person's pnt. Of view

While Adelina was busy dancing and working, what she wasn't aware of, was the sudden change in the atmosphere, as someone made their way into her office.

The intruder watched attentively as she brooms around her space, feeling as though she was secretly teasing him, by the way she moved her hips seductively from side to side.

He couldn't help the way his wolf took over, wanting to pounce on its victim, and he couldn't help his own desire to dominate the vixen that was still unaware of his presence.

Well, until he slid up behind her holding her hips that is.

And she froze.

Her breath got caught in her throat as she felt the tingles erupt from where she was being held.

And she knew exactly who it was, her body can only react to his in such manner.

She felt his breath on her ears as he whispered oh so sensually "you like being a tease?" Then he kissed, and nipped the tip of her ear, and a gasp involuntarily escaped her lips.

"I- I- Don't-"

"Shh, don't talk." He suddenly commanded, his voice taking on a new deeper tone, as his grip became firm, just as she felt his erection on her backside.

He started leaving soft kisses on her neck, and she couldn't fight the urge as she leaned her head to the side giving him more access.

Then she felt it, his lips landed most perfectly on the spot where he was to mark her, and her eyes widened.

She started struggling, not wanting to give into the temptation, "Demitrey I- I can't- "

"STOP FUCKING TALKING!" He ordered, and her lips sealed shut.

He roughly turned her around, and using his speed, they found themselves on the wall, as Demitrey held her hands above her head, and stared daggers into her eyes.

He appeared to struggle for a moment then he said "why are you doing this to me? I don't want you. Why are you torturing me?"

Adelina stared in his eyes as tears welled up in her own as she said, "you did this to yourself." Then she took a deep breath, allowing herself to bask in the sensation of being near her mate, for it would be the last time.

She allowed the tingles to warm her shattered heart, she allowed his warmth to envelope her, and she allowed herself to feel pleasure from his touch and presence, and then she opened her eyes and declared "I, Adelina Veraso, reject you, Alpha Demitrey Jackson as my mate."

Chapter 7- "Denial"

Third person's pnt. Of view

Demitrey stared blankly into Adelina's eyes, as they held their earlier position. His eyes scanned her face, pausing at her lips, then back to her eyes. He squinted his pupils, as if he was observing her, and debating whether she seriously just rejected him.

When he noticed that she was holding her ground, he laughed.

He let go of her hands, as he laughed resulting in tears welling in his eyes.

He held his side as he laughed, while Adelina stood confused on the wall, wondering what was so funny.

But her pondering didn't last, as she quickly found herself being slammed against the wall with Demitrey's death grip secured around her neck, and on instinct she tried to pry off his fingers, but her effort was to no avail.

His eyes became dark and angry as he questioned "do you really think that I would allow you to reject me? Do you really think that I will let you get away so easily? From the day I landed eyes on you, you've consumed all my thoughts. I can't focus how I used to, and I constantly have a hard on just thinking about you writhing under me as I pleasure you to the farthest extent. You have possessed my mind, and you've hypnotized me, and you think that I would allow you to leave me? THE ALPHA?! I don't think so!" And just like that he possessed her lips.

He kissed them harshly, nipping and tugging, and Adelina was sure she would bruise.

She was paralyzed by fear, couldn't move, and couldn't think.

He pulled away when she wasn't responding, and he punched the wall inches from her head as he demanded "KISS ME BACK." Then he dipped his head claiming her lips once again, this time it felt as though he was branding her.

She tried to keep up with him, but the way he dominated her actions was out of this world. His hand released her neck, and hoisted themselves unto her waist, as he pulled her unto him, so she could feel his erection.

And she couldn't lie, it was erotic, and she felt hot.

He finally ended his onslaught on her lips, just to move to his next torture target.

He kissed her neck then he whispered, "this is what you do to me." He pulled her bottom half harshly as a gasped erupted from her, and she felt his member harden at her core.

"You make me lose control. But I don't want you to... I don't want you to make me lose control. But I won't let you get away either. NO ONE CAN HAVE YOU! YOU'RE MINE!" He declared possessively, and Adelina stood frozen.

He then nipped her neck, a few inches above her marking spot, leaving a very visible mark, then he looked into her eyes as he said, "say it."

"S- say wh- what?" Adelina stuttered her question.

"You're mine. Say it."

"I- I'm... no." she said, turning her head away from him as his eyes doubled to pitch black. Oh, he was angry.

"WHAT?!" He yelled, then he breathed as he captured her arms once again, "what did you say?" He questioned curtly, as though he was restraining his anger.

"No." Replied Adelina, as she managed to turn her head and hold eye contact with the ruthless Alpha.

"Why you little-"

"Hey Adelina- OH MY GOOOD! I am so sorry. I'm- so sorry." Stuttered Cilia, as she quickly closed the door that revealed this scene, cutting off Demitrey.

He stared at Adelina for a few more seconds, released her arm, then he backed away from her, until he was by the door.

Then he said "No matter what you do, no matter how many times you deny it, you are going to be mine Adelina, that is a promise. I may not like losing control because of you, I may not want a mate, but you belong to me. Like it or not."

With that he walked out, making eye contact with Cilia, who quickly bowed her head, as her cheeks heated in embarrassment.

Adelina's pnt. Of view

As soon as the door closed, I broke down.

Tears flooded my eyes, and my sobs came out harshly, as they ran to escape my bruised and battered soul.

He was cruel.

He didn't want me, yet no one else could have me.

What kind of fate was this?

I couldn't handle it. Not this time.

My attraction caused me to fail. I know I couldn't deny him, at least not for long.

Neither could I escape him, not unless I ran away.

And that is something I couldn't do.

If I run away, the treaty between my pack and this pack will be over. Not that I care about my "dad's" pack, but I do care for Peter and Clarissa.

If the treaty is broken, Alpha Demitrey will kill my pack, and I can't risk Pete's and Clarissa's life, I'd have to warn them, make sure they're safe then run away.

Yes. That's exactly what I will do, but I would have to be stealthy, I couldn't let anyone know of my plan.

I wiped my tears as a flutter of hope warmed my heart, I was going to escape Demitrey, even if it was the last thing I did.

"Adelina? Are you okay?" Came Cilia's soft voice, as she wrapped me gently, and just as I thought I was done crying, a new set of fresh tears erupted, and I once again broke down.

"Shh, it's okay. I'm here for you. Take your time." She cooed.

And that's all I needed as I collapsed, my feelings unraveling, my tears flowing from my eyes.

I didn't know how long it took for my tears to dry up, but around that time I was knocked out, because I woke up to find myself in my room, with Cilia sitting across from me, reading a book.

When I shifted on the bed, she looked up and smiled as she said, "You're awake." Then she stood up as she said, "I'll be right back." Then she exit my room.

She soon came back with a tray that held a bowl of soup, a bowl of fruits, and a glass of orange juice.

"Here you go. Crying takes a lot of energy." She said placing the tray on the table next to my bed.
"Oh trust me I know." I drawled out, my eyes burning every time I blink.
"Oh and wash your face, it'll help cool your eyes, and lubricate them." She informed me.
"Okay that I didn't know." I managed to smile.

"Trust me, I know from experience." Cilia confirmed as a somber look slithered across her facial features but disappeared as soon as it came.

"Come on now, eat. Then we can talk later, or whenever you're ready. I-" she suddenly froze as her eyes glazed over, and I had a feeling she was mind communicating with someone, then she snapped back as she said, "sorry Aden, I have to go." She suddenly seemed in a rush.

"Wait? What? Why?" I asked, surprised at her sudden mood change.

"Can't explain now, but I'll see you later." She yelled, as she practically ran out of the room.

Well okay then.

I took her advice anyway, washed my face, ate, then I got ready for bed.

Just as I slipped under the covers, sleep was soon to meet me.

My limbs became heavy, just as my eyelids started giving way, and that's when I heard it. My door opened and closed, but I couldn't seem to control my body. I felt weak, I couldn't even lift a finger.

Then I felt my bed dip, someone moved in the bed with me, wrapped an arm around me, then kissed my head, and before I could think twice, I was gone.

Chapter 8- "New Friend"

Third person's pnt. Of view

I woke up once again to an empty bed, when I could've sworn that last night someone was in bed with me.

Who knows? Maybe it was my imagination playing tricks on me.

Nevertheless, I shook off the thought and headed to the shower, to get ready for another day at my job, and hopefully this one would end on better terms, I mean all I had to do was avoid looking out the window and avoid the nightmare of a mate that haunted my dreams.

Yeah, easy peasy.

By the time I was dressed up and ready to go, I once again had 30 minutes to get to work, so I didn't waste any more time, and quickly ran off to work.

When I got there, Diana was already waiting for me, she greeted me with a warm smile as she said "Good morning dear, I can't believe you made it today, you seem in a very bad state yesterday. How are you feeling? You can take the day off you know."

"Good morning, no it's fine really, I was just a bit overwhelmed, that's all." I smiled.

"Well I figured, which is why I hired someone to sort out the office and take care of the paperwork. You are now my assisting nurse, and I already have a patient waiting for you." She smiled.

"Sure, where?" I asked excited that I finally get in on the action again.

"Third door to your right." Diana said, as she sauntered off to another patient.

With a smile on my face, and a pep in my step, I made my way to my very first patient in this pack.

I gave a warning knock before I opened the door to find my eyes connecting with two steel grey colored ones. He had sand blond hair, and a charming smile.

"Good morning, my name is Adelina, I will be your nurse for today, may I ask what you are in for?" I greeted, as professionally as possible.

"Um, good morning, name is James, and I'm in to clean up my wound and get a new dressing." He spoke with a deep voice.

"Okay, well, may I ask why your wound has yet to be healed, I mean you're a werewolf." I made conversation, as I paced around from cabinet to cabinet looking for all the needed materials.

"Um wolfs bane, I got shot by a bullet covered in wolfs bane. Auntie D took the bullet out, but the effect still remains, however I've been making progress, especially when I shift into my wolf, my healing accelerates." He explained.

" I see, well can you take the bandages off on your own, or do you need help?" I asked after retrieving everything that I needed.

"Yeah, I'm going to need help, especially taking my shirt off." He said, smirking when my jaw hit the floor.

"Riiight." I said, shaking my head, and making my way to him.

Not only did I get nervous being around him, things had to get worse, see I had to stand at a near proximity to take off his shirt.

I mean seriously take off his shirt.

I breathed in softly, my cheeks on fire, as I slowly drove the shirt up, and over his head, revealing a fit and tight body structure.

I couldn't stand looking in his eyes as I backed away to retrieve the new bandages, alcohol, the tape and the disinfecting gauzes.

When I made my way back to him, he still held that smirk, and I had to break the awkward silence by saying "what?"

"You're her aren't you?" He stated.

"That depends." I said with a raised eyebrow.

"Depends on what?" He asked, still trying to catch my eyes.

"Depends on which "her" you're referring to." I said, my turn to smirk.

"The new "her" that just arrived, that has our Alpha in a mood." He stated so bluntly.

"I don't have him in a mood." I lied through my teeth, knowing that he could see perfectly through my lie, and my blushing didn't help the situation either.

"Right, so why can't he focus anymore? And why does he get mad at anyone mentioning you?" He questioned.

"What do you mean?" I asked, all the while focusing on taking care of his wound.

"Well for one, when we practice, his mind seem to be somewhere else, before you came, we couldn't even get one hit on him, now we get three to four punches in before he can even respond. He's weak, mentally and physically, like he's missing a part of himself. Plus, whenever one of the guys ask who you are, what's your name, he asks if we want you or something, it's as though he's overprotective you." James concluded.

I chuckled shaking my head as I said, "you have no idea," before I could catch myself.

"Wait a second..." exclaimed James out of nowhere as he captured my eyes in an intense stare then he continued "You're his mate, aren't you?"

"Me? Pfft... NO... why would you think that?" I asked, my cheeks flaring.

" Oh I don't know, maybe because his scent is all over you, and concealer never hides an Alpha's mark." Smirked James as he referred to the mark on my neck.

I found myself playfully punching him as I said "you jerk! Leave me alone."

He himself laughed as he said, "it's okay kiddo, your secret is safe with me, but come on patch me up, I have to go."

"Yeah, yeah, don't call me kiddo." I said shaking my head and rolling my eyes at him.

"I like you." He said after staring at me for a bit, "you remind me of the sister I never had. Hey, let me get your phone number." He said.

"Sure, when I'm done." I said, as I wrapped the tape around his shoulder one more time, then I backed away taking the dirty bandages, gauzes, and other materials.

After making sure everything was in place, I picked my phone from my purse, and handed it over to James.

I didn't mind giving him my number, I mean he seem like a cool guy, and to be honest he does feel like a brother I never had, I mean yeah, I didn't know him for long, but he still carried this familiar aura around him.

Anyway, after he placed his number on my phone, then took a "handsome" picture as he so put it, he handed it back to me, and got off the bed, then made his way to the door.

When he got there, he turned around just as I approached him, ready to go to my next patient. And With absolutely no warning, he engulfed me in a bear hug as he said, "thanks for your help kiddo." And with my tiny arms, it was impossible for me to hug him back in the same manner, and I even forgot to reprimand him about calling me kiddo.

Just as he was about to pull away, the door burst open, and there stood a seething Demitrey.

His angry pupils traveled back and forth between James and me, as his nostrils flared.

When James finally dropped his arms, it took all my willpower not to run back to James and use his arms to shield me from the angry Alpha.

James lifted his hand in acknowledgment as he said "Alpha."

Demitrey gazed over at James darkly as he said in a low tone "Get. Out."

And James subtly said "welp, that's my cue to go, thanks

again kiddo, I'll catch you later." And he winked at me smirking, knowing exactly what he did.

When he walked out, he made sure to close the door behind him, and the ruthless Alpha turned back to me with an icy glare, and all I could think was... I'M SO SCREWED.

Chapter 9- "Stubborn"

Third person's pnt. Of view

Adelina stood frozen, paralyzed by the icy glare of the Alpha, she couldn't move, and it was slowly becoming hard to breathe.

Demitrey gazed down at the girl in front him, the one that wreaked havoc on his life without even knowing it.

The minute he met her he knew she was the one... but would he succumb to his feelings? No, of course not.

Not if he wanted to keep her safe.

He learned from his father that being an Alpha meant having no weaknesses, and SHE was his weakness.

She made him *feel*.

He was never allowed to feel, "an Alpha is not supposed to feel" quoted his father.

Ever since he came of age to know, he found out that his father was the leader that he was because he didn't have a mate, well he did, but after his mother gave birth to him, Demitrey learned that his father rejected her, which caused her to go mad, and end her life.

Without a mate in the picture, his father ruled ruthlessly, as a pack leader and as a father.

His father made sure that Demitrey grew up as cold hearted as he, he made sure that he rid himself of the thought of having a mate.

His father made sure that he-

"Um..." Demitrey's thoughts were suddenly cleared, and he realized that he spaced out on Adelina.

"M-may I help you?" Questioned Adelina faintly, and Demitrey just wanted to run over to her and wrap her in his arms.

She appeared so fragile, yet he knew there was an ass kicker under those soft features on her face.

Demitrey couldn't hold back, he had to hold her, at least for once, then he would back away, pretend she doesn't exist, but just once, that's all he needed.

So Demitrey approached her, and she went to step back but he quickly said, "don't do that, please, just don't move." He begged in a quiet and soft tone.

And Adelina found herself obeying, mostly due to the surprise from the way Demitrey addressed her ever so softly.

When Demitrey stood, leaving little to no space between their bodies, he cupped her face, he softly brushed the pad of his thumb on her cheek, staring deep into her eyes, and Adelina found herself leaning into his touch, as she shyly looked up at him.

He allowed the top of his thumb to travel on her bottom lip, and Adelina absent-mindedly opened her lips in invitation.

Demitrey found himself leaning into her, his eyes aimed on his target, her lips.

Adelina was caught in the moment, but then his earlier actions revived in her memories, and she placed her hands on his chest to push him away.

She pushed and struggled, but he wouldn't budge, so she did the only thing possible, she slapped him.

The sound echoed throughout the room, then faded, until their heavy breaths were the only sound resonating around the walls.

Demitrey slowly turned his head, and stared deep in her eyes, and started to lean in again, and once again she aimed to slap him, except he caught her arm, so without thinking twice, she slapped him with her free hand, and this time Demitrey smirked, but it quickly faded when she aimed to attack him again.

So Demitrey captured both her arms, and he couldn't help but softly growl as the tingles erupted throughout his body, and by the way Adelina's eyes dilated, he knew she felt it too, and he couldn't help it, he wanted to kiss her, softly, just for once, he wanted her in his arms, then he would be done.

He would ignore her, just for her safety. It was as though she was a beautiful rose, and he was a deadly vine, he could spread and dominate all around her, but he would avoid taking her over, because once he did, she would be his everything, his main weakness, his main prize, she would be on his mind every second of the day, and she would be his main weak point.

Others would use her to get to him, and he couldn't allow his reputation to place her life in danger, so he would enjoy this moment, because after those minutes were up, he would be as stubborn as a mule, she would be non-existent to him, and it would stay that way.

So Demitrey leaned in, just as Adelina leaned back but he softly whispered "please, just this once, allow me. Please."
And Adelina found herself leaning into him, she couldn't control her actions, his soft pleas, his caresses, his touch

was enough for him to have her wrapped around his fingers, and so they kissed.

Their lips met halfway, and they danced softly against one another, as though it was a ballad at a grand ball.

Adelina wrapped her arms around his neck, as he wrapped his strong ones around her waist.

He caressed her body in his warm embrace, and in one quick motion he hoisted her body unto the patient bed, and moved in between her legs, their lips not once disconnecting.

He caressed her thighs through her scrubs, as he moved his lips to her neck, marking her once again, yet this time he moved softly, sweetly, and Adelina found herself leaning into him in bliss.

Before she knew it, a short sound of pleasure erupted from her lips, and Demitrey froze.

She was beautiful, but he couldn't go on.

So, he pecked her lips one more time, then he backed up.

Adelina blushed, flustered due to the actions transpired between them.

He couldn't help but smile at the effect he had on her, but then his smile faded, and he sighed as he said "We can't keep on doing this, you have to stay away from me. From this day on don't seek me out, don't talk to me, you are non-existent to me." Then he turned and headed for the door, not wanting to see her heartbroken face.

His heart was tearing, and his wolf was stirred angry and aroused, and he was growing up a storm in the back of

Demitrey's head, but he was doing it for his mate's safety... Yet he couldn't help but wonder…Why did it feel wrong?

When his hand reached the door knob, he heard a broken voice resonate from Adelina as she demanded "why don't you just reject me then?"

And Demitrey froze, his anger rose, partially from his wolf, but he breathed, calm himself and said, "that is out of the question." And with that he walked out.

She was his mate, no one could have her, he may be keeping away from her, but that's because he didn't want to be the cause of her getting hurt, however that didn't mean that he would let her go just so someone else could have her.

The moon goddess destined them as mates, they were meant for each other, and that is exactly how it was going to stay.

Adelina found herself frozen on the bed, tears silently streaming down her face.

Shattered, that's all she felt.

She saw something in his eyes, she saw something flicker, the way he touched her, the way he spoke, how could he deny the attraction? How could he be so stubborn? Because she could've sworn, there saw something in his eyes.

But maybe it was her imagination, maybe it was just her want for him to want her. Her desire to be wanted by him could've easily clouded her judgement, but lesson learned.

He wanted her to stay away, then she would stay away.

Adelina angrily wiped off her tears, then she jumped off the bed, and picked up her phone. She was tired of sulking.

She dialed the number, and he answered after the second ring, and she couldn't help her smile as she said, "Hey James, want to hang out later?"

Forget you Alpha, she thought as she made plans to meet up with James.

Chapter 10- "Moving on..."

Adelina's pnt. Of view

"Good night Diana, see you on Monday!" I waved off with a smile as I made my way out of the clinic, meeting James.

As soon as I saw him, I ran and gave him a hug as he returned it with his usual sly smirk.

"Hey there kiddo? Had fun at work?" He asked as he and I sauntered side by side, to our destination, "the castle", which is the nickname Cilia and I came up for the Alpha's mansion.

"Yeah, I did, actually you won't believe what happened today!" I giggled over-excitedly.

"Umm... you found out that you're actually a boy and not a girl?" He pointed out goofily, earning a punch from me that caused him to wince.

"No you jerk." I glared at him.

"Are you sure? Cause your punches are deadly. I almost have to do a double take, or else I strike you back." He smirked, as my glare turned deadly.

"I'm positive, but anyway I got to help Diana deliver a baby today! Plus, I got paid!" I said jumping up and down like a 5-year-old child on Christmas morning.

"Hey how about that?" James said in fake marvel, and I once again found myself laying a punch on his shoulder as he chuckled.

This was our usual routine, ever since that day that the pack's Alpha, whom I refused to mention his name, decided that I would be non-existent, James would pick me up from work, and over time we started hanging out, and we became close friends, so far he and Cilia are the only ones who knew for sure that the ruthless asshole- I mean Alpha, was my mate, and to be honest, they have been by my side since he warned me off, and they have been an even bigger help at getting me over my attraction for the Alpha.

I mean my feelings are not completely gone, but I hardly reflect on them because I have those two that keep me occupied most of my days, and if they're not around Peter and Clarissa are one call away.

I hardly found myself thinking of that son of a biscuit, and if my mind was to wander down that road, I quickly switched gears and start thinking of other things, and in fact that method allowed me to gain training with Cilia and James.

Now, every night, the three of us trained, well James trained us, because throughout the day we each had something to do, but for 2 hours each night we trained.

I found my daily routine to be quite distracting, and I couldn't be happier.

I mean yeah, I know bottling up my feelings about the Alpha, refusing to think of him, and avoiding him as much as he avoids me could result in consequences, but I didn't care, at least not right now, but little did I know that I would have to pay those consequences soon enough.

"Hey, hey! Kiddo? You're zoning out on me, bring it back in." James firmly pressed his hands on my shoulder, a worried expression lazing on his facial features.

"Sorry, my mind just wandered a little." I said, an embarrassed blush creeping up on my cheeks.

"Oh trust me I know, I mean we've been standing in front of the castle for good minute now, but I asked you if there is anything you want to tell me, like if today is a special day...?" James said, drawling his question out slowly.

"Um... no?" I said, confused, I don't think I missed anything.

"Are you sure?" He asked slowly again, like what the heck

was his problem.

"Um, yeah, I'm sure." I said looking at him as though he has grown two heads.

James sighed and shook his head, then he gripped my hand and dragged me up the castle stairs, once we were inside, he practically hauled me up the stairs, his firm grip not loosening one bit.

"Hey um James? Want to tell me what all this is about?" I questioned, as I tried to pick up to his pace.

"Wait and see." And that's all I received.

When we finally made it up to my floor, he started heading in the direction of my room.

Now to anyone who could walk upon this scene of James dragging me, it would seem like two lovers rushing to privacy just so they could get involved in a very long sexual session, like those scenes you see in a movie, well at least that's what I think we looked like.

And my suspicion was confirmed when one of the pack members spotted us and blushed looking away.

When we finally reached my room, I opened the door and there came a loud "SURPRISE!" causing me to shriek, and step back bumping into James.

"What the-"

"HAPPY BIRTHDAY!" Came Cilia's over excited voice as she leaped out at me, embracing me in an overjoyed hug.

"Um... thank you." I found myself saying, tears suddenly welling up in my eyes.

To be honest I was shocked, my birthday was something I only celebrated with Peter and Clarissa, and since they weren't around, I didn't think on telling anyone, I mean who was I going to celebrate it with? But then I realized, I had friends here, and it was going to be okay.

"OMG! You're 21! Can you believe it! I finally get to take you out to my favorite spot!" Exclaimed Cilia as she bounced up and down, like a kid high on sugar.
"Oh yeah? And where is that?" I asked, my heart finally slowing down to its usual pace.
"Uh huh, it's a surprise. Just get ready. I set out your outfit on your bed. James and I will come pick you up in exactly one hour." And just like that Cilia was out the door, and I was left alone, with my mouth agape.

It took me a moment to gather myself, then I made my way to the big red birthday bag that occupied my bed.

Inside I found a pair of high-waist white jeggings, with a black laced flowy crop top.

I looked over the outfit, trying to figure out what Cilia was planning, and then I dug further in the bag.

I fished out a shoebox that held some hot red laced peep-toed stilettoes, and below that was a bag of makeup.

I smiled thinking about Cilia and trying to figure out what was up her sleeve, and with that thought in mind I stripped, took a shower and got ready.

By the time my hour was up, Cilia came rushing and banging at my door, when I opened it her jaw dropped to the floor, same as James'.

They looked me up and down as James wolf whistled and said, "moon goddess bless me now and let her be my mate."

I giggled and threw a pillow at him as I said, "boy you wish."

And Cilia shook her head laughing and said, "alright let's go."

"Where are we going though? I don't like surprises" I said picking up my purse.

"The club." Cilia simply added, and turned, heading for the door.

"WAIT! YOU go to the club?" I questioned, my eyes bulging out of their sockets.

Cilia simply turned, in her short back dress, and black heels and smiled as she said "yeah." And with that she turned and left.

Once she said so, I gathered my wits, I shook off the surprise from Cilia, and I looked at myself in the mirror one more time.

I looked over the top and how it flowed perfectly into my high-waisted jeggings, ending with my red stilettos.

My hair was pinned back in thick brown waves, while my makeup was natural, my red lips and big eyes coming to life.

I winked at myself in confidence then stepped out of my room, it was my birthday, and I was going to enjoy it, and watch out Alpha, because I'm moving on.

Chapter 11- "...Or so I thought"

Third person's pnt. Of view

As Adelina descended the stairs, what she didn't expect was for the Alpha to be standing at the bottom of the stairs, taking part in a make out session with Serena.

The Alpha hearing footsteps from the stairs, pulled away from Serena as his eyes connected to that of his mate, Adelina.

For just a split-second Adelina froze, she felt her heart beat pick up pace, and her breathing lost its pattern, but then she remembered, his cruel words, his treatment, his teasing and joking, and she cleared her mind.

Her memories of his ruthless actions felt as though a dagger drove straight through her heart, but she wouldn't succumb to that weakness. Not today, not ever, not when she made the effort to move on from him.

She broke their eye contact and walked straight passed Demitrey and made her way out the doors.

Demitrey watched Adelina's every movement until she disappeared behind the doors, and he couldn't deny, he had a beautiful mate, and he wanted to cherish her, but he also couldn't place her in danger, he had to stay away.

Or so he thought.

When he noticed who followed Adelina out those doors his blood boiled, it was James', the pack's #1 player, and Cilia.

He had no problem with Cilia, but when it came to James, he didn't want him nowhere near Adelina, heck he didn't want any one of the male species to approach her, and knowing Cilia and James, he had a feeling he knew exactly where they were taking Adelina.

He was quick to follow them out the door, just as they got in a car and sped off.

Demitrey quickly dialed his Beta's number and ordered him to meet up front with the car.

Once Kade arrived with the car, Demitrey jumped in and they rushed off after Demitrey's mate, not even sparing Serena a second glance.

Meanwhile, the trio soon found themselves parking in front of "Dynasty", the hottest werewolf club in town, with the longest lines in the street, but with James having connections, they didn't have to wait in line.

The scene was vibrant and alive. The music boomed in the speakers, while the bass enchanted your heart into beating into the perfect rhythm. Bodies bounced, grinded, and whined against one other, while the colored lights danced over the skins that occupied the dance floor.

The scene was hot and erotic, you couldn't help but get involved in the action.

James led the ladies over to a free table, and then went to the bar for drinks.

When he came back with six shots, Adelina was about to refuse when she remembered that she was 21, and it was time to let loose.

Heck, she needed to let loose. The image of her mate kissing another woman made her blood boil, filling her up with red rage, and green envy. She wanted to hurt them both, but most of all she wanted to forget them both.

No in fact she just wanted to forget Demitrey.

He didn't want her, and she has been trying to move on, and tonight was the perfect night to test her limits as a free woman, so in the blink of an eye, Adelina threw back all six of the shots, leaving both James and Cilia speechless, then she took Cilia's hand and led her to the middle of the dance floor.

Tonight, Adelina was going to forget, she was going to stop thinking about Demitrey, and she would stop fantasizing about them ever being together. She was going to let go.

And just as she made her decision, the DJ dropped a reggaeton mix and the crowd went wild.

The girls were quickly ripped away from one another, as two strangers tore them apart.

Adelina didn't seem to mind, the alcohol buzzed in her system, and the music seem to hypnotize her, as her hips moved in sync with that of the mysterious stranger that seem rather excited to dance with her...

The girls were ready to dance the night away, and to them the fun was just beginning.

Soon however, Demitrey and Kade made their way into the club, they were quick to spot Cilia dancing with a random dude, that seem more interested in leaving kisses all over her, and Kade didn't seem very happy about that.

In the blink of an eye, the guy was ripped from Cilia, and Kade took a possessive hold of her as he whispered possessively "MINE" and just like that he swept Cilia off her feet, literally, and carried her out the club.

Cilia was speechless, Kade was her mate... The Alpha's Beta was her mate, and she was ever so happy.

The way he held her and captured her eyes with his made Cilia's heart flutter, and she completely forgot about Adelina and James.

James on the other hand was busy flirting and making out with one of the girls in the club, and he walked out leaving Adelina on the dance floor.

It didn't take long for Demitrey to spot his mate; however, he wasn't too happy at the guy clinging on to her like a second skin, but what sent a dagger right through his heart was the fact that his mate appeared to enjoy herself being in the arms of another, and soon his pain turned to anger.

He took measured step towards the intoxicated couple, and in a matter of seconds the guy was ripped away from Adelina.

"Hey bro, fucks the matter with you?" The guy said, aggressively pushing Demitrey, and Adelina gasped, waking up from her trance.

Demitrey stepped up to the man and landed a punch square in his face as he said, "keep your hands off my girl."

The guy quickly got to his feet as he said "her? She not your girl, in fact," the guy added as he pulled Adelina to his body embracing her "this pretty young thing is all mine, and" the guy spun Adelina, flushing her back into his front as he kissed the spot where she was supposed to be marked "she is not marked, which means she is not your girl." The guy smirked smugly, and kissed Adelina's marking spot again, and Demitrey saw red.

Before anyone could suspect, the guy went flying across the room, landing against one of the electrical pipes, as his body convulsed with thousands of electrical volts frying his insides.

Everyone stood stunned at the sight.

The Alpha just claimed Adelina as his, yet they all questioned the fact that he didn't want a mate.

Adelina stepped up to him, her fists balled as she said "What did you do that for? Huh? You said you didn't want me! I was moving on! I was trying to forget you! And the chance I get to finally have fun, and escape from you, YOU RUINED IT!" Adelina was seething in anger as she stared daggers at the man who tortured her so, and Demitrey turned his dark face on her as he simply said, "let's go", totally ignoring her angry outburst.

Then he turned and started making his way for the exit, but when he sensed that his mate wasn't following, he turned around and found her standing with her arms crossed in defiance as she said "no."

And the crowd erupted in gasps followed by whispers as they gossiped "did she just say no to him? Omg she's his mate! Oooh she just defied the Alpha."

"No?" Was Demitrey's question.

"No." Was Adelina defiant answer.

Demitrey shook his head then took three long strides towards Adelina, and before she could register what happened, she was hauled off the dance floor and onto Demitrey' s shoulders, then in a cool stride, not caring about the peering eyes, Demitrey made his way out the club, carrying his struggling mate with him.

Demitrey struggled to place her in the car, and Adelina being a fighter was quite the challenge, she kicked, punched and scratched him, she was angry and relentless.

When Adelina landed a strong blow to Demitrey' s head, causing him to see stars for a few seconds, he threatened her and said, "keep struggling, and I'm putting you in the trunk." And just like that Adelina froze, the shaking her head defeatedly, she got in the car, and soon they drove off.

What they missed as they drove away from the club however, where the prying eyes that followed Adelina from the moment she stepped foot in the club. They missed the way their encounter in the club sparked an interest among a few of the individuals in the club, and most important, they missed the figure that moved and lurked in the shadows, observing their interaction.

Meanwhile, Adelina sat staring out the window, anger waltzing in her veins. Her mind was buzzing with questions such as "*how did he know where I was? Why did he come for me? Why did he call me his girl? I thought he didn't want me.*"

The effect of the alcohol seems to start fading from her system, and soon she became very sleepy, but before she fully drifted off to sleep, the last thought on her mind was that "I moved on... or so I thought."

Chapter 12- "Anger"

Adelina's pnt. Of view

I found myself being shaken awake by a firm hand that belonged to none other than Demitrey.

He shook me until I was shoving his hand away while I said "okay, okay, I'm awake, jeez."

His cold glare just penetrated my own as we locked gazes in a fierce stare down.

One of us was bound to look away first, and I would be damned if that was me.

With one simple breath, and no blinking he simply stated "Get. Out."

With a huff, I smiled sarcastically as I said "gladly." And with a roll of my eyes, I opened my door and stepped out of the car, but by the time I was closing the door, I found myself wedged in between the car, and the solid chest of my mate.

His glare was cold, domineering, and unforgiving. My mind begged for me to look away before I got affected, yet my pride willed me to stay put.

"Did you just roll your eyes at me?" He questioned, his tone low, sending shivers dancing across my entire being. "And if I did?" I mustered the courage to ask.
He chuckled, his glare unwavering, then next thing I knew, his fingers were caressing my cheek with feather light touches, and I forced myself to turn away, unwilling to give into him, unwilling to give into my feelings.

I was trying to get over him for heaven's sake.

His eyes became hard at my actions, and he placed his hands on both sides of my body, caging me in, as he moved his body closer to my own.

He smirked once he felt my racing heart, and he simply asked, "feeling feisty today, aren't we?"

"Go to hell." Was my heated reply, and he gripped my chin firmly, not enough to hurt, but enough for me to know he was stronger.

He leaned in, his lips brushing softly against my own, and before even realizing, I found myself leaning in, but he pulled away teasingly as he said with a lust filled tone "that mouth of yours, those lips, they're going to get you in a lot of trouble."

His eyes were dark with lust, his voice giving away his feelings, but I forced myself back, I wouldn't succumb, nor would I submit to my feelings for him.

He seemed to read my mind for my eyes held a glare similar to his own, so he backed up, and gave me enough space, then he turned around but before making his way inside he ordered "you're sleeping in my room tonight."

And just like that he left, leaving me standing speechless.

That arrogant bastard!

I was steaming! Livid at his actions, and he had the absolute audacity to say that I'm sleeping in his room?!

We'll see about that.

I stomped my way up to my room, slamming and locking the door shut, then I stripped and headed for a shower.

"What a perfect way to end our birthday." I noted the sarcasm in Aden's voice.

"Tell me about it." I replied.

"What are you going to do?" She asked, a tone of

excitement slightly visible in her voice.

"What do you mean?" I asked, confused.

"Well... are you going to go to his room?" She asked giddy, and I could tell, my wolf is in my head, and she has been nonstop bugging me about that asshole, and she seem to have forgotten that he rejected us.

"No! How can you even ask something Like that? Did you forget already what he has done to us?" I asked suddenly fuming, the mere thought of him made me angry.

"Well, technically he didn't actually reject us, he just wants to stay away from us, and maybe he's trying to protect us or something." Aden tried to reason. Wait... Was she defending that asshole?

"PROTECT US? HA! FROM WHAT? He's my mate, when we know each other, yet we stay away, that only makes us weaker, and it hurts! Okay? I hurt because of him, but nooo, he wants to stay away! FINE let him stay

away!" And with that final outburst, I blocked Aden from my thoughts.

My mind cleared, just to reveal my white knuckles, choking my towel.
I shook my head and jumped in the shower trying my best to cool off.

When I finally could breathe normally again, and my mind was filled with happy thoughts and memories, I made my way back to my room with the towel wrapped around my body, but as soon as I opened the door, I froze.

There, lying on my bed was the Alpha, shirtless, with his eyes closed.

I stood frozen, contemplating my situation in my mind, while my eyes seem to access my situation of a mate that seem to lie comfortably in my bed.

It appears my eyes developed a mind on their own, as they seem to study every inch of his perfectly toned structure, as if they were memorizing every sculpt of his wide shoulders and fit chest, the way he laid carefree made it seem as though he had all the time in the world.

If only I could lay next to him, drive my fingers slowly over his built being, if only I could ki-

Woah! Woah! Woah! Woah! WOAH!

Get your mind out of the gutter Adelina.

"Or leave it there... I don't mind." Came Aden's sultry voice in mind.

How the heck did she get back in?

"Enjoying the show?" Came Demitrey' s voice, pulling me away from my thoughts.

"I've seen better." I shrugged, looking away, trying to avoid the heat that washed over me.

He stood up, and sauntered his way over to me, and it took all my will power not to run and lock myself in the bathroom.

Wait a second, lock.

"I locked the door! How did you get in?" I demanded, anger slowly rising in my blood stream.

"Have you forgotten, this is my house, I can go wherever I want." He replied coolly, as though he was the king of the world.

"Yeah, whatever." I huffed, tightening my hold on the towel.

His eyes seem to catch my actions, and his pupils dilated, as his voice took a deeper, darker note, and he breathed as he said "I thought I ordered that you sleep in my room tonight."

"Mmh, you did, but see I don't usually take orders from pompous, arrogant, assholes, and plus," I added, making my way by the bed " I like my bed a bit more, so, I'll have to decline that offer, but you can surely see your way out."

I could've sworn I saw steam coming out of his ears, as his whole stance screamed: ANGER.

Mmh, guess the Alpha is not used to people turning him down, if anything a girl.

But then he turned and smirked.

Wait he's smirking... why is he smirking?

He once again took calculated steps towards me, until he was standing just a few feet away.

He shrugged and placed his hands in his pocket as he said "you're right. My bed only belongs to me and my mistress, what was I thinking by inviting you in there?"

And I saw red.

Before thinking twice, my fist went flying, but in quick reflex he managed to catch it, seconds before it connected with his beautiful jaw.

But that didn't stop me, I sent my other fist flying, but to no avail he also caught it, except this time, using his strength, his pulled my arms closer to him, then slammed our bodies on the bed.

And just like that, we ended up in a very compromising position.

I found myself laying on my back, a flimsy towel the only thing keeping my body from the eyes of the ruthless

Alpha. Both my hands were held captive on either side of my head, while my knees were propped up, apart from each other, with the Alpha lying right in between my legs.

Chapter 13- "Heated Jealousy"

Adelina's pnt. Of view

We laid still in that position for a few, not a word travelling between us. Our locked gazes, and heavy breathing was our only mean of communication.

The tension developed its own language, and the environment translated it perfectly.

I don't know what was going through his mind, but for all I know, I would stay as still as log, just to avoid any more awkwardness.

I knew the towel wasn't doing much to conserve me. I could feel the breeze bathe my upper thighs, and his breath tickled the revealed skin through the towel's opening at my belly button.

His breathing became slightly heavier, his eyes growing darker, and slowly, almost torturing, his burning gaze started gliding down my skin, over my exposed cleavage that was saved and cut short by the towel.

His scrutinizing slow, yet heated glare started nearing the towel opening, and I couldn't help the excitement that tingled my dirty mind, but the proud Adelina inside wasn't going to succumb just because a sexy Alpha male was lying on top of her, adoring her body with smoldering gaze.

I found myself snapping my fingers as I said "hey, buddy! My eyes are up here."
And his gaze suddenly met mine, as he smirked and said, "I've seen better."
For some reason that hurt, but hey, that's all he has been doing to me since we met, so I sucked it up and said, "you've seen nothing yet."

Then a mischievous idea popped into my brain and I smiled almost sweetly as I said "James, however, has seen a lot more."

And his eyes darkened, his grip tightened, and his breath was coming out clipped and short.

"What did you just say?" He growled out angry.
"You heard me." I said, smirking, keeping up the act.

His eyes flashed as various emotions danced in his eyes. And for a flicker of a second, I could've sworn I saw hurt, but maybe it was a figment of my imagination, because as soon as it came, it was replaced by anger, his usual emotion.

"Well, then, if he has seen so much... How much has he done?" He bluntly questioned, as one of his hands suddenly started caressing my side.
"Wh-what d-d-do you m-m-mean?" I asked, suddenly

nervous, and totally forgetting my act.

"Oh you know..." He stated almost suggestively, as his skilled fingers slowly sneaked under my towel, his eyes never leaving mine "if you show, you might as well give, so how much as he done? Did he caress you? Was he gentle?" He started whispering, his lips teasing my own with feather light touches, and his fingers, although moving softly against my skin, igniting a fire that only spread by the second.

This was a bad idea... teasing the monster.

My breathing was no longer under my control. My heart beat began to thrum to a different rhythm. My mind turned to mush, and my body became hypnotized, as if it no longer belonged to me.

His soft caress was playing my body and nerves like a skilled violinist telling a story on his instrument.

Then his gentle touch turned rough, as his palm caressed my outer thighs, kneading my skin, while his other hand possessed my neck, showing full domination, as his eyes became stormy dark and he firmly demanded "Or was he rough? Was he harsh? Did he give it to you how you liked it?"

He dipped his head, in a measured slow tempo, and nipped on my earlobe, as he teasingly whispered, "tell me, how do you like it... mate?"

His anger was taking over... but was it just anger? Or did I sense a little jealousy?

He changed from hot to cold in the blink of an eye. It was hard to keep up.

One second rough, the next gentle, a sensually teasing pattern.

His hold became aggressive, almost possessive.

And I found myself paralyzed.

"D-Demitrey, stop." I whispered.

"TELL ME!" He suddenly roared.

"Did you enjoy having him? DO YOU LIKE BEING DOMINATED BY HIM? ANSWER ME!" Oh, this was getting serious, this is what I get for playing with fire!

"N-no, I don't like it, in fact I've never been taken by him, or anyone." I succumbed to telling the truth.

"You're lying." He stated, his eyes darker than complete oblivion.

"N-no, I'm not, I've saved everything for my mate..." then my eyes turned boldly to his as I said, "for you."

He froze for a minute, then before I could register anything, he kissed me, and not the romantic kiss, but instead the "you're my girl, and you belong to me" kind of kiss.

The kiss that is so mind-blowing, possessive, and the one kiss you will never forget.

The one that causes you to wake up with swollen lips the next morning.

I was barely able to keep up with him, my wolf was encouraging my actions, while my logical side was screeching at me for not being able to resist.

Then I snapped out of it, I couldn't allow this, he just insulted me.

I placed my hand on his chest, to try and push him away, but he only kissed me harder, and it was suddenly becoming very hot, and very hard to breathe.

My stomach turned into an acrobatic all-star, doing all types of flips and tricks, and my treasured place seem as though it was a good time to start feeling more moisturized than usual. I had the sudden urge to be touched there, or just have something there, something big, warm, and satisfying.

Wait! No! No! No! No! No!

NO! Get a grip woman!

I scolded myself.

I tried to close my legs, but my hunk of a mate was making that impossible, and when his hips started grinding sensually against my own, I lost it.

"Aah, Demitrey." The moan escaped before I could control myself.

He finally moved away from my lips, but his hips kept it's teasingly slow yet very sensual rhythm.

He moved down to my ear kissing it as he whispered oh so sexually "that's right baby, only I can make you feel this way, only my name gets to come from your mouth in that way. Your body, your needs, your sounds of pleasure, they all belong to me. Let me hear it, sing for me baby."

"Ooh Alpha." I voiced out in an alien tone, as he thrust his hips into me, causing a friction to build up somewhere near my uterus.

"Who's Alpha?" He growled out possessively. As his rhythm picked up pace, his lips leaving heated pecks on my marking spot.

"Aah..." Was all I could muster now. My brain was a goner, as well as my body.

"WHO'S ALPHA?" He gruffly whispered, his hip rhythm

unforgiving and pleasing.

"MY ALPHA." I declared, and I felt myself explode.

My body was in a frenzy, I was floating, I was high, and breathing for me was non-existent.

There was no intercourse. I was still physically a virgin, but that was a mind-blowing orgasm.

My first ever orgasm, given by my one and only mate...

The mate who didn't want me.

My foggy mind was suddenly cleared, taken over by anger, and before anything, I mustered up the strength, and pushed him off me.

"Get off me! And stay the hell away from me!" I raged.

He landed a cool gaze on me, and he shrug and said "as you wish... mate, but do me one favor, the next time you think to get me jealous, think again. Because I don't like sharing."

"You can't share something that you don't own. I don't belong to you."

"You sure about that...? Because that wasn't what I heard a few minutes ago." He said smugly as he turned to leave, but then he paused after opening the door as he said, "Oh and put some clothes on, wouldn't want anyone walking in on such explicit image." Then he winked and was out the door before I could hurl more of my anger at him.

    Instead, I laid still staring daggers at the door which the asshole just exit from, and the only thought that seem to circulate my mind was that I hated him... But then again... did I really?

Chapter 14- "Not a Date"

Adelina's pnt. Of view

I've been standing at the Alpha's office door for about a few good minutes now.

I wanted to go in there and talk to him, well technically ask for permission, but the thing is I haven't seen him since that night he walked out of my room, and that was about two weeks ago.

I didn't know what he would say or do.

I admit, I was curious, but then I was also proud, and over the past few days I've worked even harder to get him out of my system, and I think I've made progress.

He hasn't crossed my mind for a while the past few days, and him being out of my sight has helped him disappear from my woman intuition-based fantasies.

So that says something.

I stood there biting my nails, and soon, I started pacing back and forth.

I mean, I don't know why I was so nervous, I could care less about what he thought of me, and all I had to do was go in there and tell him my weekend plans, which involved me leaving the pack boundaries for a few days.

With shake of my head, I breathed to calm my nerves, then I lifted my fingers, and I knocked.

It took a few seconds before he finally said to come in, and once he did so, all ounce of bravery was gone, vanished from my system and into thin air.

With instant moist fingers, I gripped the handle, turned it and opened the door. When I stepped in, I made sure to focus my eyes on anything but him, lending me enough courage to close the door, instead of running out of his office like a mad woman.

When I turned however, our eyes made an instant connection, and my breath who seems to always act funny around him, got into its comical routine.

His gaze burned and penetrated my eyes, and it was a raging war on going within me.

My submissive side begged that I look away, but my proud side was daring, no, challenging him to look away.

Once he realized that I wasn't going to succumb to his lethal glare, he cleared his throat as he said, "and what do you want?"

"Well, good morning to you too." I muttered sarcastically, and all I received in return were a pair of cold eyes.

Very sexy cold eyes, you could stare at them all day, you could even-

WOAH! Stop right there!

Get a grip!

"Anyways..." I drawled out, clearing my thoughts "I was wondering if I could go back to my pack territory for a few days. My best friend Peter and Clarissa finally decided on doing a traditional wedding celebration, and I am invited... please." I quickly blurted out, and he just sat there... staring.

Then, without a flicker of emotion, he simply said "no."

"WHAT?!" I exclaimed before I could restrain myself.
"You heard me." He said calmly, then he returned back to doing his work.
"No, wait, please. I won't be alone, James has agreed to go

with me, and Cilia well she can't go because she's a bit... busy... With her mate, but at least I won't be alone." I tried to reason with him.

"Oh James is going with you eh?" He asked almost as if he was mocking me, "the James who abandoned you at the club, where any harm could've happened to you?" He asked, and it was almost invisible, but I still managed to detect of tone of worry in his voice.

"Look you don't have to worry, I spoke with him and Cilia, they apologized, but please, this is my best friend, a brother that we are talking about, you have to let me go, I'll only be gone three days, I promise." I froze after those words fluently left my mouth.

Did I just say that to him? Why did I sound like a wife promising her husband to be home soon?

I didn't need to promise him anything!

And well it was to no avail, because his eyes only got darker as he said "No."

"Come on! Okay, fine! If it's James you don't want to go with me, I'll find someone else, but all I'm asking is your permission. I'm trying to be faithful to you and the pack! Why can't you just let me go?" My chest was heaving with anger.

"BECAUSE IF I LET YOU GO YOU WILL NEVER COME BACK!" He roared, and that shut me up, but only for a few seconds.

"So what? You suddenly want me around now?! Shoot I find that hard to believe, since you IGNORE ME MOST OF THE TIME!" I shot back, but I wasn't done "and you know what? That wouldn't be such a bad idea, to leave and never come back! Especially if it meant being away from you!"

And in the blink of an eye, using his speed, I found myself pinned against the wall by none other than my mate.

His heart was beating erratically, his hard breathing a perfect match, he looked down at me, as I looked up at him, in low yet very commanding tone he said " You will do no such thing. You will not be leaving the pack territory, nor will you be leaving Me."

"Then come with me!" I matched his tone, our staring contest unwavering.

He chuckled then said "me? Go with you? Nah, I would never go on a date with you."

And I would lie if I said that didn't hurt as if it were a knife plunging in my heart, but I shook it off, he could be an asshole all he wanted, because right now my main care was to go see my best friends. I missed them so much, and this was the perfect opportunity for a visit.

"Look," I sighed, looking away not letting him see the hurt in my eyes " if you don't trust me enough to go beyond the pack territories on my own, then just escort me, or get one of your men to do it, and when the celebration is over, I'll head straight back here, but please... sir, may I please have your permission to go."

He stared at me, but then shook his head and said "fine, I'll go with you. But this is not a date." He quickly warned. But I couldn't help the smile that settled on my face, and without thinking twice I hugged him and said, "thank you."

Then I pushed him away and headed for the door, but before I left, I said "and by the way the feelings mutual, I wouldn't want to go on a date with you either. See you later!" And just like that I exited the office with a triumphant smile on my face.

Chapter 15- "Road trip"

Adelina's pnt. Of view

The day arrived faster than I expected, and Demitrey and I soon found ourselves taking a road trip back to my old pack.

The car was as quiet as a ghost town, he didn't seem interested in talking to me, neither did I, but there was something I wanted to discuss with him.

So I cleared my throat and I said faintly "so, here is the thing, Pete and Clarissa have a spare room for me, and I can crash at their place, but um, I contacted the nearest hotel, and they are checking a room out for you, free of charge, since your reputation seem to travel."

No response.

That was it, he said nothing, so I cleared my throat again and continued "so, when we reach the pack territory, you can drop me off by the bus stop, and Peter will be picking me up, and the wedding starts at 3 tomorrow, so I'll see you at the church, then after we have the reception and celebration, we can either rest and head back home tomorrow, or if you don't want to stay we can leave as soon as you want."

Still no response.

Okay, guess that's my cue to stop talking.

We kept the quiet air until we crossed my old pack's territory, and we were quickly approaching the spot where Pete had agreed to pick me up, so I had nothing else to do but speak up.

"Hey um, you can drop me off here, Peter will be picking me up shortly."

And once again, no response, so I pushed my limits, I placed my hand on his thigh, and slightly squeezed my fingers to get his attention, and he stiffened.

"Can you hear me? I just need- OH MY GOD!" I screamed out as he swerved off to the side of the road, in the blink of an eye, my seatbelt was ripped off, and I found myself beings captured by two strong arms that impaled me onto a very strong man in a straddling position.

Noticing the situation, the temperature suddenly went up, my cheeks burned, my heart raced, and my lungs, well it was their time to put on their comical act.

I was breathing as heavy as he, and his eyes burned into my own.

"I-"

"JUST BE QUIET." He ordered, he breathed in and out, as if in a pattern to calm himself, when he finally appeared calm enough, he looked up at me and said, "do you know how hard it is for me to be in this car with you right now?"

"I-"

"You what? Here," he said, pressing my body on his, more specifically the treasured spot in between my legs, he held on to my hips and guided them into a grinding motion as he said "You feel that? This is all I've felt since we step foot in this car, and you just had to talk, I tried to control myself, but no, you had to push it."

His voice was so hard, hot, yet chilling cold.

The way his eyes never left mine as he spoke was so dominating, I can't fail to admit that I was most definitely turned on, but I didn't do anything wrong.

"I- I didn't do anything." I whispered, not trusting my vocal cords to come out strong.

"Are you sure?" He asked, his voice suddenly strained.

"Yes." I said, my voice sounding breathless.

"Well, your hips don't lie." Was all he said with a smirk.

"Wha-?" I looked down to find his hands gone, my hips seeming to have developed a mind of their own, as I found myself grinding against his hard member.

The friction caused by my actions sent continuous jolts of pleasure throughout my body, and I couldn't find it in myself to stop.

My mind was begging to stop, but my body was begging for something else, before I could think twice, I stared dead in his eyes and I said, "kiss me."

He looked as if he was taken aback, but that emotion only flashed in his eyes for a second, because his expression was suddenly replaced by that of an arrogantly sexy jerk.

"Why? I thought you hated me... mate?" He said with a smirk, and I knew I was going to regret this later, but I just opened my mouth and said, "just shut up and kiss Me."

"Mmmh, I don't think I like your tone." He said, playing with me, in one of my most heated moments.

The jerk! I was going to murder him!

But then an idea popped in my head.

I stop moving my hips, and his smirk vanished, guess he enjoyed that.

I placed my hands on his chest, and I felt his heart leap against my hand.

I teasingly yet skillfully started unbuttoning his shirt, and occasionally, I let my fingers brush against his skin.

Once his chest was fully exposed, I leaned down and started landing some soft pecks against his hot skin, and I could tell he was affected... just what I wanted.

I slowly slid my fingers down to his abdomen, and further down until I reached my target, and he went stiff as I rubbed my palm against the bulge in his pants.

I leaned my head down to his neck, and kissed his marking spot, which earned me a hot and possessive growl, then I brought my lips to his ear as I whispered "well then, since you won't give me what I want, and we're back at my old pack, maybe I can find someone else to do the job for me." And the tables flipped instantly.

A possessive arm slid around my waist, and I quickly found myself locking gazes against my mate.

His eyes were dark with lust and the natural possessiveness, he placed his hand around my neck and held me in place, his lips brushing against mine as he said, "You will do no such thing."

And before I had a chance to reply, his lips crashed against mine. His tongue was roughly thrust into my mouth in a very erotic way, and the moan that escaped me was not unintentional.

My hands started exploring his body, as his did mine.

Soon, his skilled fingers were finding their way to my treasured spot, and I couldn't help but encourage him as I pushed myself into him even further.

Before I knew it, my pants were unbuttoned, and his fingers found his way to my most precious gift.

He pulled away from the kiss, and started kissing my marking spot, and once again a moan freely waltzed from my mouth.

When he was done nipping at my skin, he whispered in my ear possessively "you're MINE, to kiss, to please, to punish, and to dominate. No one else touches you, and if you ever mention being with someone else, I will hurt you myself. Now, say it, say that you're mine."

His fingers slowly rubbed the entrance of my essence, and just as they were about to slide in, something snapped in front of my face.

"Hellooo, earth to Adelina, girl!" Came Cilia's voice snapping me back to reality.
"What?" I asked, as I cleared my head of my daydream.
"The Alpha is waiting for you outside, better get going before he changes his mind about going with you." Cilia informed me, and I quickly shook my head hugging her as I said, "see you later."

As I made my way to the car, I couldn't help the embarrassed blush that settled upon my cheeks, I hope the Alpha didn't notice my discomfort, since I was literally daydreaming about him, but when he gave me a quizzical look, I already knew this was going to be one heck of a road trip.

Chapter 16- "A kind of Deja Vu"

Adelina's pnt. Of view

So far, the road trip has been uneventful, and by uneventful, I mean there has been absolutely no interaction between the Alpha and me.

However, deep within me has been a total turmoil.

My mind and heart couldn't seem to get over the fact that I wanted the asshole so much to the point where I was day dreaming and fantasizing about him on explicit levels, and my body couldn't get over it either.

It has been hours into the trip, yet I can't seem to calm down. My cheeks were flushed, and I was just praying that he didn't notice. My stomach was performing endless acrobatics, while my treasure seemed to tingle every time an erotic image of the Alpha and I flashed in my eyes.

I couldn't dare to look at him, I mean hello, I was hot and flustered because of him, however, I did have to talk to him, and as soon as I opened my mouth, I felt a sense of Deja vu wash over me.

But anyway, I cleared my throat and I said faintly "soo, here is the thing, Pete and Clarissa have a spare room for me, and I can crash at their place, but um, I contacted "La Belle Hotel" and they are checking a room out for you, free of charge, since your reputation seem to travel."

No response.

Why did this feel so familiar?

That was it, he said nothing, so I cleared my throat again and continued "so, when we reach the pack territory, you can drop me off by the bus stop, and Peter will be picking me up, and the wedding starts at 3 tomorrow, so I'll see you at the church, then after we have the reception and celebration, we can either rest and head back home tomorrow, or if you don't want to stay we can leave as soon as you want."

Still no response.

Yep, this most definitely was Deja Vu.

Since he decided today was his day to be mute, I decided on keeping quiet as well.

We kept the quiet stance until we crossed my old pack's territory, and we were quickly approaching the spot where Pete has agreed to pick me up, so I had nothing else to do but speak up.

Funny how my thoughts were exact to those in my day dream.

"Hey um, you can drop me off here, Peter will be picking me up shortly."

And once again, no response, so I tried to get his attention in a more effective way, I placed my hand softly on his leg, and I slightly squeezed as I said "Can you hear me? I just need- OH MY GOD!" I screamed out as he swerved off to the side of the road, in the blink of an eye, my seatbelt was ripped off, and I found myself beings captured by two strong arms that impaled me onto a very strong man in a straddling position.

Oh yeah, this definitely felt familiar.

He was staring daggers at me, and I stayed frozen, feeling as though I was in trouble.

"Why are you in such a hurry to leave mate?" He questioned darkly.

"Um, just excited to see my friends is all." I answered honestly yet very faintly.

"Oh I bet you are, I could smell your arousal the moment

you stepped foot in the car. Waiting to meet with a lover?" He demanded, his eye growing darker with each word, his grip becoming steel like.

"What? No! Of course not!" I quickly defended myself.

"Oh really? Then tell me, why are you aroused? Is it because of another? And don't think to lie to me." He demanded.

"Why do you care? What does it matter if it was because of another?" I asked, my temper suddenly rising, but that was quickly replaced by fear the moment his hard grip latched around my neck, and he pulled me close, as his lips brushed my ear and he threatened "I will kill him, and I will hurt you, if you think for one minute that I will allow you to fantasize about another. Now tell me," he asked darkly, his grip becoming a bit pushier "who is it?"

It was becoming hard to breathe, and stars started to float in my vision. My heart was pounding as though I was running a marathon, my nerves on over drive, and mind screaming for me to do anything to survive, so I succumbed.

"It's you! I have been fantasizing about you!" I managed to declare, and his grip slightly loosened, as his eyes became wide with shock.

But such expression only lasted a few moments before his grip once again became firm around my neck, and his eyes focused into slits as he said, "you're lying."

"No! No! I'm not." I quickly blurted out, tears forming in my eyes, my head shaking frantically.

"Then," he once again pulled me close, his lips softly touching mine as he continued "prove it."

And just like that he let go of my neck, and I greedily breathed in as much air as I could in one gulp, held it, and released, and then I continued this pattern, until my heart was once again beating at a normal pace, and my nerves became calm.

"Well?" Came Demitrey's impatient tone, "what are you waiting for?"

I nodded, and breathed in, my head was on the line, and all I had to do was prove that he was the one I was fantasizing about.

So I took a deep breath, opened my legs further, and lowered myself in the straddling position, until my core met with his already bulging member, then I reminisced on my fantasy, and started moving my hips in a back and forth motion, earning a hiss from the Alpha male that seemed hell bent on making my life miserable.

His gaze became hooded with lust, and my arousal just hiked up, and my actions became more vixen-like and less timid.

I found the courage to lean down and land a kiss on his jaw, then down to his neck on his marking spot, then I started going lower, my fingers working to open the buttons on his shirt.

I suddenly felt his hands grasping my hips, as he brought them harder onto his own, and each time our hips would collide, he thrusted his hips up, and I found myself throwing my head back in ecstasy, a moan voluntarily leaving my lips.

He starred kissing my neck, my marking spot, and then my jaw and finally my lips, then his thrusts became more powerful, and faster.

I found myself panting, as the build-up in my uterus started to form, my claws came out, and I found myself scratching and gripping into Demitrey' s skin, earning an aroused growl from him.

He starred nipping at my marking spot, and I came undone.

I was flushed against his body, my heart beating erratically, yet in rhythm with his own.

When the stars finally returned to space, and out of my vision, he hoisted me up, and back into my seat, then he smugly said in a bored tone "fair enough." Then he continued driving.

For the rest of the drive I kept to myself. I sat, leaning against the window scolding myself. This time it was no day dream, this time I didn't wake up, or snap back to reality, this time it was reality, and it was a kind of Deja Vu.

The rest of the drive was quiet, I was numb, and at the moment I didn't care for anything, I just wanted to be in bed and cry. So, when he passed the bus stop, where Peter's car was waiting, and when he pulled up to the hotel, all I could do was stay silent, and cry inside, but on the outside, I was boiling in anger, and it was all directed at one individual, and I vowed to make him pay.

Chapter 17- "Happy ending"

Adelina's pnt. Of view

I was angry at myself, I was angry at him. I should've never acted the way did, I shouldn't have anything to prove to him, or anyone for that matter.

How dare he make act this way?

I huffed and puffed all the way to the room that Demitrey was supposed to sleep in alone. I received weird stares from passersby's and in return I growled menacingly, and they would quickly look away.

When we finally made it in the room, as soon as he closed the door, I caught him off guard by slapping him on the cheek as I demanded angrily "how dare you make me act this way? I shouldn't have to prove anything to you! You're my mate! How dare you accuse me of lusting after another?!"

He slowly turned his head, his eyes dark as he stared at me, but then he smiled.

He just smiled, and I would be lying if I said that my anger didn't melt a little.

Key word: a little.

"What are you smiling at?" I asked, anger still evident in my voice.

"You're cute when you're angry." He simply stated as he pinched the tip of my nose, and I quickly slapped his hand away, my anger suddenly rising.

Then he chuckled shaking his head and walked passed me.

And I became delirious.

I turned and jumped on his back, my short self clinging onto him as I started throwing punches at him, but all received was laughter.

He was laughing at me!

I wrapped my arms around his neck, my legs around his waist as I tried to choke him while clinging to his back.

"I hate you! I hate you!" I said trying my very best to choke him.

And when I thought I was winning because he staggered back, the last thing I remember was him latching his strong hands around my arms then flipped me over his shoulder and onto the bed as he said, "play time is over."

When I could shake the dizziness off, I found myself being held captive by my mate, as he pinned both of my hands on each side of my head and laid in between my legs.

You know for some reason I just keep finding myself ending up in these positions, I just didn't get it.

Anyway, I looked up to find his eyes dark with lust, yet there was a bit of amusement dancing there too, but it was faint.

He smirked down at my flushed cheeks, then he nuzzled my neck as he said, "never mind that, you're cute, and hot when you're angry, for a sec there it makes me want to take you." And his words sent me struggling.

I tried to wiggle free, kick my legs, free my arms, but all I was doing was making the situation worse, because he pressed himself down on me, his eyes becoming dark as night, and I finally froze.

I didn't breathe, I didn't blink, I didn't move.

He stared, focused on every detail on my face, and all I could do was stare back.

He leaned down, feathering his lips against mine as he whispered "you, are something else. A little fireball, yet sensitive, a little hot head yet very fragile. You're addictive you know." He chuckled, then he once again teased me with his tempting lips, and I couldn't help but open in invitation.

My nerves were going haywire, my wolf purring sensually at the feeling of her close mate. My heart once again began to harmonize with his own as my eyes stared deeply within his.

He leaned down, and his lips connected with mine so softly, unlike the rough way he has used to kiss me.

I was caught off guard.

My heart started palpitating, and my mind started freaking out.

His lips danced softly against mine, non-invading, and I melted under him.

I shyly started kissing him back, earning a soft growl from him, and I would be lying if I said I wasn't affected.

He slowly freed my hands, and I latched my arms around his neck pulling him closer. His hands started exploring my body, his fingers leaving a trail of fire bursting on my skin, and for once I truly welcomed it, while red flags were going up in my mind.

I shouldn't be this easy, or weak, I shouldn't allow myself to be so vulnerable.

But then he left my lips, to nuzzle my marking spot as he whispered, "my mate." And I lost it, my walls just burst, and before I knew it, I found myself opening up to him, submitting to him, but before it got further than just kissing, there was a knock on the door, and he groaned aggravated, as if he wasn't finished with me yet, and when he stared at me with promise in his eyes, I knew, he was nowhere near done with me.

Nevertheless, he got off me, and headed for the door, while I stood up and straightened out the sheets.

And when he opened the door my back went stiff as a very familiar voice that I loathed sounded at the door "hi baby!" Screeched Serena.
"Babe? What are you doing here?" He asked, his voiced slightly hushed.
"I missed you babe, and I didn't want to stay away from you for a whole three days. I wouldn't survive." She said overdramatically as she invited herself in, but then froze when she saw me.

"You? The fuck are you doing here?" She asked addressing me, but then she turned around and faced the player himself "what is she doing here?!" She asked anger evident in her voice.

"I should be asking you the same question." I spoke up, my anger taking over, while my wolf growled menacingly in the back of my mind.

She faced me surprised, in fact perplexed, but then she stalked her way towards me, her fist balled, and I stood my ground, waiting to attack.

"What did you say?" She asked coming to stand in my face.

I lifted my head and met her gaze Head on as I said "you heard m-" ***SLAP***

I felt my face turn at the impact.

Did she just hit me?

I breathed through my nose, and out through my mouth, and when I turned to face her, she didn't expect it when my fist connected with her jaw, sending her staggering backwards.

She turned her head spitting out blood as she attacked while saying "Why you little bitch!" But I was quicker.

I grabbed her arms while tripping her leg landing her on the floor on her back.

I didn't hold back as my fist connected continuously with her face. She screamed out, as she tried to claw at my face, so I took her off the floor by the shoulder just to slam her back against the floor while straddling her.

All I saw was red, and I was going to murder that bitch.

She managed to land a blow to my temple, causing me to lose focus a few seconds, but it wasn't enough, I snapped back to reality quick, my punches becoming more furious.

She seemed ready to pass out, but then just as I was about to knock her out, I found my body being wrenched off her by none other than Demitrey.

He hauled me off her and threw me against the wall as he held my throat in a threatening grip.

His eyes dark, deadly, and dangerous.

It started becoming very hard to breathe, and his nostrils were flaring.

He leaned in as he said "how dare you put your hands on Serena? I will hurt you pup, keep trying my patience!"

WHAT?!

I tried to speak, but I could hardly breathe, and I found myself clawing at his hands, just to ease his grip.

In my peripheral vision, I noticed Serena stand ever so wobbly, and she made her way to us.

When she reached us, she wrapped her arms around Demitrey, and smiled a very bloody and evil smile as she told me "get this you little hoe, he will always choose me over you."

At that exact moment something flashed in his eyes, and his grip loosened, until he finally let me go.

He dropped me to the floor, then wrapped his arms around Serena.

He looked down at me then turned as he made his way to the bed with Serena.

He held her in his arms as she snuggled against him, both totally dismissing me, and with the speck of pride and dignity I had left, I held my head up high, took my suitcase by the door, and walked out, but as soon as I was a few feet away from the closed door of their room, I shattered.

My tears blinded me, my hurt suffocating me.

My chest heaved as I tried to breathe but the pain was too much.

My wolf howled in pain, and I crawled to the nearest wall, placed myself in a ball against the corner, and cried my eyes out.

I wasn't sure for how long I stayed there, but the agony was deafening, leaving a splitting headache for an aftermath.

When I finally had enough strength, I dialed Peter's phone, and when he heard my voice, he already knew that something was wrong, and soon enough, he came and picked me up.

When I saw him I didn't even have the strength to get up, and when he wrapped his arms around me, I thought there weren't any tears left, but I was sadly mistaken, because it was a though a da broke through, and tears flooded my eyes, as if they were trying to escape my numb and miserable being.

I was stupid. I opened up, I let my walls down, and that was taken for granted, trampled upon, dismissed and discarded like trash.

But no more.

Truly no more.

I was tired, I was done, and I would leave, if it's the last thing I did.

I managed to get up, and Peter took my suitcase. As I made my way by the door, my super hearing picked up the sounds of pleasure erupting from Serena, and the last piece of my heart just dissolved.

I was done with Alpha Demitrey, and he could rot in the depths of hell for all I cared.

I was done Alpha, you proved your point, I wasn't wanted, nor was I needed, and its okay, I'll leave, I'll get out of your hair, you won't have to worry about me anymore, I was moving on, I was no longer your obligation.

I would get Peter and Clarissa to safety right after the wedding, then I would escape.

Leave to never come back.

Congratulations Alpha, you've had your happy ending, and now, it was time to make a new beginning for myself, one where a mate was no longer in the picture, a mate was no longer my priority.

From this day on, Adelina Veraso was moving on, and hell would have to freeze over before I would think to let myself be fooled by that jerk of an Alpha, or any other male for that matter.

Chapter 18- "Marked"

Adelina's pnt. Of view

When Peter and I reached their house it was about time, I was so ready to see my best friends, and spend time with them. I wanted to forget, and just live my life.

As soon as I stepped out the car, I was slammed against the car while Clarissa suffocated me in tight hug.

"Hey. Missed you too hun." I croaked out, in order to express the fact that her hug was secretly murderous.
"I missed you so much! You idiot! You bitch! You never called!" She suddenly pulled away shaking me, making my eyes play ping pong in their sockets.
"Her "mate" didn't allow her such freedom." Explained Peter with disgust.

Clarissa's lips formed and "oh" as she took my hand and led me inside.

Being used to them, it was easy for me to get settled, and after we've ate, laughed, joked around, it was time to get serious.

I explained to them everything that has transpired between Demitrey and me, up to this day.

I explained that I was moving on, and that my leaving would most likely start a war, and I explained that I wanted them away from danger.

At first, they were slightly reluctant to leave, but then they thought about our pack, my dead beat of a father, and the evil that spurs in the hearts of the pack members, and they were instantly on board.

We planned to escape while everyone thought they were going on their honeymoon. When we reached the airport where we would separate, we would change our phones for new ones, and new numbers, and we would go in opposite directions.

Wherever we land, we would manage to keep in touch, but no one else would be aware of our whereabouts.

Once everything was settled, we called it a night.

I laid in bed that night, finally allowing myself to revise the day, even if it meant going over every single detail.

Thinking about my situation I realized that I had a weak moment, but that's okay, because what doesn't kill you makes you stronger.

I thought about my mate, how he could be hot and cold all at the same time. How he could play you for a fool, hurt you, and yet you still find would yourself falling for his tricks.

He was sculpted physically in the most perfect way, such an alluring image you can't help but be drawn in.

He was cold, calculating, dominating, and the mere thought of him demanded attention. His presence could silence an entire room, and he knew it.

I even reminisced on one of the days where I begged him to reject me.

Flashback

Adelina was standing in his office, when she no longer could handle it, she ran over to Demitrey and got on her knees.

"Please Demitrey, reject me, let me go and you can be with Serena forever, I can tell that you want her, and you

hate me, so just do us both a favor." She begged tears streaming down her face.

So she wanted to leave me? I bet it's for another man. Well over my fucking dead body, thought Demitrey.

"I don't think so Adelina, you're not leaving, and just for speaking such words, YOU WILL BE PUNISHED!"

End of flashback

That day was the worse day of my life. He locked me in the room and starved me for hours, then when he came back, he was as cold as ever.

That was the first draw that influenced me into plotting an escape.

He was so intense, yet intimate. He could make you feel loved, wanted, needed even, and just so he could crush you like dirt under his feet.

I let my mind drifted over to what could happen after he realized that I would no longer be coming back.

There would most definitely be a war, and I know for a fact that my "dad's" pack wouldn't survive, hence the reason why I would make sure Peter and Clarissa were safe.

They are the only ones that truly has shown care and love for me, and I wouldn't be cruel and leave them in the line of fire.

Finally, I thought about what I was going to do after my escape, where would I go? I'll probably check out Europe, most likely Italy, or France I've always wanted to visit there.

Yep, France it is, then I could move around to Italy, probably even check out Greece.

With a smile on my face I drifted off to sleep, instantly dreaming about dancing baguettes and pizza.

The next day arrived quicker than I expected, and Clarissa was losing her mind.

The wedding party only included the fiancées, the maid of honor, yours truly, the best man, which happened to be Clarissa's cousin, and four of our high school classmates.

Came preparation time everything was chaotic. While the bride was being hunted down by the wedding planner, I took the liberty to pack our bags secretly, for no one was to be aware of our plans.

Once everything was prepared, our getaway car has been disguised as that of the newlyweds' car, it was time for the wedding.

Once we reached the chapel it was there I met Clarissa's cousin, and boy was he Gorgeous.

Dark brown hair, unique turquoise eyes that had a hint of green, tall and well-built posture, and most charming as ever. Yet he carried this powerful aura and there was a slight tone of danger that followed him that kind of rose red flags, but I figured that's just the way he carried himself.

"Adelina this is Valinick Monteroso, he is my cousin, and he will be your escort for the evening," started Peter, as he introduced me to his cousin, "Valinick, this is Adelina Veraso, she is the lovely lady I spoke to you about, and my best friend." Concluded Peter.
"Pleasure to meet you." I spoke up, a genuine smile on my rosy cheeks.
"Oh gorgeous," he said with a thick Italian accent, "the pleasure is all mine." He finished, as he leaned down,

landing quite a charming kiss on the top of my hand, causing my blush to deepen.

He kept me entertained until the wedding began and I even managed to come up with a nickname for him, Val.

When we made our way down the aisle, my elbow locked with his own, I felt two daggers hunting down my back, and when I reached the altar and took my spot, the twin daggers belonged to none other than my mate himself, glaring in anger.

Usually, at a time like this, I would be worried that I did something wrong, but this time there was nothing. I was immune to him, well I tried my very best to be immune to him.

I stared him down, then with a smirk I looked away, this was going to be a fun day.

The wedding ceremony was beautiful, when Peter was saying his vows, I could tell he was trying his best to not cry, and Clarissa looked gorgeous in her dress.

Everyone was happy, even my "family" was here, but I avoided them like the plague, I could care less for them.

We had a few minutes before the wedding party would head to the reception hall, and while the bride and groom were receiving congratulations, I made my way to the bathroom to freshen up.

Except I never made it there.

On my way to the bathroom, I was suddenly snatched off my course, and stuffed into a closet, with none other than my mate holding me captive.

He looked murderous as his eyes glared at me, but it was no match to my icy gaze.

"May I help you?" I asked my voice clipped.

"Yes, you may. Can you tell me what the heck was that you pulled back there? Leaving the hotel? Just for me to find you in the arms of another man the next day?!" He demanded.

"No," I simply answered, then I added "fuck off." I went to open the door, just for my body to be wrenched away, and for my back to make contact with a firm chest.

He was breathing hard and deeply, his strong arm latching around my waist, keeping me pinned to him.

I wanted to struggle, but I wasn't going to, there was no more fight left in me for him. I was done.

He kissed my marking spot, and it took all my willpower not to succumb to his seduction.

When he realized that I wasn't going to react, he sighed then said in my ear "you're leaving me aren't you?" And my heart stopped.

The pain was evident in his voice, and my wolf howled, knowing that her mate was emotionally hurt.

She wanted to comfort him, be there for him, but no, Adelina wasn't going to allow it.

I was tired, battered and bruised, and I wouldn't stick around for such degrading and cruel treatment.

I was worth way more, so much more, and I knew my self-worth.

So, with a proud and relieved sigh of my own I spoke up with a smile and said "yes, yes I am." And just like that, I opened the door, and pulled myself from his grip, because I knew if I stayed there for another second, my plan would've been forgotten, I would've stayed with him, and there would be no going back.

But again, I was pulled back, as he pushed me against the door, closing it.

He stared at me, while in his eyes I could see hurt, pain, regret, anger and possessiveness.

The tingles from his touch caused by the mate bond was nagging at the wall I built around my heart, and it was becoming irritating.

He leaned down, once again nuzzling my marking spot, and I felt my eyes close while I absentmindedly started to enjoy his touch.

One more time.

No, one last time.

I'll allow him to hold me, just one more time.

I felt his lips brush over the spot, and a moan got clogged in my throat, and then I felt it.

The scorching pain caused by his canine teeth puncturing my skin.

I was about to scream out when he placed his large hand over my mouth muffling the noise.

I struggled against him, but he wouldn't relent. Instead his teeth sunk deeper into my skin, and tears pricked my eyes.

No, not like this.

It hurt, my heart hurt, but then, as soon as the marking was complete, I was taken over by pleasure.

I felt good, I wanted to get even closer to him, and I wanted him on a much deeper level.

He finally retracted his teeth, and kissed his mark, then he kissed me, it started out soft and sweet, but when I didn't respond, it turned rough, branding.

He kissed my salty tears, he kissed my shattered heart, he kissed my hurt pride, but most definitely he kissed a defeated Adelina.

When he finally pulled away, he smirked and said, "have fun on your escape, but just know, you will always belong to me."

And just like that he left. He moved me over, straightened his jacket, opened the door, and left.

Out of the closet, out of my life, and out of my heart.

Chapter 19- "Motives & Reasons"

Demitrey' s pnt. Of view

What did I do?

What did I do?!

I lost control! I marked her!

I couldn't even blame it on my wolf! This was all my doing.

I hurt her, branded her, forced her into my claim, and now she must really hate me, and I couldn't blame her.

The mere thought of her leaving me made me feel paralyzed, I didn't, no couldn't get too close, but I didn't want her so far away either.

And now... she was leaving me for good.

My mind flooded with images of her, my beauty, my sweet, my hothead, my vixen, my mate.

I reminisced on and on about the moment she walked into my life, while I drowned my sorrows in vodka and gin, and anything else strong enough to numb the pain I was feeling.

I thought about the sweet smiles that would pop onto her lips as she slept.

Yes, creepy, I know... but I couldn't help but sneak into her room just to watch her.

I would want to hold her, but I restrained myself, as much as I could.

Until I was hit by the wave of having a mate in my life, the thought of having one repulsed me.

I used to think that mates made you weak, they were easy targets, and easy preys.

They could manipulate you, play you for a fool, control you until they had you crawling your knees, and I promised myself I would never let any mate degrade me in such a way.

The funniest of all, they declared that it was all because of love.

Love...

Such an abused word.

So many fools, lost their lives for love... not me, not this time.

I grew up hating and repulsing the idea of a mate, and my father played a major role in making sure that I would never stray from the idea that mates were deadly... But then came along Adelina.

CHRIST! She kills me.

I mean I became her slave.

She demanded my attention every second of the day, when I was training, working out, working, eating, or in the shower it didn't matter... She demanded it every single time.

And when I was sleeping? Oh, even worse! She was the star of my every fantasy.

I couldn't escape her, nor did I want to, until I realized how easily she made me lose control, just for it to be handed back to me.

She drove me crazy, and it was addictive.

Once second, I loathed her for making me feel all, everything, every emotion, anger, weakness, jealousy, pain, and the next I loved her for making feel all, everything, every emotion, pain, anger, jealousy, and weakness.

She made me feel alive, human, instead of just the known ruthless monster, with a reputation that seems to travel, as she so put it.

She is a tease, sometimes pure at heart, and sometimes guilty as charged.

I can read her like a book, I know when she is lying, I know when she gets an idea, I know when she is aroused, and her emotions are so raw, it's a thrill.

I love teasing her because it's so easy to tell what she was feeling, it was alien, unique, and absolutely beautiful. Not only that, but her emotions are like oxygen to my cold soul, they make me feel warm and tingly, makes my heart leap.

She is my kryptonite.

I love the way she turns me on just by a simple action, and I like how she is just clueless of the way makes me feel.

But then again, I don't really play fair in that department. I hold this mask on my face, and a wall around my heart.

I have seen some of the greatest Alphas fall because they let someone in, and I didn't build a reputation just so a mate could come and destroy it all.

There are were when I didn't want her around. She is lethal, a ticking time bomb, and I wouldn't take part in setting her off.

Yet... I can't seem to let her go. Just the mere thought of her with someone else is just, I don't even know what word I can use to describe the feeling.

I would happily murder anyone who dares to look at her with lust in their eyes.

And that fucker Peter is lucky she actually sees him as a brother, because he sure as heck sees her for more.

And the cousin, who escorted her is even worse, and it's sad, my mate so pure, so innocent, so oblivious and immune to their lust.

She never noticed the glances of pure lust that Peter sent her way on his own wedding day. She was so caught up in the whole charade that she missed how he looked at her when he so called "declared his love."

My wolf was angry because it was my fault that she left the hotel in the first place.

I was moody, jealous, angry, foolish, and selfish, an asshole, and I was stupid, and so I hurt her by marking her.

Tying her to me till death do us part.

She can never love someone over me, she will never feel the same towards another as she does me, and although my actions were wrong, I am damn proud.

I'm happy because Adelina Veraso is mine, all mine, it was sealed forever, and nothing, and I mean nothing would change that.

She is my girl, to love, encourage, correct, and she was my forever, whether she liked it or not.

I claimed her as my own, and I meant that.

So, go ahead and call me an asshole for playing with her, loving and hating her simultaneously, and making her mine.

Hate me for marking her, but it won't change a thing, that girl is mine, and I loved it.

Chapter 20- "Dance of confusion"

Adelina's pnt. Of view

Throughout the entire limousine ride to the reception hall, I was as quiet as a mouse, there was no laughter in my heart, no smile in my eyes, and no light on my face.

Val seemed to notice my change in demeanor, and although he didn't question it, he tried his best to turn my frown upside down. Plus, when I noticed that I was starting to draw attention from the newlyweds, the actress in me came out, and I plastered a practiced smile on my face, which turned out to be convincing.

When we reached the hall, my smile became genuine. Why? Well there was an amazing dance floor just calling my name.

I mean yes, there was food, and drinks, but the ballroom dance floor was the only thing that caught my attention.

The night became light soon enough, everyone was laughing, having a good time, and my cloud of rain was lifted for a bit, until of course the devil himself walked in with his slutty demon trailing in after him.

I tried my best to avoid them though, if they went left, I went right, if they were going up, and I'd make sure that I was down, yet somehow, his eyes just kept on finding me. I know it was his eyes because now I'm officially tied to the bastard, so I could feel him from a mile away, but I wouldn't let that fact dampen my mood, at least not yet.

Plus, Val was a huge help when it came to keeping me company.

He had me laughing my butt off, not to mention that he was a flirt.

When he noticed that throughout the night my eyes kept on sending love notes to the dance floor, he offered to dance.

He took a very dramatic yet sophisticated bow as he held out his hand silently asking me for a dance, and when I accepted, his firm grip clasped around my hand and he directed me to the dance floor, just as the band started playing an Argentine tango.

Now, mind you, I was already a big fan of ballroom dancing, so imagine having an Alpha male lead you to the dance floor, and one of the most passionate dances of all time start to play.

So yeah, you can understand, I was on cloud 9, my current situation completely forgotten.

We took our position center stage, and the moment he clasped his arm around my waist, hoisting me into colliding with his chest, with eyes burning in dark emotion, I knew this night was going to be a very memorable night.

And boy did I wish I was wrong about that.

We started with some easy movements, letting the music get in sync with our bodies, then, when the time was right, the music erupted into staccato perfection, and the games began.

It was erotic, the way his hands caressed my curves. There was a seductive glint in his eyes that hypnotized my brain into doing exactly what he wanted. He guided me but didn't demand that I followed, but instead he invited me to dance, and he handled me like a true gentleman.

He composed and performed my body as though he had decades to practice.

His touch was firm, yet his strokes of guidance, his fluid movements were that of an artist creating a perfect masterpiece of heated passion.

My limbs moved in harmony, my hips swung bravely and fiercely, as though I was unstoppable.

My heart danced to the rhythm of my feet, my body floating in his arms.

We glided across the dance floor, the other guests forming a crowd of admiration at every corner.

Yet no matter his charm, his chivalry, I couldn't help but feel the cold stare state of my mate, my Alpha.

The man that held me was truly a prince, an artist, a gentleman, but the 15 seconds of fame in his arms couldn't compare to excitement I felt the moment I made eye contact across the room with my mate, while in the arms of another man.

While our staring contest only lasted 5 seconds, there, in that exact moment I saw something in his eyes.

Well there were multiple things, there was anger, main obvious, then there was jealousy, and there was something else burning there, hot and mixed with rage, but I couldn't pin point it, and then there came something clear.

A promise.

A promise for what? That I do not know, but it was there.

And before I could dwell more on the subject, the dance ended with a professional bow, and the crowd erupted in cheers, breaking our connection.

Val once again pulled me close and landed a kiss on my cheeks, surprising me, but that was quickly washed away because I could've sworn I heard a growl travel from my mate, but it most likely was my imagination.

He had no right to get jealous... He's the jerk who has mistreated me, took advantage of me, teased me, hurt me, made me cry, marked me on purpose for his sole arrogance, and now because of him I would never feel the same intensity for another as I do for him.

I would have to live my life getting over him because I would never love another as I would love him.

I made my way to a small secluded hall just so that I could have some quiet time. My staring contest with Demitrey left me speechless and flabbergasted, why must he have such an effect on me?!

"You never know, maybe he had a reason for his actions, have you ever stopped to think of his reasons? I mean come on Adelina, no mate is that cruel, and something has to be forcing his hand." Came Aden's voice in the back of my head, and I couldn't help my scoff. **"Really Aden, you are still trying to protect this guy, have you seen what he's done? He marked us, on purpose might I add!"** I fired back, my wolf was ridiculous.

Before she could reply, a hand was suddenly placed on my shoulder, startling me, but when I realized that it was Peter, I quickly calmed down.

He looked happy as his eyes scanned my face, which made me slightly uncomfortable, but then his eyes became dark when it landed on my marking spot.

"Aden? What is that?" He asked carefully.

"What is what?" I asked playing dumb, this wasn't going to end well.

"Don't play dumb with me, what is that on your neck?" He asked, his voice becoming hard, his eyes darkening, as I started feeling uncomfortable.

"Mosquito bites." I quickly answered, trying to back away from him by shuffling my feet, that way it wasn't so obvious that he was freaking me out.

"Oh really? A mosquito bite that looks quite identical to that of a mate's mark." He said taking a threatening step towards me. Yeah this was most definitely freaking me out, and the fact that we were in a secluded area didn't comfort me either.

"It's a mosquito bite! Jeez Peter, did you think that I would let that asshole of a mate near me after what he's done, better yet mark me?! And to think that you actually thought better of me." I said anger actually taking me over, I mean yeah I was lying to my best friend, who was currently freaking me out, but then again I finally caught a glimpse of what he actually thought of me.

"I do think better of you baby, it's just I don't like the image of you with him at all, it's infuriating, knowing what he has done to you. Plus, you don't belong to him, YOU BELONG TO M- eh hem, sorry, something caught in my throat." He said as he faked cough again and walked away, while my eyes stared wide as saucers.

What was he going to say? That I belonged to him? Didn't he just get married? If anything, wasn't he in love with his mate? Even worse, did he just call me baby?!

Oh my, this just confused everything.

My head felt hot, I felt nauseous, the room was spinning. I was finding it hard to breathe, and the dress felt like a giant hand suffocating me. I had to get out of here.

Run. I had to run.

Too many questions, too many voices. I had to escape, that was the only thing left to do.

So, I bolted out the reception hall and into the woods, I ran and ran until my lungs in human form started burning, so I leaped into the air, transforming into my white furred wolf.

The thing I loved most about my wolf was that if I stood in the light of a noon sun, the tips of my fur would reflect an aura of light neon pink, but if standing in the light of a rising or setting sun, the aura became golden like.

I landed on the ground with a thud as my legs started pumping faster.

I had no idea where I was going, but I just needed to run, get away.

My life became upside down.

I could've sworn Peter was going to say that I was his.

It made no sense, he was acting strange towards me, he hated my mate, or the idea of me having a mate, and now that I think about it, whenever Clarissa wasn't around, he was always too close for comfort.

I suddenly had the urge to empty my stomach, and before I could make it any further, I threw up all the consumed contents from my stomach. My wolf yelped as ragged coughs pushed the foul-tasting bile up my throat and out of my mouth.

Aden was panting until she could control her breathing, the we took off in a bolt.

I wasn't sure where my destination was, but all I knew is that I needed to get out of America.

They say don't run from your problems, but as of right now, I wasn't even sure what or who my problem was.

Oh Adelina, why do you always find yourself in these situations?

Chapter 21- "Mystery Letters"

Unknown's pnt. Of view

I stared from the shadows as the girl ran out the hall, leaving a few startled guests behind, including her mate, which was my main target.

He looked ready to run after her, but then hesitated.

Smart guy.

I made eye contact with my partner who winked with an evil smile.

We got him.

He was trying his best to not show that he was into his mate, but he was failing badly.

All that was needed for the plan to be completed would be verbal proof.

I needed him to say that Adelina was his mate.

I already knew that she was, and so does my partner, but no one else knows.

My blood was raging in my veins with need for revenge, a revenge that could either land me dead, or the ruler of America's most powerful pack. Alpha Demitrey's pack.

Never undefeated but carried death wherever they went.

I would never win a duel against Demitrey alone, but if he became weak because of his mate, she would be the key to my success, and a good sex toy if anything.

I just needed to push Demitrey just a bit more.

My plan has been going quite well, while the big bad Alpha was acting as though he didn't want a mate, he was pushing her away and right into my trap, and the moment he realized that he would lose her by my bare hands, he would have to succumb into picking either his pack or his mate, but either way he would lose both.

I had to be patient though. Now I had to track her down and keep the Alpha on edge.

I disappeared in the shadows as I made my way up to the secret office that dwelled in the walls of the reception hall, I took my time to write out my thoughts, and seal them in my signature envelope.

Once that task was completed, I headed back to the hall, making sure that my whereabouts were not perceived to be mysterious.

Once I blended back into my corner, I called over one of the waiters, and handed him the envelope.

I explained it was to be delivered precisely to Demitrey, no one else.

And as the waiter headed towards his target, I melted into the shadows, changed courses, and finally blended back in the crowd, all the while keeping an eye on the man I loathed and envied most.

Demitrey' s pnt. Of view

I was standing by a window, looking out over the way Adelina ran off to, hoping she would come back, but to no avail.

Serena was busy chatting away with some of the guests, which gave me plenty of time to go look for her, but I wouldn't risk it.

The enemy was here.

I felt it, or rather him.

And my premonition was proven right soon enough, because minutes later, a letter was delivered to me.

And no, it wasn't just any letter, it was a unique letter, in an anonymous beige envelope, quite similar to the one I received the day I found out that Adelina was my mate.

A letter familiar to the ones that kept on coming after Adelina became part of my life.

The letters that held the key to everything.

With no other choice, I opened it, already anticipating what it was going to say.

Dear Alpha,

Oh my, it seems as though there is trouble in paradise. Your mate has disappeared. Ran away it seems. Aren't you curious? Shouldn't you be looking for her? But then again no, the big bad Alpha does not care for a mate, oh no no no, tsk, tsk, tsk, the Alpha can't have anyone finding out that he has a weak spot for his mate. That would make the lethal Alpha weak, and maybe vulnerable. Well Alpha, if you don't care to look for her, I will do the honors, and once I do, I will take her, rape her, and torture her until she becomes my willing slave. Ah, imagine, the deadly Alpha's mate is my willing slave and whore. The thought itself sends chills of pleasure and wicked happiness down my spine. Oh, how I love this game, and you are trying so hard to show that you're not affected by her, it's actually cute. Well Alpha, until I feel like tormenting you again, ta ta for now.

Sincerely yours, and with love and honor, your worst and biggest enemy.

I wanted to crush the paper in my hands, no, in fact I wanted to crush and murder that bastard by my bare hands, but no, I wouldn't react now, not when the enemy was so close.

I plastered on my straight face mask as my eyes scanned the crowd. I wasn't going to show emotion, but God! My insides were raging with emotion.

I did care for my mate, and my wolf was restless not knowing her whereabouts.

I wanted her in my arms, I wanted to kiss her, hold her, but no, the danger was too close.

If I showed that I cared, she would die.

If I showered her with love and compassion the way I wanted to, she would die.

I couldn't, no, wouldn't place her in such danger.

Not only so, once she died, I would no longer be the strong leader, my pack that sheltered widowed women, and orphaned children would be taken over by evil rogues, and so many innocents would lose their lives.

My warriors in the pack and I, we carry a reputation, but this reputation holds a proud banner. We take over packs that are being misguided and mistreated by their Alpha's. We give those oppressed a new homes and hope.

Yes, we are ruthless, our strategies are cruel, but only towards evil Alpha's and rogues, no women or children were ever hurt during our attacks, and my men honor me, so yes, I have something worth fighting for.

And my mate, she is now my main priority, and she was being threatened, that did not sit well with me.

I admit, yes at first I didn't want a mate, I can't lie, the life of a bachelor is a blast, but once I met her, I was ready to make her mine, until that letter arrived.

The first one arrived the day her dad announced the marriage to seal the deal.

Initially, I thought it was a prank, but once the second letter arrived with threats of my mate being hurt, and a picture to show that both her and I were being watched, I had to be cautious, hence the arrogance and the attitude of a jerk.

I thought If I acted careless, the threats would stop, but hey I had to admit I made up excuses to see her, I acted mean and attacked her just so that I would have an excuse to kiss her, all the while letting her think that I was ruthless.

But no, this time it has gone too far.

As soon as I got home, I would seek this asshole out, end his life once and for all, then, then I would shout it out to the world that Adelina Veraso was my mate, my love, my heart, my everything.

Chapter 22- "Explanations, and Ambush"

Demitrey' s pnt. of View

When the wedding ceremony finally concluded with the bride in tears for her missing best friend, I couldn't be happier. Not because she was worried about her best friend because trust me, I was worried too, but because it means I was going home sooner in order to start tracking down my number one enemy.

I didn't even think to wait for Serena because since she found her way here on her own, she could find her way back home on her own. On my way there however, I sent a message to my beta Kade telling him to wait for me in my office because we had a prey to hunt.

While on the road, I found myself reminiscing about my mate. I thought about how easy it was to tease her, how her heartbeat would change the second I got close to her. I remembered her soft seductive lips on mine, how they always had my heart running a thousand miles per hour. I thought about her eyes, and how they could take my breath away, and I also thought about the situation she found herself in now, all because of me. I admit, I shouldn't have marked her, but I just couldn't handle the idea of her with another man, especially when she seems relieved that she was finally leaving me.

But then again, who could blame her, I have been nothing but an asshole, and no excuse I can make could ever change that, no reason I have could ever make up for my mistreating her, but once I've taken care of whoever is trying to get rid of her, I will explain the reasons for my action, I'll ask for her forgiveness, but I will not be selfish enough to ask her to be with me, she will be free to choose on her own will what she wants to do, and if she rejects me,

I'll accept, because I've come to the realization that I don't deserve her.

I reached the pack territory faster than I expected, and I didn't waste any time as I dashed up to my office where I found Kade patiently waiting for me with two glasses of scotch. I smiled taking it from him as I shook my head, this is why Kade was my best friend and beta, because he knew me like the back of his hand, as I knew him.

After sending my scotch back in one gulp, we got down to business.

We sat down on one of the couches as I explained to him what was taking place and how it all started. I explained what took place on the trip, I told him about the letters, and how my mate ran away.

By the time my explanation was over, all that Kade could muster was a "wow," but then he seem to think about something then he said out of the blue " Okay, so I understand that you being a jerk was to keep up an image, but it still doesn't explain why you continued having sex with Serena, because I know for a fact, the moment I found out Cilia was my mate, I couldn't even think of another woman in that way. "

"well," I began "I started to resent Serena, and I avoided touching her for a bit, but then she caught on, she started saying that it was because of Adelina that I stopped being attracted to her. I initially brushed her off, I could care less what she thought, but then another letter arrived." At my words, I stood up to retrieve one of the many letters sent to me by this anonymous, from my desk.

It read:

Dear Alpha,

I'm surprised, you're no longer attracted to your mistress. My, my, my, that's not a good sign. I wonder, does it have to do with a certain girl that arrived at your pack few weeks ago? Because if it does, you know what that means, I have you where I wanted you. Well, whatever your reasons, you just proven to me that the ruthless Alpha has a weak link.

Sincerely Yours, and with love and honor, your worst and biggest enemy.

P.S. If you're wondering how I found out about your intimate relationship status, don't bother wasting your time tracking anyone down, I have well-hidden eyes in your pack.

"So that night, I found Serena going up the stairs, and I started making out with her, the same night we had to go get our mates from the club. Since then, I made excuses to avoid her without raising suspicion about the fact that I lost all interest in Serena, and only had eyes for my mate. But in total honesty, the last time I actually slept with Serena was the night before I met Adelina and found out that she was my mate." I explained.

"Wait, really? Because everyone still thought that you guys fooled around." admitted Kade.

"Oh, I know, a simple hug to Serena means that you're her fuck buddy, and since she can't keep her mouth shut, all I had to do was play my cards right. Cuddling, hugging, shunning other females over her, everything worked out as planned, especially when I received this letter." I said, then went to retrieve another letter that read:

Dear Alpha,

So maybe I was wrong, maybe you aren't falling for Adelina after all, no matter, I will still find your weak link if it is the last thing I do, and once I do, sweet victory will be mine.

Sincerely yours, and with love and honor, your worst and biggest enemy.

"Okay, I see, but one more thing, why didn't you try to fish out who the inside man was?" Kade asked.

"Don't you mean woman?" I asked with a smirk.

"Huh?" Said a confused Kade.

I called him over to my desk, as I started to skim through more of the letters, our backs to the door.

Big. Mistake.

"See at first I did want to go all S.W.A.T. team on this, but then I found a clue in one of the letters. See I know Serena, she happily brags about who she has been with, but one thing she would rather die than mention is when she has been rejected by someone, so the only way for this person to figure out that she and I were having problems was if she told him herself. But I must admit, I wasn't fully convinced about the idea, until she showed up at the hotel room. I never told her where I was going, nor did I leave any clues." I explained.

"You're right, you didn't leave any clues." Came a voice from the door, and before I could turn around and attack, I felt something pierce my neck as I fell to the floor disoriented, while a paralyzing pain shot throughout my entire body. Next to me, Kade landed in a thud, and soon my vision became blurry. Before darkness could really consume me, I saw a shadow of a figure, but before I could make out who it was, I was gone.

Chapter 23- "Secret plan" - Part 1

6 months later

Unknown's pnt. Of view

My secret plan was finally complete.

When we managed to paralyze Demitrey, who I refuse to call an Alpha, it was just the beginning.

With Demitrey being held in captivity, everything just fell into place, the pack warriors and Demitrey are all being held in the dungeons with chains bathed in wolfsbane, so their strength was minimized, and with their mates being held away from them, their weakness only multiplied.

But the weakest of all Is Demitrey himself, so now, I run the pack, and that is all I've ever wanted.

To be clear, I never actually went in a duel with Demitrey, and yeah, I cheated my way to the top with some help, but who cares, the top is where I belonged.

The female members whether mated or unmated from Demitrey's pack where all placed in one wing of the castle, however two different rooms.

My guards and warriors consisted of rogues who were ruthless when it came to clearing out packs, we killed, and murdered. Everywhere we went we left a river of blood.

I also changed the pack name to the Blood red pack, instead of the Red moon pack.

That name suited us better.

Anyway, ever since Demitrey's mate ran away 6 months ago, she hasn't contacted anyone, which is just fine by me, because well, as much as I wanted her here, to be my personal toy, it's better that she was far away, because once destined to be a Luna, always a Luna.

She would try her best to free her people, which would wreak havoc and destroy my plan, so I just let her be, to the point where I didn't even know where she is.

My pack had yet to be disturbed by anything or anyone for that matter, and I wasn't going to let my years of hard work to go to waste, well at least I thought I wasn't.

With no mate, I had nothing to focus on but my hunger for power and I only wanted more.

After getting rid of my mate, I didn't lust after anyone, but every now and then my warriors and I force some of the unmated she-wolves into pleasing us, in any way that we want.

The mated she-wolves were way deadlier, we would never get away with touching them inappropriately.

But as you can see, I now had complete reign over this pack, well over my rogues, the women and children. As far as the men go, they were all being held captive.

Every once in a while, when I feel like it, I send someone there to feed them, and that is probably like once in a full moon, however, I do so make sure they are always being injected with serum, which gives them the strength to stay alive, but not the strength to fight.

Plus, I send down pictures of their mates all bruised and battered, just to add to their torture, knowing that they couldn't even do anything about it.

My victory was pure bliss, and I was loving every moment of it, until someone burst through my door telling me that my second in command had been attacked.

I bolted to my feet and dashed to the clinic, where I found the sight on a gurney, bloodied with gashes on the neck that could've only been made by canine teeth, you could tell there was a lot of blood lost, and the consciousness wasn't fully there.

I sent someone to fetch that old hag of a nurse, I think her name was Diane or Diana, whatever, and once she got there, I ordered her to fix my second in command, and I threatened to kill her if she let my commander die.

Once the old hag got to work, I held the guard who told me the news by the throat dragging him outside as I said, "who is responsible for this?"

He tried to pry my fingers off as, as he strained to breathe, but I wouldn't relent, instead my grip became tighter as I lifted him off the ground by the throat, and he seemed ready to pass out, but he finally managed to say, "the Alpha."

And I saw red.

He must have realized his mistake because he quickly stuttered out "I I m-meant Demitrey. H-h-he did it."

In one motion I threw him away as though he weighed nothing.

His body hit a near tree then crumpled to the ground.

"Take him to the dungeons, he dares disrespect me. Make this an example to everyone who witnessed this, I AM THE ALPHA! And make no mistake, I will not be so nice the next time someone dares call another an Alpha in my presence."

After my announcement, and the disgrace was taken away, I made my way down to the dungeon, making sure I placed my mask firmly on my face, my identity has yet to be revealed to these people, and I wanted to keep it that way.

Once I entered the underground, the smell of blood, sweat, vomit, along with other bodily discharges I wish to not mention and the heat hit me like a she-wolves' slap to the face, and those are strong.

After taming my urge to throw up and managing my sudden upset stomach, I made my way straight to the last cell in the dungeon. The custom-made cell made to hold the strongest of strongest wolves.

Once I reached it, I cringed at the sight in front of me.

There on his knees, sat Demitrey, his mouth and neck bloodied, his breaths coming out hard as though he just completed a marathon that he ran for days.

"My, my, my, what a sight, the big bad Alpha at my feet, this is just wonderful." I smirked.

"I am not sure I approve of your act of violence earlier though." I stated in a scolding tone, as I sneered down at Demitrey.

"Go to hell." Was his simple, bored reply.

Without thinking, my foot lashed out, landing a perfect blow to his head, his body swayed violently to the side, but the chains wouldn't relent, and just pulled him back to the center, while the wolfs bane in the cuffs dug under his skin.

He grunted in pain, but he wouldn't scream.

He never screamed.

He never willed himself to do so.

And I wanted him to scream.

I wanted to hear his pain loud and clear.

I wanted to see his defeat.

Without thinking, I pulled out the baton I carried in my boot, and relentless started striking him.

Each hit echoed through his bones, the bruises singing the proof of his torture, but the strained veins in his neck and forehead displayed his arrogance, his will to not give up.

He wouldn't give up!

And that only fueled my anger. I attacked and battered him until the chains were the only limbs holding him up, then, then I took a breather.

I stood up straight, brushed off the wrinkles on my clothes, and then looked down at the bloodied Alpha.

I spit on him and smiled, then I walked out, feeling victorious. Although he had yet to admit defeat, my hunger to humiliate and destroy him had been sedated, until next time of course.

With a nod of my head to the guards, his cell was locked, but before I could really exit the dungeon, I heard a very dangerous and powerful growl erupt from deep within the dungeon, followed by many others. Yet the first one, it held the power of a true king, a true leader, and it also held a promise.

And I hated myself for feeling a sudden cold snake of fear and nervousness slither down my spine.

I shouldn't be afraid, the Alpha has no way of escape, and as everyone knows... I AM THE ALPHA!

Chapter 24- "Secret Plan" -Part 2

Demitrey' s pnt. Of view

I laid quietly and still in my own pool of blood, as I gave my body time to recuperate. I didn't want to continuously use my excessive wolf healing because my wolf needed strength too for when the battle was to come along.

I have no idea who that maniac is, and although I attacked the second in command to see if I could pry out some information, it was to no avail. One thing I do know for sure is that he is one angry individual.

I tried to pick my brain to figure out which one of my enemies is coward enough to ambush me just to take over, but not one could add up to the criteria of the one that seems hell bent on torturing me, and the ruckus caused by the pack's mind link in my head wasn't making it any better.

Everyone was constantly complaining, some even arguing amongst each other.

See the mind link is our only mean of communication, and I could easily block each of them out, but that would risk us missing a clue about who we think calls himself "the Alpha."

Pathetic. Absolutely pathetic. I mean how arrogant can you get when you go flaunting yourself around, demanding that everyone calls you "the Alpha"?

I am an Alpha, but I earned that name. I didn't just wake up one day and started demanding that you give me the title. I worked for it.

Anyway, everyone was constantly complaining... *"Oh my, we are going to die."*

"Where is the Alpha?"

"Oh he abandoned us."

"Maybe if he found his Luna, she would've given him the strength to fight."

"Wait, I thought there was a rumor that that girl, what her name was again?"

"Adelina."

"Yes! Her, there was a rumor that she was his mate."

"Well where is she now?"

"I don't know."

"Well the Alpha better man up, or give us a plan, I'm ready to take on these m***********s."

At some point I became tired of them, but then that's when I got an idea, although I didn't like the way my plan was, I'd have to do it.

I growled a menacing "**Quiet**" in the mind link, and it became as quiet as a cemetery.

"**Now, I've been patient with your bickering, but thanks to you, I've figured out our battle plan, however, first, we have to recruit a special someone. So, for now, I'm going to go over my plan with my warriors, then give each group your part to play. Until any further announcements, please act as normal as you've been acting over the past 6 months and try to keep quiet in the mind link.**" I declared.

Then a United "*yes Alpha*" followed, and then the mind link became quiet.

Finally, I opened my mind link to both Kade, and sadly James.

"*What's the plan Alpha?*" Came Kade's voice.

It was time to get down to business.

I explained my plan to both James and Kade.

Now because Kade is my beta and best friend, he gets the easiest job. Meanwhile, James was my messenger, he was going after the one person that would give us the strength to fight.

My Luna, Adelina.

See, as much as I hate to admit it, James is the one that spent enough time with Adelina to know exactly where she could be, and I must say, I am very jealous of their relationship, and I was very irritated by that part of my plan, but it was time for our pack's redemption, and we were going to do it as one.

After explaining my plan to my two main players, it was time to lay low, and formulate a battle plan for the entire pack, because this time, the warriors weren't the only ones attacked, no, this time it became personal to each member of the pack, and we were all going to fight back.

Third person's pnt. Of view

As Demitrey started focusing on his plan, it was time for James to get the ball rolling.

He thought over what the Alpha told him.

The Alpha tapped both Kade and James into a secret mind link as he went over his plans, first he said "guys, do you remember our training in the wolfs bane field?" "Yes, sadly." Came Kade's voice, as James agreed silently. They hated that week of training, they spent days learning to overcome the wolfs bane effect, even if it was for a small minute, and now, the training was going to come in handy. "Well, it's time to put that training to work." Declared the Alpha.

So, James took in the Alpha's advice, and channeled his energy into doubling his skin, using his wolf as a backup, then, he wrapped his hands on each of the chains, where they connected to the ceiling, and yanked as hard as he could, and the chains broke free. Although his palms were burning from the wolfs bane that bathed the chains, the effect wasn't a paralyzing or painful as it used to be.

Then he waited.

The noise was to alert one of the guards, and just as they planned, seconds later, a guard came to check out what caused the noise.

But he really shouldn't have, because the moment he noticed James, he instantly found himself being strangled by the chains, and the wolfs bane dug under his skin, while James muffled his screams until, there was no life left to scream for.

The guard's body fell limp to the floor, as James searched him for the key.

He freed his hands of the shackles, then passed the keys to Kade, who had his own plan to execute.

Then, James took the rogue's clothes, and dressed himself up, once his makeover was complete, he saluted the Alpha, then made his way to the dungeon's entrance.

Once he reached the other guard, he lured him to the dungeon's dark entrance and punched him dead in the face.

The plan wasn't to knock the guard out, but it was to rouse suspicion, and eventually chaos.

James landed punch after punch until he felt the guard close to losing consciousness, then James released him, and made a run for the woods.

James was one of the fastest runners in the pack, and the Alpha ordered him to run until he crossed the pack's territory, because he knew the rogues wouldn't dare risk losing their lives by stepping out of the pack boundaries.

It took a few minutes for the pounded guard to gain enough understanding to yell "we have an escaped wolf! We have an escaped wolf!"

He got to his feet and sounded the alarm.

Minutes later, James heard the thunder of paws gaining on him, and he smiled as he allowed himself to transform, and his wolf took over.

With a victorious howl, and a devious growl, James was gone.

He pushed himself to reach his max speed, and although his limbs complained and struggled from not being used in a while, they quickly got up to the challenge, and soon James was zooming through the forest.

It took a good hour before he reached the pack lines, and once he crossed it, he announced to the Alpha that he succeeded, but he didn't stop running.

He ran until he finally reached another civilization. There he managed to clean himself up, steal a few wallets, get some new clothes, blend in with the crowd, and make his way to the nearest airport, where he used his new platinum card to book a flight.

James had a feeling he knew exactly where Adelina would be, and that was his destination.

Chapter 25- " Secret Plan" -Part 3

Third Person's pnt. Of view

"Have a good night Katharina, see you on Monday." Waved Adelina with a smile, as she exit the clinic. It has been over 6 months since she moved down to Italy, and she has managed to settle down quickly.

She found a family-owned clinic who welcomed her with open arms the minute she signed up to be a nurse, and since then she has been living her life in Italy.

The reason why Adelina chose Italy over France was because it was where she landed first. When she stepped out of the airport and into the open air of Italy, she fell in love.

The colors, the food, the textures, the food, the culture, and the food, all lived up to her expectation and more.

Especially the food.

When she started wandering in Italy with no definite destination in mind, she absentmindedly bumped into Katharina, who that day was rushing off to work.

She remembers Katharina quickly apologizing and explaining that she was late for work, and that she would have to cover two shifts because they lost one of their nurses, and that was Adelina's opportunity.

After mild complications with her identity, and what she was besides human, she was hired.

There aren't many packs in Italy, so the family promised to keep Adelina's secret. They welcomed her as though she was their own daughter, and over the past 6 months, Adelina and Katharina formed a sisterhood bond that is unbreakable.

So, between her newfound family, her newfound job, and her newfound home, Adelina hardly had time to think of what she left back in America, and because the mating process wasn't complete, she didn't even feel anything when it came to her mate. I mean yeah, she would always be attracted to her mate, but without the complete mating process, she couldn't feel whether he was in pain, or in danger, or anything for that matter.

No other man caught her attention, and even though she was in Italy, where some of the most gorgeous men lived, she still couldn't find herself to be attracted to anyone, except of course Demitrey.

She did miss home sometimes though. She missed James and Cilia, she missed Clarissa and Peter, she missed the pack Clinic and Diana, and she missed her wolf.

She hardly transformed into her wolf, and whenever she and Aden communicated through their mind link, it would end in argument because Aden wanted to go back to America, confront Demitrey and demand an explanation for his actions, but Adelina wanted no part of it.

She believed that everything Demitrey did was because he wanted to, that it had nothing to do with him protecting her or anything of the sort.

In all honesty, any thought of Demitrey infuriated her, yet appeased her.

She hated to think about the effect he had on her even before he marked her, yet she loves reminiscing the way his voice would caress her, the way he demanded her attention even if he didn't utter a word.

She hated how she was always so desperate to see him, yet she loved the end results of their encounters.

She loved the way he would hold her so possessively and captivate her with his eyes. The way he could instantly make her lose control of her body, just to let her believe she had the upper hand, and she hated yet appreciated how he could read her like an open book.

She despised the way he drew her in and teased her, yet she admired the way his actions made her heart leap, and made her feel appreciated.

She absentmindedly touched her lips, while she reminisced about his lips on her.

She despised the fact that he was hot and cold all at the same time, yet she adored that about him, because it kept her on her toes, always in suspense.

She hates missing him, she hates the feelings that wash over her, and the feelings that make her want him, the that make her yearn for his touch.

And she hated her heat and mating seasons. For 6 months in a row, she had to spend countless nights under a cold shower during the mating seasons just to appease her arousal, and no matter how aroused she felt, she couldn't even bring in another male to do the job.

She couldn't help but admit, she missed her asshole of a mate, but would she go back to him...?

HELL TO THE NO.

Adelina hated the fact that he made her feel worthless, like she wasn't important. He even proved to her that he didn't care by having Serena around.

Serena... just the thought of that she-wolf made Adelina clench her fist. She wanted to murder that bitch.

She did worry sometimes though. Because she hasn't heard from anyone since she ran away.

Not that she wanted to though, especially not from Peter.

Not after what he did.

She couldn't believe what was revealed the night she ran away.

She was so sure that Peter was going to say that she belonged to him, which wouldn't make any sense because, well yeah, her and Peter dated in the past, but as soon as his mate came in the picture everything romantic ceased between them.

Whenever Clarissa was around it was as though she hardly existed to Peter, but that's the point, whenever Clarissa was around, she wasn't in the picture, but as soon as Clarissa stepped away from them, or left them in a room or secluded area, even for a minute, Peter somehow always became too close for comfort. Almost like her father.

Not only so, Adelina thought over that fact that even during the wedding, when Peter said "I Love you" he wasn't staring at Clarissa, but Adelina had tears in her eyes, and she wasn't sure who he was staring it when he said it.

Even though Adelina wasn't present consciously, she soon found that her legs absentmindedly brought her in front of her apartment.

With a shake of her head to clear her thoughts she fished for her keys and made her way into her vintage-style apartment.

When she got in however, she felt a change in the atmosphere, and she knew for a fact she wasn't alone.

She closed the door softly and obtained the baseball bat behind the potted plant right by her door, then she took slow and measured steps as she furthered into the apartment.

She reached her living room, and as far as her enhanced sight could tell, there wasn't anything out of the ordinary, then she heard a rummaging sound echoing from the kitchen.

She slipped off her shoes, and patted her way across the floor, trying to be as quite as a mouse.

When she reached the kitchen, there she saw a figure rummaging through her fridge.

She took a deep breath and charged her way towards the person, with her weapon raised.

The bat was seconds away from making contact with its victim, when the person turned around and screamed "whoa whoa whoa whoa whoa! Stop! Adelina it's me!"

Adelina's pnt. Of view

"JAMES? Oh my God what are you doing here? In my fridge if anything?"

He looked back at the fridge then back at me and smirked as he said, "I was hungry."

I shook my head and brought the bat down as I looked him over.

He had bags under his eyes, he looked as if he had lost weight, and the bright fire and his eyes seemed to have dimmed, and I didn't miss the red skin that surrounded his wrists.

"Is everything okay?" I managed to ask after my observation.

He looked over at me, a sad air suddenly masking his face as he replied softly "No." Then he shook his head looking down.

"Okay... well, let me cook us something and you can rest

on the couch for now, I'll wake you when dinner is ready." I spoke, trying to appease the sad atmosphere.

He looked at me as though I didn't have to tell him twice. He trudged his way to the living room, where his body just slumped on the couch, and soon enough the walls started shaking with James' snores.

I shook my head once again and made my way to the kitchen to whip up some dinner. Meanwhile, I couldn't help the way my mind started to wander and buzz with questions.

Is everyone okay?

What happened?

How did James find me?

Did Demitrey send him?

How is Cilia?

These questions amongst others circulated my mind as my hands worked around the kitchen, collecting needed ingredients for pizza made from scratch.

When the pizza was ready, I cut 5 slices and placed them on a plate, along with some salad, and juice. I then made my way to James and placed the pizza on the coffee table.

Then I tapped his shoulder as I said "James, James wake up."
"Mmmh, just five more minutes." He murmured as he turned away from me, the couch struggling under his size.
"James, wake up!" I tried again, shaking his shoulder, yet he just shrugged my hand off.
"James... I have pizza." And just like that he was fully

awake, he turned around and sat down as he devoured his meal.

He was done and seconds, and yet he still looked famished, so I gave him the rest, then I traded his juice for water, since he appeared dehydrated.

Once his hunger was sated, he leaned back against the couch and breathed with his eyes closed.

He sighed again as though he was finally relieved from years of oppression.

"James, what happened?" I asked again carefully, worry slowly taking over my entire being.

He didn't answer for quite a while, and I figured to give him space so he could gather his thoughts, but as soon as I stood to leave, in a low, almost pleading tone he said, "You have to come back to save the pack Luna."

And I froze.

Chapter 26- "Secret Plan" -Part 4

Adelina's pnt. Of view

I stood frozen in my spot for a few seconds before I turned and faced James as I asked, "What did you say?" "Please..." He breathed again as he said "come back with me Luna. You have to save the pack." He said, his eyes silently begging me, along with the pleading tone coating his voice.

He never addressed me as Luna before, in fact, no one has.

"Save the pack from what?" I asked carefully. "We were ambushed, the day you ran away, everyone was drugged, and when we woke up, we were being held captive. The pack warriors along with the Alpha are being held down in the dungeons. And everyone else is being held somewhere else. I managed to escape, sent by the Alpha, but the Alpha and the pack are weak without you, which is why you have to come back with me Luna." He explained.

"Wait, so Demitrey sent you here, just for you to tell me that I should come back to save the pack? Unbelievable!" I exclaimed at the absurd situation.

"Well, he also said that he needed you, personally." Explained James, a sudden blush fixating on his cheeks.

Wait, was James blushing?

"What do you mean by "personally"?" I asked carefully.
"Um... You know..." he said shaking his hand in sign as though I'm supposed to figure out what he was talking about.

"Um... no, I don't know." I said, completely confused.
"Really Adelina?" He said exasperated.

"Well, I'm being honest, what do you mean?" I asked, suddenly becoming irritated.

"Well, when an Alpha and A Luna know that they are mates, they have to seal their connection through both marking and sexual intercourse, so when the Alpha says he needs you personally, it means that he needs you on a level that no one else can fulfill." He said, trying to avoid my eyes.

Then, it clicked.

"Oooh," I said as it finally came clear "I see, well I'm not sure what to tell you. I mean why should I help him? He has been nothing but an asshole since the day he walked into my life. He's teased me, hurt me, made me cry, and make me feel things that I never felt before, then he marked me without consent when his ego got the best of him and he was afraid that I would find another man, and now he has the AUDACITY to ask ME to help HIM?!" I snapped, my breathing heavy and angry.

"Well... yes." Said James simply, "You should help him, because once you do, it's not only him that you are helping, but you're also helping the pack, me, Cilia, Kade, And-"

"And Serena." I growled angry cutting him off, my hands curling into fists.

"No, actually, you get to kill her if you want, we suspect that she plays part in the opposing team." Explained James anxiously as he witnessed my angered state.

"Wait, what?" I asked, my fury currently forgotten.

"Oh yeah, Demitrey suspected her since the first few letters arrived." Explained James.

"What letters?" I asked surprised and confused.

"Uh... did I say letter? I meant um... I think I've said too much." Said James.

"What. Letter." I said again, my tone suddenly becoming authoritative.

"Oh come on, don't use that tone with me." He said, almost pleading.

"James, I really hate to do this, but I am your future Luna, and if you want my help to save the pack, you will tell me everything. Is that clear?" I said calmly, knowing he wouldn't resist my command.

"Yes Luna." He bowed respectively.

Then with a bright and childish I said "okay!"

And just like that he rolled his eyes, and I sat down waiting for him to talk.

Third Person's pnt. Of view

While James managed to track down Adelina, the pack back home had a bit of celebration.

Demitrey received the signal from James that he found Adelina, as a wave of relief washed over him, and he gave James permission to do anything it takes to get Adelina to come back to the pack, even if it meant telling her everything that took place since the moment he knew she was his mate.

His heart skipped a beat at the sound of her name, and he couldn't wait to see her, well, if she decides to come back and help that is.

And as said before, if she didn't come back, he would cope with it.

Demitrey then announced to the pack that James found their Luna, and the pack link became alive with thoughts of rejoice.

But that moment was short-lived because the Alpha warned them to keep quiet so "The Alpha" and his rogues wouldn't find out the plan.

Now, all they had to do was sit tight until the Luna was back on pack grounds, then it would be time to execute part C of the plan. Since part A and B are based on Adelina's decision.

Demitrey' s pnt. Of view

After the pack link managed to quiet down, I finally went back into my mind, where I found my relief, Adelina.

She was engraved in my memory, and she was my strength that kept me going.

Her beauty was unique, both inside and out, she was a fireball when the situation called for it, as well as she was submissive.

I hated that I let my fear of putting her in danger, and partially my ego, get the best of me.

I hated how I pushed her away, even if I was trying to protect her.

But I have to be honest, I was afraid.

I was afraid of losing her, and I was also afraid of her.

The minute she walked in my life she had total control over me, and my wolf.

There wasn't a minute when I was with her that my walls didn't crumble, even if she did nothing.

Just her presence was enough for me to succumb to her will.

I hated how I would try to put up a front, just so that prying eyes could see that I didn't want to claim her, yet, that mission always failed. The moment the hurt flickered in her eyes, I was defeated.

Her eyes, the portal to her soul, so captivating, hypnotizing.

She captured me with the fact that she didn't mind being vulnerable. She didn't try to put a mask on, nor did she try to hide who she was.

Her eyes, her facial features, and her body language said everything.

She left herself open to me, and Lord knows I loved it when she opened herself to me.

I love how no matter how mad or hurt I get her, the moment I showed her affection, she was willing to forgive me.

But would she be willing to forgive me now?

I mean I most definitely overstepped my boundaries.

My regret, my main torment, is the fact that I marked her.

I took away her will to ever fall in love with another but me, and now, now, I was willing to beg and grovel for her forgiveness, not just for the pack, but for me.

I fully declare it, I am in love with Adelina Veraso, my mate, my queen.

And I just hope, I pray, that she would be willing to forgive me.

I know I shouldn't have pushed her away, but can you blame me?

I mean, what would one do? How far would one go to protect someone they love and truly care for?

Unknown's pnt. Of view

I held the pathetic rogue by the throat as I throttled him, and he tried his best to explain what happened with minimal air to breathe.

"He-he-he managed to get out of his chains, and he ambushed me. He dressed like Luke, and almost knocked me out. We tried our best to get to him, but he was too fast." Said the rogue.

And I saw red.

I threw him to the ground as I said, "You Idiot!" Then I relentlessly kicked him, until he was too battered to move.

"Get him out of my sight." I spat on his bloodied form and made my way back to the dungeon.

I couldn't pinpoint the reason why he would escape, but I wouldn't leave any loose ends.

I mean the Luna probably was a reason, but why would they waste their breath knowing that she most likely wouldn't help him?

Either that, or they had something up their sleeves, and if there was a plan amiss the pack, I was going to find out what it was.

I made my way straight to the main cell in the dungeon.

When I opened it, I found Demitrey chained up, but healed since our last encounter.

He looked at me, then rolled his eyes looking away, as though my presence alone bored him.

"What do you want?" He asked, his tone matching the bored expression settled upon his face.

"I'm supposed to be asking the questions here." I muttered menacingly.

But all Demitrey did was smirk and say smugly "yet, I am asking the questions. What. Do. You. Want?"

"You already know why I'm here. One of your pack warriors escaped." I said, as I started pacing his cell.

"Okay, and?" Was his reply.

In the blink of an eye, using my super speed, I had my hand wrapped firmly around Demitrey's throat, yet he didn't even flinch.

With gritted teeth I declared "I want to know exactly what your plan is or else I will destroy your pack member by member until I get to you."

Then he breathed, blinked, and out of nowhere burst into laughter.

He laughed as though he just witnessed a comic act, tears started forming in his eyes, and I backed away from him, my anger surfacing.

Without a second thought my hand connected with his jaw, and his laughter stopped, well for a few seconds.

Then he just doubled back laughing.

"C-come on man, is that all you got?" He said, his laughter taking a whole new level, then to his right, his Beta started laughing, and soon the entire dungeon was booming with laughter.

I couldn't handle it, they were all in the face of danger, yet they were laughing.

With a growl, I marched out of his cell and towards the entrance of the dungeons, when I reached it, I stripped one of the guards from their bow and arrow and made my way back to Demitrey.

When I was halfway there, I aimed and shot the arrow at his shoulder, to show who is in power as the arrow penetrated his skin.

The laughter seized immediately, and I smirked in victory.

Demitrey gazed at his wounded shoulder, as though it was alien, then out of nowhere, his laughter returned, followed by hundreds of other laughter, and I stood there aghast.

When he managed to stop laughing, his eyes met mine in a fierce glare as he said to me "your days are numbered, keep trying your best to bring me down, but just know in the end there will be only ONE true Alpha, and I AM THE ALPHA!"

And the laughter of the dungeons switched out into howls of agreement and praise for their Alpha, and that's when I felt it again.

A cold snake of fear slithered down my spine, causing shivers of doubt and uncertainty to rattle my entire being.

With a sharp turn, I made my way out of the dungeons, but as I walked away, their laughter returned, and I couldn't help but think that I was screwed.

However, would I let anyone know of my fear, of course not.

It was time to get down and dirty, and if I was going to be victorious, I would have to play dirty.

Chapter 27- "Secret Plan" -Part 5

Third person's pnt. Of view

Adelina and James sat in a very tense silence, both somehow trapped in their own minds.

James was anxious, he explained everything that Demitrey told him, from the moment he met Adelina, to finding out that she was his mate, from the letters, to their ambush.

He explained that the Alpha suspected Serena but before they could really pinpoint who was behind all of it, they were ambushed.

He sat quietly, allowing the Luna time to absorb and digest everything, all the while he was anxious on the inside, not sure what the final response will be.

Meanwhile, Adelina sat quietly, trying to process everything that James told her. She never expected what she heard.

There were too many voices in her head, too many memories playing back all at once, too many reasoning, too many encounters between her and Demitrey, and there were too many questions.

She needed air.

Adelina abruptly stood, and James was quick to follow, but Adelina shook her head and said "no, it's okay, I just need a breather. I'll be back."

But James wasn't having it, he stood and blocked her, Adelina stood with eyebrows raised in surprised.

"I'm sorry Luna, but the Alpha gave me specific directions to not let you out of my sight." Explained James.

"What? Why? Is he afraid I'll leave again?" Asked Adelina, her anger slowly surfacing.

"Yes." Was James' simple and blunt reply.

"Wow." Was all that Adelina could muster.

Then she breathed and once again shook her head, holding her temples as a headache slowly creeped on her brain.

"James look," sighed Adelina with eyes closed, "I really need some space to think all of this through, so can you please just let me go, I promise, I'll be in the park across from here." She opened her eyes, trying to reason with James.

"Sorry Aden, look, just go in your room, and I promise you won't even know I'm here." James said, giving an ultimatum.

"Come on." Whined Adelina.

"Either that, or you sit here while I keep an eye on you."

Said James, not letting up, then he saw a mischievous glint flash in Adelina's eyes, but before she could say anything, he said "and don't even think to use your Luna tone on me, the Alpha will have my head if he finds out that I let you out."

"Uuugh, FINE!" Adelina said giving up, and stomping all the way to her room, where she slammed the door shut.

James chuckled and shook his head at Adelina's childish behavior, he really missed her, it was like the little sister he never had, although if he had a sister, he most likely wouldn't have brought her to the club, but then again, maybe he would've.

James found himself taking off his shirt and settling on the couch. He sent a message to the Alpha, giving an update about Adelina, and how she is handling the situation through their mind link, as a sweet slumber started to caress his body.

But just as he was about to fully commit to sleep, there came knock on the door.

He was going to be quiet and pretend that there was no one home, until the knock came again.

With a low growl, he trudged his way to the door, and with an angered "WHAT?!" He opened the door, then he froze.

There, in front of his eyes, stood a surprised beauty, who, just like James couldn't keep her eyes off the tall figure standing in front of her.

Her eyes observed his face, then slowly started traveling down his naked torso.

Then just as her eyes started to zero in on the growing bulge in his pants, she heard a low yet very possessive voice claim "MINE." And just like that she was engulfed in his arms, his lips claiming hers.

Demitrey' s pnt. Of view

I sat quietly after receiving the news from James about my mate.

According to James, she wasn't taking it very well, well, I'm assuming she's not taking it well, especially since she begged James for space.

But then again, I didn't expect her to take it well, especially since it's a lot to take in.

I mean, I'm pretty sure that before today she thought of me as an utter and complete asshole, and after today she might either think even worse of me, or maybe not.

But it didn't matter, I knew in my heart she would come to help save the pack, but what would come after that? Well, that was all up to her, and fate.

But whichever came first, I would do anything to get her back, no matter what it takes.

Adelina's pnt. Of view

I slammed my door shut and made my way to the bed.

I sat down, as my brain became alive, but then I became too excited to sit, so before I knew it, I started pacing back and forth.

Questions where flying all over my brain.

Why didn't he tell me?

I could've helped!

Is that why he tried so hard to keep away?

Or is that why the tables always turned with him? From cold to hot and back?

Why?

Who?

How?

I had a headache.

I couldn't focus on any particular thing, since everything was trying to mash up in my mind.

The pieces of memories and encounters where binding together as though they were all part of one big puzzle, one big picture.

I breathed and closed my eyes, as my fingers massaged my temples, as the headache worsened.

"*Okay, you need to calm down.*" Came Aden's voice in my head.

"How? How Do you expect me to calm down after all I've heard?" I demanded, angry.

"*Because I've been keeping an open mind about our mate situation, and why he did what he did. I tried to warn you, or at least get you to see things my way, but nooo, you were being stubborn.*" She snapped back.

"Well maybe I didn't want to keep an open mind, maybe I just wanted him to love me, sweep me off my feet, take care of me, see pass my flaws and just love me. I'm just tired! Okay? I'm tired because from the moment I was born, I could never find someone to love me on that level. I had no parental love, and love from my friends had their limits. All I dreamed of, was a mate, a mate that loves me! All he had to do was love me!" I didn't realize I was crying until I felt the drops fall on my chest, and I quickly used to the back of my hand to clear the streams on my face out of anger.

"How can you be so blind? He DID love you. Heck, he DOES love you. If he didn't, why do you think he tried so hard to stay away, to control the urges he felt for you? He knew the moment he showed that he cared. You would be in trouble! I can't believe you!" Snapped Aden, then she zoned out of my mind.

I sighed as I sat on the bed again.

She did try to reason with me, but I guess my yearnings made me blind.

Too blind in fact.

I sighed, knowing already what I had to do.

But if I were to consider doing this, then I still had some questions that needed answering.

I made my way to the door so I could speak with James, but just as my hand reached for the knob, I heard some shuffling around, just as I heard one of my vases crash on the floor.

I opened the door in haste, and made my way to the living room, which I instantly regretted the moment I witnessed the scene that would scar me for life.

Chapter 28- "Secret Plan" -Part 6

Adelina's pnt. Of view

"WHAT IS GOING ON? JAMES?! Oh my Gooood!" I snapped, my hands clasping over my eyes, to block out the explicit scene taking place in my living room.

"Oh! Adelina! I'm sorry, I just... I'm sorry" said a soft voice.

Wait, I know that voice.

"Katharina? What in the world are you doing?" I asked, my vision still blinded by my hands.

"Um, well, you see, what had happened was-"

"She's my mate, but I apologize Luna, I should've controlled myself." Said James, cutting off Katharina's babbling.

"What?" I asked in d disbelief.

"Yeah, I guess I had a mate after all... um, you can uncover your eyes now." He said awkwardly.

Slowly and carefully, I brought my hands down, and slowly peeled back my eyelids, as they landed on James and Katharina, whose both cheeks' were tainted with a dark blush.

"Um, Kat, what are you doing here?" I asked finally breaking the silence.

"Well, I came by so we could have a sleepover, I got home, and I was bored, so I thought to come by, but then when I knocked, he opened the door, " she explained her eyes flashing over to James, who's eyes met hers halfway as she continued, "and well, something just came over me, he said 'MINE' and I couldn't control the wave of lust and want that washed over me, next thing I know, I'm in his arms, and I'm actually determining that he's the best kisser I've ever had."

She said, her eyes looking at him all googly like, his eyes mirroring hers.

Without any warning, they started kissing again, and the moment they melted in each other's arms, a pang of sadness, hurt, and pain resonated in my heart, and although I felt happy for the new couple, I still found myself envying what they had, and wanting what they had.

Tears suddenly welled up in my eyes, as my nose tickled with unspoken emotion. But before I allowed them to fall, I cleared my throat, and once again, they snapped back from their romantic exchange, but I didn't want to keep them from that, they deserved their happiness.

"Okay, well I know how this mate thing works. Kat since I've given you the lesson of werewolf 101, and I'm pretty sure that you are both aroused, just know that there is a guest room down the hall and to your right. You can use it for as long as you need, and not just for physical encounters, you guys need to talk in private" I said with a smile, and James gave me a grateful look as he took Kat's hand and led her to the room.

I already knew what was going to happen, so instead of sitting and sulking in my thoughts, I occupied myself by cooking.

Though, at some point and time, I still found my mind wandering to the one and only Demitrey.

I was, now, so confused about him.

He hurt me, he teased me, yet he made it looked as though he loved me, as though he couldn't resist me.

But then were those actions fake, or real?

Did he act a certain way to hurt me, even if his intentions were good?

Do I just believe everything James said and move on?

Forgive and forget?

There were too many questions, each needing an answer, so I'm making my decision. It's my heart first before anybody else, I could care less if of my decision leaves a negative impact on some lives, or if others disapprove of my decision.

I was taking charge of my independence.

Demitrey' s pnt. Of view

I haven't heard anything from James since we last communicated, and to be honest I was really beginning to worry.

I had two plans set up, and everyone had a role to play, but Adelina held the secret to which plan we would use, she was the center of all of this.

I got down into a sitting position, although my body protested, and my wrists became numb from the wolfs bane. The pain was there, but I shut it out, I had to focus on something else.

I closed my eyes, and soon enough, pictures of my Adelina started flashing in my vision.

I smiled and breathed, she was always my relief.

I smiled as my memories of her played over and over, except, it wasn't supposed to happen like this.

I grew up under my father's hands, and he made sure that he engraved the idea that mates were a no no.

He gave me the idea of having a personal mistress, to keep my lust at bay and sedated, but after that, a mate was to never catch my eye.

I mean, after his mate, my mother, birthed me, he killed her, and although he didn't do it by his bare hands, his actions and intentions were clear enough.

But how could I resist such a pull?

My father explained the connection of two mates, but his words never truly compared to what I felt the moment I knew Adelina was my mate.

I remember, whenever I asked questions about mates, and when would I meet mine, my father would beat me and flog me as punishment, then he sworn that the moment he found out who my mate was he was going to kill her.

So, I had to take a drastic move.

I killed my father.

No, it's not the way one might think.

I didn't poison his drink, or food, nor did I kill him in his sleep.

No, instead we had to battle it out for the position of Alpha of our pack.

Everyone was there to witness it, even our worse enemies.

I killed my father in that duel, and although I am not proud, I am happy that my mate was safe from the fate of being in constant danger.

Or so I thought.

Unknown's pnt. Of view

It has been over three days since that warrior escaped, and he has yet to return. The rogues didn't pick up anything as far as whether Demitrey had a secret plan or not, and my questioning session with Demitrey didn't go so well, so now I'm back at square one.

Unless, the warrior escaped because he couldn't handle the humiliation.

Many might wonder why I held on to the pack for 6 months, and if anything, why didn't I just kill Demitrey and take over the pack, well the answer to that is quite simple.

Claiming to have captured the most powerful Alpha in America, and having living proof of it, is two different things.

Many have claimed to achieve what I've done, yet none of them had proof, but every second of every day that Demitrey spends in misery is living proof of what I did, and that is way more satisfying then just ending that bastard's life.

Chapter 29- "Acceptance"

Adelina's pnt. Of view

I waited for hours before James and Katharina came back, and when they did, there was no denying what went down between them in those few hours.

Though they lacked their mating marks, there was no denying that they were both happy to have found each other.

Katharina was wearing one of the spare shirts I keep in the guest room, while James was currently fixing his own clothes.

After fumbling around with their outfits, James cleared his throat awkwardly, while an identical blush tainted both their cheeks.

I laughed and shook my head as I said "relax guys, I know what happens between mates. Anyway, here's the thing. I-"

"Aden wait, before you say anything, James told me about what happened and what is taking place back in America, and I think you should go." Said Katharina as she cut me off.

"But- "

"I know that you're stubborn, and I know that your mate hurt you, but he had a reason, and I'm pretty sure as soon as everything is over, he will cherish and love you." Continued Katharina, cutting me off again.

"Kat I-"

"No, I know what you're going to say, I won't allow you stay here, I'll drag you back to America myself if I have to, you're helping your pack!" She once again cut me off.

"But Kat, I'm trying to te-"

"Nope, I don't want to hear it unless you're saying that you will go back to him. Look Adelina, I wouldn't have given it a second thought if Demitrey didn't have a reason for what he did, but now that you know why, you can't still be mad at him. Heck I just met my mate, and I can't bear the thought of being so far away from him." She continued on, not allowing me to speak.

"Kat look-"

"Just give him a chance. Please Aden-"

"Will you just shut up and let me talk?!" I boomed, cutting her off, and her lips sealed shut out of surprise.

I sighed shaking my head and looked at her, I made a move to speak, but instead paused, and making sure she wouldn't cut me off again.

Once I was satisfied with her silence, I smiled then breathed and said "what I was trying to say earlier was that I'll go. Though I have many questions, the only person able to answer them is in captivity, and I cannot live without feeding my curiosity. I decided to play my part as Luna and save the pack. And I would've said that earlier if you didn't keep cutting me off." I fixed Kat with an annoyed glare, which she completely ignored.

"Oh, well okay then, good, I'm proud of your choice." She said looking away, and completely dismissing my accusations.

James on the other hand, in a quick stride, engulfed me in his famous bear hugs as he whispered over and over "thank you Luna."

"Thank me when we win this battle." I said pulling away.

"So, when do we leave?" Demanded Katharina.

"Tomorrow, since it's already too late to leave now. We need to get some rest." Explained James.

"Kat, what are you going to tell your parents? I mean you can't just up and leave." I tried to reason.

"Don't worry, I know how to handle them." She said with a smile.

"Okay, it's settled." Said James as he and Kat made their way back to the guest room, while I made my way to my room.

For some reason, declaring that I have accepted the Luna position felt like a breath of fresh air, a release and a relief.

If twenty-four hours ago someone told me that I would willingly be going back to the pack, I probably would've laughed and tried to place that person in an asylum for such absurd thoughts, yet here I am.

Now, once we win this battle, what was going to happen? I wasn't sure how long it would take for me to forgive Demitrey, but then again, is he even in the wrong? I mean all he was doing was to protect me, even if he went a far distance to do it.

Do I just say "hey, so we're mates, the threat is gone, so kiss and make up?"

Ha! As if.

In all honesty, I wasn't sure what the future held, and for once, I was more curious then scared, if scared at all.

Third person's pnt. Of view

James was sure to contact the Alpha and tell him the good news.

And good news it was indeed.

When the Alpha announced to the pack that their Luna was coming back to help save them, the mind link roared in rejoice, but once again their excitement and chatter was hushed down by the Alpha.

It was time to get serious.

It was now time for Kade to execute his part of the plan.

And as the Beta he had to play his part.

But as the Alpha's best friend he was pissed off. He knew this was one of Demitrey's childish jokes, and he would make sure to get back at him for it.

This time, it was easier to escape the dungeons, Kade didn't have to follow the same process that James did because Kade had the keys from the first rogue that James ambushed.

He silently maneuvered his way out of his shackles and his cell, then he planted the keys somewhere were Demitrey would have easy access to once needed.

With one last look to his best friend, and a slight nod in show of respect, Kade made his way to exit the dungeons.

Easier said than done.

The guards have been doubled since James' escape, and even if he took out the ones guarding the entrance of the dungeons, the struggle would probably alert the others.

But then again, that wasn't such a bad idea.

Rogues loved scenes, violent scenes, so seeing two rogues fight could be the perfect distraction Kade needed.

He managed to scavenge a few small pebbles on the dungeon floor, then he blended into the shadows.

He kept his breathing as quiet as possible, so quiet that he could hear his heart beat resonate in his eardrums.

With a quick release of a breath, he launched the first pebble.

The small rock landed on one of the rogues' neck, and he shrugged it off.

Then Kade did it again, and once again the rogue shrugged the pebble off.

Suddenly frustrated, Kade sent another pebble flying and this time the rogue felt it and turn to his partner saying, "hey asshole, stop bothering me."
His partner looked over at him as though he'd grown two heads and said, "the fuck is wrong with you?"
"Nothing will be wrong if you stop throwing stuff on me." Said Kade's victim.
"Whatever." Huffed his partner, who went back to ignoring him.

Kade watched in silence for a few seconds while the rogue kept his eyes on his partner. When the rogue was sure his partner wouldn't do anything, he looked away with a grunt and an "I thought so" facial expression.

Kade gave him another thirty seconds before he once again sent a pebble into attack, and the rogue with an angry grunt shrugged it off.

Kade repeated his actions, as so did the rogue, though his body began to show evidence of his annoyance, and his anger.

But once again, after giving the rogue a few seconds to cool down, Kade sent the last pebble he had left flying, and that's all it took.

"Alright wise guy." Said the rogue as he stood and met his partner with a fist to the face.

His partner startled for a few seconds, took a moment to register what happened, and when he did, boy was he angry.

His partner's fist connected with the rogue's jaw, and soon enough, they were full on fighting, and the other nosy and curious rogues were quickly leaving their post, and eagerly becoming an audience to the ongoing boxing and wrestling match.

With all the noise, and all their backs turned, Kade managed to set foot out of the dungeon, and tip toed his way across the yard, hiding occasionally.

He kept up his stealthy march until he reached the castle, where using the secret passageways, he managed to make it to his destination, the mated she-wolves' room, without being discovered.

Once he reached the room, his mate was waiting for him.

He embraced Cilia lovingly and kissed her possessively. He missed and loved his girl so much, but he had to stop.

Some of the other she-wolves were becoming a bit agitated.

He cleared his throat and asked if everyone was okay, once he received positive feedback, he said "Alright ladies, make me one of you."

And the girls happily gave Kade a makeover.

Kade was now known as Kadie, and he couldn't hate his best friend any more than he did now.

But now, it was also time to prepare.

While everyone anticipated the Luna's return, each pack member had to be ready to play their part, but for now, they were all playing the waiting game.

But little did they know, they didn't have to wait long.

Demitrey' s pnt. Of view

"I'm in, and fully camouflaged." Declared Kade in the mind link, or should I say Kadie.

I knew he didn't want to play this part, but he was the only one fit for the job, especially because of what he would have to do next.

After receiving the news from James, my heart skyrocketed, the thought of my mate coming back stunned me.

To be honest, I didn't think she would even consider coming back. Well maybe she would for the pack, and maybe for me as well, I don't know. And although she now knows the reasons for my actions, I didn't think she was coming back specifically for me.

My mate is sweet, kind hearted, forgiving, but strong willed, so I had to at least hope that part of her coming back was because of me.

I chuckled at myself and shook my head. I couldn't even sound sure in my own thoughts.

"*Now why would she come back for you?*" Said my wolf, breaking my train of thought, though he hadn't spoken to me since the night Adelina left.

"**Oh so you actually do exist. I thought you were just an imaginary friend that I made up.**" I replied to him sarcastically.

"*Shut up Demitrey.*" He said

"**Shut up Trey.**" I fired back at my wolf.

"*Look, I just miss her okay? And I feel like you've ruined the chance you had to make her fall in love with us, with you.*" Said Trey, the sadness and worry evident in his voice.

"**I know, but what would you have me do? Put her in danger of getting hurt, or worse?**" I demanded, my anger and regret pumping and raging through my veins.

"*Of course not, but I just miss her, she was perfect for me, for us.*" He said.

"**I know, I'm pretty sure that's why once in a while you took control and became the romantic mate she wanted.**" I said.

"*Hey, don't even think to use you that card man, you know majority of those times, you were fully in control.*" Defended Trey.

And he was right. When I lost control, it wasn't my wolf who took over, I willingly gave up my control, and just to gain the satisfaction that I had willingly pleased my mate.

"**You're right.**" I said.

"*Of course I'm right. Now you have till tomorrow to get your wits together, we're going to fight to get our mate back.*" Was all he said, then he faded to the back of my mind.

In silent agreement, I nodded to no one in particular.

I was going to get my mate back. I don't deserve her, yet she is my destined mate, I've mistreated her, even if my intentions were good, so I will do whatever it takes to get Adelina back.

In silent promise, I nodded.

I promised it to myself, I promised it to my wolf, and I promised it to my pack.

I will get my mate back.

Chapter 30- "Inner Voice"

Third Person's pnt. Of view

"James, I can't believe you're making me do this." Whispered Adelina harshly as she addressed James.

"Luna, you are aware that I was the one who did the lifting right?" Said James exasperated at Adelina's behavior.

"Doesn't matter how or by whom it was done, this still feels wrong!" Argued Adelina, as they stood huddled over a kiosk, currently in the process of booking last minute tickets back to America.

"Look Aden, we could've done right by the law, get placed on the standby list, and pray that three people just don't show up for their flight today, but I already spoke to the Alpha and he said to get you back to the pack ASAP, so, desperate times call for desperate measures. Plus, it's not so bad," added James with a sly smirk, "all I did was lift the wallet off a very rich individual, I'm positive that few grands won't be missed by him."

Appalled by James' words, Adelina struck him in his stomach.

James doubled over coughing, as Adelina seethed "James, I am already irritated by the fact that we are currently breaking the law, and I am just seconds away from breaking your neck, if you want to keep forcing my hand, please be my guest, but make sure you are well aware that I will hurt you!"

James took a breather, he looked over at the woman he considered a little sister, and chuckled, then he straightened himself up and scuffed her hair as he said "calm down kid, you know you love me, but I got to tell you, that's a mean punch you got there, so I have to ask you again, are you sure you're not a man?"

Adelina made a move to grab his neck, but Katharina quickly stood between them and said "Aden, he's just trying to get a go at you like the pest that he is."

"Ouch." Exclaimed James as he feigned hurt.

"Anyways," said Katharina rolling her eyes at James' childish behavior, "Just get the tickets booked, ignore him, and save your anger to use as motivation to kick some rogues', a crazy male who calls himself the Alpha's, and that thirsty she-wolf's arse." Reasoned Kat, and Aden smiled.

What would she do without Kat?

Adelina shook her head, pushed aside her guilt, and managed to book the last-minute tickets, and soon enough, they were on their way back to America.

Adelina's pnt. Of view

This is it.

It's official.

I was going back to the pack.

But I couldn't even determine how I felt, I just hope I made the right decision.

Every intuition that I have, my gut feeling, my mind, they are all saying that I made the right choice, yet my heart is silent.

What does it say? Why can't I hear nothing from deep inside? Is it because my heart is confused? Silent? Or broken with no hope of repair?

My heart learned to protect itself by building walls around it. Since the minute my mind could register how cruel the world could be, my heart armored up, yet right there nipping at the wall was hope.

My hope of a loving mate.

Soon enough he came in the picture, and my heart became unsure.

She was torn, she couldn't decide.

Let her walls down, and let him in? Or keep my eyes on him and let my heart decide which path to choose?

It was all up to her, my heart.

She slowly started to let him in, allowed him just enough space to test the waters.

Or so I thought.

Maybe my heart allowed too much space.

The countless moments made it difficult for my heart to choose.

The switching of gears and directions made it impossible to see which way we were headed.

One second my heart feels broken with harsh words, tears, and emotional havocs.

Yet the next, she feels warmth as she gets mended by the littlest acts of love, passion, kindness, and the sweetest of words.

One second hot.

The next cold.

And repeat.

Then, then, after all the ups and downs of the rollercoaster called a supposed "relationship", there came another individual.

Not a stranger to my heart, but his declarations, his feelings and his actions became alien to me.

At first, when I ran to get a breather from being marked by my mate, and being cornered by my best friend, I was confused.

But deep down inside, I knew.

She knew.

My heart knew what Peter was going to say.

But how could I come to terms with that?

How could my heart come to terms with that?

Peter had a mate.

He just got married.

And his mate, the sweetest person, understood that Peter and I were close, and she never got jealous, or felt uncomfortable because of the connection Peter and I shared.

But that night, I felt betrayed.

My heart felt betrayed.

But it felt equally the same at being the betrayer.

Hearing Peter's confession made me feel as though I was betraying Clarissa.

I could still remember that night, as though it was yesterday.

Flashback

He looked happy as his eyes scanned my face, which made me slightly uncomfortable, but then his eyes became dark when it landed on my marking spot.

"Aden? What is that?" He asked carefully.
"What is what?" I asked playing dumb, this wasn't going to end well.
"Don't play dumb with me, what is that on your neck?" He

asked, his voice becoming hard, his eyes darkening, as I started feeling uncomfortable.

"Mosquito bites." I quickly answered, trying to back away from him by shuffling my feet, that way it wasn't so obvious that he was freaking me out.

"Oh really? A mosquito bite that looks quite identical to that of a mate's mark." He said taking a threatening step towards me. Yeah this was most definitely freaking me out, and the fact that we were in a secluded area didn't comfort me either.

"It's a mosquito bite! Jeez Peter, did you think that I would let that asshole of a mate near me after what he's done, better yet mark me?! And to think that you actually thought better of me." I said anger actually taking me over, I mean yeah I was lying to my best friend, who was currently freaking me out, but then again I finally caught a glimpse of what he actually thought of me.

"I do think better of you baby, it's just I don't like the image of you with him at all, it's infuriating, knowing what he has done to you. Plus, you don't belong to him, YOU BELONG TO M- eh hem, sorry, something caught in my throat." He said as he faked cough again and walked away, while my eyes stared wide as saucers.

What was he going to say? That I belonged to him? Didn't he just get married? If anything, wasn't he in love with his mate? Even worse, did he just call me baby?!

Oh my, this just confused everything.

Too many questions, too many voices, I was running.

I bolted out the reception hall and into the woods, I ran and ran, my lungs in human form started burning, so I leaped into the air, transforming into my white furred wolf.

After running for hours, when thought I could manage my thoughts, I found my Inner being developing a mind of its own, and while I battled with myself to remain calm, and stay strong, I lost my strength and my heart released its inner voice.

I crumbled to my knees and I cried my heart out.

My inner voice expressed itself through my tears, my pain, and my hurt.

Before I realized it, I was shouting off the top of my lungs, screaming out of fury, while the ground withheld the relentless beatings from my fists.

Soon however, I had no more tears, and my shouts subsided when I was emptied of emotional strength.

End of Flashback

I wasn't sure how or when I made up my mind to leave, or officially leave America, yet here I was on my way back.

And now, now I'd have to face the monster that took away my inner voice, my heart's voice.

I'd have to face reality.

And when I voiced that thought in my head, it all became real.

It felt real, my decision was final, and at the realization, I felt it.

The skip and palpitation of my heart.

I was going back.

Chapter 31- "Let the Games Begin"

Third person's pnt. Of view

About approximately 11 hours and a few minutes later, Adelina was being shaken awake by James, as he announced that they landed in America, more specifically southern Georgia.

The minute Adelina was fully awake, she felt her heart skip another beat.

She was back.

With a deep breath, and a shake of tried motivation, she stood to her feet, and followed the other passengers out.

After going through their final travel procedures, they found themselves on their way back to the pack's territory, however, they made a quick stop at a hotel for Katharina, where they planned to pick her up after everything was over.

James and Adelina then took a bus, that dropped them off at the tip of the forest, and there, they went in by foot.

Once they were sure they were well hidden by the thick pine trees, and the large maple trunks, they both transformed into their wolves, and went zooming through the forest.

Meanwhile, James had announced to the Alpha that they were here, and so it was time for them to start putting their plans to work.

"Alright everyone, James and the Luna are on their way, so you all know what you must do. Try to be as subtle as you can, and let's get these bastards out of our territory." announced Demitrey.

"Yes Alpha." came the pack's uniform response.

And everyone got to work.

First, the mated she-wolves started a ruckus among themselves, making sure that the noise was loud enough to draw in the rogue in charge of guarding them.

The rogue appeared with a sneer on his hideous face as he said, "what's going on here?"
With a hidden smile, the girls already knew that their part of the plan had worked.

Cilia placed an angered face, pointed at a disguised Kade, or in this case Kadie, and exclaimed in anger "she stole my lipstick, and I want it back!"
"What would you need lipstick for? It's not like it would help you." Said Kade, while he tried to sound as feminine as possible, though it didn't help that some of the girls were quietly giggling at Kade's effort.

"Well what do *you* need lipstick for?" Said the rogue as he looked over at Kade, lust written in his eyes.

Kade surprised and angered by the man's gaze took a threatening step towards the unsuspecting rogue, but Cilia caught on to his actions and stepped in front of him and said "yeah, what *do* you need the lipstick for?" As she sent him a warning glare.

Kade caught the upper hand on his composure and said, "that is none of your business."

The rogue shook his head, but then stepped towards Kade and said "well, maybe she misses her mate, so she dolls herself up to feel better. But," said the rogue, as he stood in front of Kade "baby girl, if all you wanted was some company, you could've just asked, I would've gladly taken care of you, and your mate wouldn't have to know."

He whispered in an effort to sound seductive, though he failed poorly, and he even had the audacity to wink.

Kade's eyes widened, then narrowed in anger, he gasped over dramatically and exclaimed "how dare you?" Then following his words, his palm went flying towards the rogue's cheek, as a harsh slapped echoed around the room.

And everyone stood frozen.

The rogue's neck snapped to the side, as he blinked multiple times in order to come in terms with what just happened, but before he could fully recover from his shock, he was ambushed and taken out by the ladies, while Kade rid himself of his feminine disguise.

Part one of the plan was complete, because now, Kade had the keys to free everyone trapped in the castle, but most importantly, he had a way out of the room where the She-wolves were being held in, and with the first part of the plan complete, it was time to move on to part two.

Demitrey, with the help of the keys he withheld since Kade left the dungeons, managed to free himself from his shackles, then he snuck out of his cell, freed the nearest warriors, then handed them the keys, and they nodded in silent understanding, because they knew what had to be done.

Then, after taking care of his part, Demitrey went back to his cell, and pretended to be in his shackles, it wasn't time for the rogues to know of his freedom just yet.

The warriors moved stealthily and quietly in the dungeons, and one by one, each warrior was freed.

Now, it was time to take out the rogues that guarded the dungeons.

Since Kade's contradiction, they added another rogue to the two previous guards, who apparently had more common sense then the first two combined.

So, the warriors would have to use a different approach to lure the rogues in.

First, some of the warriors took their shackles, and beat them against their cells.

The noise echoed throughout the entire dungeon, until it reached the entrance.

The rogues heard the ruckus but chose to ignore it.

However, when the noise only intensified, curiosity got the best of one of the rogues, and he said "Look, let me go check and see what all that noise is about." And with that he made his way into the dungeon.

Big. Mistake.

The minute his body was hidden by the shadow of the dungeon, he found himself in a headlock, and before he could scream, the sickening crack of a broken neck sang throughout the dungeons, followed by an eerie silence.

In fact, it was so silent, that the second rogue was both dumb and smart enough to go check for his partner.

However, the minute he disappeared from the other rogue's sight, he was strangled to death by the awaiting chains of the oppressed warriors.

Now, all they had to do was play the waiting game.

The third, and apparently brightest of the three rogues noticed that his two imbecile companions had yet to return.

But for a minute he didn't seem phased.

When about ten minutes went by, and they were still not out, he sucked his teeth and said arrogantly "you asshole better not even think about playing a trick on me. Get your butts out here."

Silence.

"I'm serious, stop this childish foolishness, and come on out." He demanded, yet all he was met with was utter silence.

"Okay wise guys, enough of this silly rant, come out now, and I won't tell boss that you're lazing on the job." He said, his voice now unsure.

When he received no reply, he shrugged, but sadly allowed his curiosity to get the best of him.

He took careful steps towards the entrance, but eventually, he buried himself in the darkness of the dungeon, and the darkness was the last thing he ever saw.

The moment he was at arm's length, one of the warriors wrapped one of the wolfs bane' covered chains around his neck, and muffled his screams with his hand, and eventually, with the lack of oxygen and the searing pain of the wolfs bane, rogue number three was taken over by death.

Now that three of the rogues were taken out, they only had to deal with the greater number of them left, however, because of the set plan, everything had to go according to the system.

Three of the warriors secured the rogues' shaggy clothing, and disguised themselves, then one by one, they each stood at post at the front of the dungeon, while the others laid low, awaiting the arrival of their Luna.

Meanwhile, inside the castle, Kade was finally able to rid himself of the she-wolf charade and, like the others, disguise himself as the rogue they ambushed.

Then he stationed himself outside the she-wolves' doors, also awaiting the Luna's arrival.

From this point on, the Luna was the one who would get the ball rolling and set off the domino effect.

She was their secret weapon, and the most important player in this battle. She was also the element of surprise.

"The Alpha" had no idea what was coming for him. The games were just beginning, and it was going to be one heck of a ride.

Chapter 32- "Game time"

Adelina's pnt. Of view

We reached the pack's territory line just as the sun went down.

Once we were close enough, we could even see some of the rogues hanging around the yard.

I was just about to step out of our hidden spot when James pulled me back, and signaled for me to be quiet, then his eyes glazed over, and I realized that he was mind linking with someone, most likely Demitrey.

At the thought of him, my heart fluttered, then it's as though I was hit with a ton of bricks as my back, my wrists, my arms, and my legs started to ache.

My bones screamed in agony as my knees buckled.

I sucked in a sharp breath but managed to stay on my feet, when all the sudden James was back to normal.

But I wasn't.

I felt something in the back of my mind, like the whisper of a tickle, then I heard his voice.

It was faint, soft, and if I tried to focus enough, I could almost hear what he was saying.

I shook my head then tapped James as I whispered "James, I think I just heard Demitrey in my head, and out of the blue, I feel pain all over."

"I know," he said calmly "he's trying to communicate with you, and the pain, well now that you're close enough, you can feel the pain from his torture."

"Why can't I hear him clearly, and why am I now feeling his pain?" I asked frantically in a harsh whisper, as the pain intensified.

"Because, he marked you, but you didn't mark him, and the mating process wasn't completed." He explained patiently.

"Oh, okay, well then what are we waiting for? We have to go help him." Both my wolf and I said simultaneously, as I made a move to step out of the forest again.

But once again, I was pulled back by James.

My eyes snapped at him in a hard glare, and he bowed his head in respect, yet he whispered, "I am sorry Luna, but with all due respect, the Alpha already has a plan, and we must stick to it."

I looked over at him for a bit, but when I realized he wouldn't budge, I grumbled and crossed my hands childishly as I said "fine, so what's the plan?"

He smiled and said, "we wait for the signal."

So, we crouched back into our hiding spot and waited.

However, while we waited, I couldn't help the way my mind drifted off to its sole topic, Demitrey.

Demitrey' s pnt. Of view

"*Alpha, the Luna and I are in position. Whenever you're ready.*" Came James' voice as it rang in our mind link. "**Great, good job warrior, I knew you would bring her back. Alright, wait for my signal, I will alert everyone, and everything will go as planned.**" I said, then focused on the pack link, but before I could speak, I felt the urge to contact my mate.

I was dying to hear her angelic voice.

I have missed her so much that my heart was currently palpitating just at the thought that she was near.

Before I realized, I was trying to communicate with her.

I could feel her in the back of my mind, but that was as far as I could go.

The disadvantages of not completing the mating process, but then again, that was all my fault.

I sighed.

It was worth a try.

I eventually shook off my disappointment and placed my longing to the side.

I would see her soon, all I had to do was be patient.

I opened the pack link "**everyone, the Luna is here, she is just outside the pack bounds, and is waiting on the signal to move in, so let's get the ball rolling.**" I declared, then added "**Kade, you're up.**"

"*Yes Alpha.*" Came his curt reply.

It was game time.

Third person's pnt. Of view

Kade, after receiving the Alpha's command, opened the door to the mated she-wolves' door and led them out, then he directed them down the hall making sure to keep the coast clear of rogues.

When they reached the hall where the unmated she-wolves resided, there were two rogues guarding that door.

He signaled for everyone to keep quiet, then with a calm stride, he strutted his way towards the two rogues.

Once he was within eye reach, one of the rogues saw him and greeted "oh hey George."

But just as he got closer, the rogue squinted his eyes then said "hey! You're not George." But it was too late.

Kade's fist met with the first rogue's temple, and just like that, he plummeted to the ground with a thud.

Just as the rogue's body made contact with the ground, the second rogue said "hey! The hell do you think you're do-" but his words were cut short as Kade grabbed him by the arm, slamming him face first into the nearest wall, causing the rogues body to sprawl out on the floor.

Once Kade was sure they were out cold, he fished the keys from the rogue, and freed the captured she-wolves, then the ladies made their way to the kitchen and castle basement, where the Alpha ordered them to set up the needed equipment, while Kade made his way out to the yard, still in rogue disguise.

Adelina's pnt. Of view

"How long do we have to wait for this signal?" I muttered impatiently.

"Just a few more seconds." James urged.

And just as he said, a few seconds later, a figure made his way to the forest.

He stood facing a tree, his back to us, when I noticed the movement of his hands.

Soon I realize what was happening, and I quickly averted my eyes, a blush suddenly scaring my cheeks.

"Really? The signal is a guy peeing?" I asked.
"No, he just plays a part in it." Said James as he paused, then he nudged my arm and urged me to look as he added "that is the signal." Then my eyes snapped back to the peeing man, as one of the warriors I recognized, sneaked up behind the rogue, and twist his neck in a very unnatural way, causing the rogue's body to fall limp on the ground.

Then he looked directly at James and me and nodded.

James nodded back then grabbed my hand, and we emerged from the tree line of the forest, and into the yard.

The minute we crashed into the clearing, James let out a powerful growl, and just like that the rogues were alerted.

One of them ran to a bell as he yelled "trespassers! We have trespassers!"

But before even I could register what happened, James lunged me onto his back, and dashed forward, heading straight for the dungeons.

Just as we reached the entrance, waves of warriors washed out of the dungeon and into the clearing, and soon the announcing rogue was singing a different song.

He rang the bell louder and more urgently as he declared at the top of his lungs "the warriors have escaped! The warriors have escaped!"

But before he could say it a third time, he was taken out by one of the warriors.

When the last warrior exited the dungeons, there was already a full-grown war happening.

Rogues and warriors clashed in the yard.

Humans transforming to wolves.

Howls and growls resonating in the open air.

And blood carelessly painted the once dry and parched ground.

I couldn't bear to look as one of the warriors pinned down a rogue and teared out its throat with his canine teeth.

And that was just the beginning.

The warriors were fluent and agile, just like their Alpha.

They had skill, and you could see their determination, you could tell that they had a reason worth fighting for.

And at that moment, I couldn't be prouder to be their Luna, although the gruesome sight was starting to make me feel queasy.

James ducked as we finally entered the dungeons, and the smell hit me like a truck.

It took all my willpower not to spill all my stomach contents onto James' back as he led me straight down the dungeon.

I looked around me as I studied the place where my people and friends were being held in for six months, and I couldn't help but cringe at the harsh shackles, and just the unsanitary condition of the place.

I didn't notice at first, but once I looked up straight ahead, I saw it.

Or more specifically, I saw him.

There he was, on his knees, chained and bound to the floor in his cell.

But what really caught my attention was the way his eyes instantly connected with mine.

It's as though he felt my spirit, as I felt his.

My heart instantly picked up its pace.

I thought I'd never see him again.

I didn't expect to be back so soon, if at all.

My breath became quick and shallow, as I couldn't find it in myself to look away from his gaze.

I felt a sensation drive from my head to the tip of my toes, as a jolt of excitement left goosebumps on my skin as evidence.

I was back, and my mate was only a few feet away.

Chapter 33- "Cozy Picture"

Adelina's pnt. Of view

James' march finally came to an end when we were just outside Demitrey's open cell, and throughout the entire walk to his cell, his eyes never left mine.

Demitrey's eyes scanned my face, but then his gaze became confused, as his eyebrows furrowed.

It's as though he couldn't believe that I was here.

His eyes travelled from my eyes, to my lips, where he paused for a second, then his gaze started back on its travel.

But there wasn't much to see, since I was still perched on James' back, and when he noticed how my legs were wrapped around James' waist from the back, while his hands gripped under my legs, a low and menacing growl was enough warning for James to instantly drop me, bow respectfully, and make his way out of the silent dungeon, leaving only Demitrey and I.

I looked back at him and rolled my eyes.

The arrogant asshole still didn't lose his possessiveness, nor his jealousy.

I stepped into his cell shaking my head at him, then stood right in front of him, with my arms crossed, and one of my eyebrows raised.

Funny thing was, while I looked calm and collected on the outside, my insides where a total opposite.

My heart was racing, and I was struggling to keep my breathing calm.

As his eyes hungrily took in my stance and my form, goosebumps rose high above my skin, and my insides felt as though a tsunami of butterflies and a tornado of flurries were dancing the polka.

When it seemed as though he had enough, he finally stood to his feet, the chains rattling, while his bones cracked from movement as a result of being stuck in the same position for a bit.

He skillfully removed his shackles, his eyes never leaving my sight, then he bent back, cracking his spine, followed by squatting to crack his knees, and finally, finally he flexed and stretched his arms, causing his arms to crack, and his biceps to bulge, and my mouth watered.

James's mentioned that, no matter what they went through over the last few months, Demitrey made sure that they kept up their strength.

And hot damn! They did.

Mama was liking the picture in front of her, as much as her wolf was.

No. Wait! No.

I shouldn't be thinking like this!

"*Mmh, I don't min*d" pureed my wolf.

Get a grip!

I shook my head, now wasn't the time for this.

Demitrey smirked, as though he could hear my sinful thoughts, and my eternal struggle.

He then took a few steps towards me, and to my surprise I stood my ground.

When he was close enough, he opened his arms, then gave me a charming smile as he said joyously "Babe!"

And just like that I found my hand flying, and coming in perfect contact with his cheek, causing the sound of a sharp slap to resonate around the halls of the mute dungeon.

"You asshole!" I yelled, then turned from him, anger suddenly overtaking my veins.

I noticed in my peripheral vision that he slowly turned his face, then touched his cheek, that was already going red, he shrugged but smiled as he said "Okay, I deserve that." And my anger intensified.

My hand once again flew, but this time, it wasn't a slap it was a punch.

His neck turned harshly on impact, as he staggered over.

"Damn baby! What have you been eating since you been gone?" He said, then spit out some blood.

"Why didn't you tell me about the letters?" I demanded my hands on my hips, my face masked in anger.

He straightened himself up, then wiped the blood on his lip.

He looked over at me and smiled as he said, "damn I missed you."

For some reason his words caused my heart to skip a beat, but then I realized that he didn't answer my question, so I punched him again, straight on the nose.

"ANSWER ME!" I demanded, my voice booming, bringing the quiet dungeon to life.

"Because," he said, then spit out some more blood "I didn't want you placed in any danger. If anything, any more danger. My reputation alone already placed your life in jeopardy, and as your mate I would do anything to keep you safe." He said, then he touched his nose and pouted as he said "oww, that hurt." He touched his nose again, then close his eyes as he healed himself. When he managed to touch his nose without wincing or flinching, he smiled and said "there, all better."

I couldn't help but chuckle at his childish behavior, but I soon started scolding myself for being affected so easily.

I was supposed to be mad at this man, not feeling more and more attracted to him.

My anger was slowly diminishing, but I felt like hitting him one more time, just for old time sake.

Before he could register what happened, my hand landed against his cheek, and this time he said "hey! What was that for?"

I looked over at him and said, "that's for everything you put me through idiot, when all you could've done was tell me what was going on."

At my words I felt my anger rise again, and this time, with a mind of its own, my hand attempted to get another shot at him.

Key word: Attempted.

My hand was inches away from his cheek when he suddenly grabbed it, but that was just motivation, as my other hand went into attack.

Too bad he knows me so well.

His other hand captured my own in no time, he used one hand to hold both of my hands behind my back, then he snaked his free arm around my waist, and hoisted me close him, causing my chest to collide with his own in a very erotic manner.

My breath came out of me in a whoosh, and my eyes were suddenly captured by his own.

"Now that's better." He muttered in a low tone.

His eyes travelled from my eyes to my lips, and he started to lean in.

His actions and our current position had my heart going haywire.

Where our hands made contact tingles erupted, and my cheeks flushed.

He held me possessively, then continued to lean down, until his lips reached their desires target, my mark.

Before I could stop myself, a soft moan escaped my lips, and I found myself leaning my neck on the opposite side, to give him more access.

No. No. No!

Stop it right now! Screamed my mind, but my heart had developed a mind of its own.

I closed my eyes, and I felt myself being engulfed in flames.

My breathing became short, and occasionally, when he kissed my mark, or slid his tongue over it, a gasped would escape me, and I wasn't even trying to fight it.

Well, at least, I don't think I wanted to fight it.

I suddenly felt a sensation starting to build in my lower region, and the friction caused when my chest heaved against his own caused my twin buds to stand at attention.

I wiggled my hand from his hold, and tangled my fingers on his hair, pulling him closer.

When his canine teeth nipped at my mark, an alien sound escaped me, and I found myself wrapping my legs around his waist.

He turned us around and pinned me against the concrete wall of his cell, as the bulge in his pants came in instant contact with my core.

Before I could control my urges, I managed to grind myself against him, and he growled.

It was dark, possessive, scary, and erotic, but I wasn't scared because it was mine.

He was mine.

All mine.

He suddenly bucked his hips against my own and I gasped.

He did it again this time a whimper was all I could muster.

I felt hot.

I felt needy.

I needed something.

Actually no.

I wanted something.

Something only he could provide.

His actions sent various jolts rushing and heating up my entire being.

I wanted more.

So much more.

Yet, for some reason, deep within all that layer of arousal, there was still a sane part of me, saying that this shouldn't be happening right now, that I shouldn't be allowing myself to get seduced by my mate.

But his actions, the constant nipping of my mark, his grinding against my core, and his possessive hold on me were sending me spiraling down a tunnel of lust, want, need, and something else.

But, that sane part of me was right.

This shouldn't be happening.

I snapped back to reality, and struggled as I said "Demitrey, we need to stop. We can't keep going. You know, in fact I'm still mad at you." Though my attempts weren't quite as convincing, given that my voice sounded breathy and moany.

He paused, then pecked my mark one more time before he pulled away, as he gently placed me down, but he didn't let go, which I was thankful for, because my mind was somehow still in a haze, and my knees buckled under the pressure of the heated environment.

He smirked at my flushed cheeks, and my weak attempt to calm my breathing, then he sighed and said, "I know you're still mad, but I missed you so much."
"Well, if you told me about the letters in the first place, we wouldn't be here now would we." I muttered sarcastically.

His eyes suddenly became dark, and I can promise that it was not from lust.

"I already told you, I didn't want you in danger." He said, his voice low.
"But I'm your mate, we're supposed to deal with things together." I argued back.
"You're right, we are mates, " he said as he took a step towards me, his eyes dark, and I found myself taking a step

back, but there wasn't enough distance between the wall and I, and soon he was on me, and had me caged in by placing his arms on either side of my head.

He looked deeply in my eyes, and there I saw sincere emotions.

There was hurt, pain, anger, sorrow, remorse, and something else.

Something special.

Unique.

He then said "I also know that as your mate, I'm supposed to care and protect you, and if it means going through all that we went through then fine! But look, I admit, I should've approached the situation in a different manner. And for that I apologize."

Then out of nowhere, he dropped to his knees and wrapped his arms around my legs, as he placed his chin on my belly, his eyes locked with mine.

"Adelina, baby, I'm so sorry. And I know that my words probably mean nothing, but I will stop at nothing until I earn your forgiveness, I will go through hell and back, I will grovel, and I will beg until you forgive me. You probably couldn't determine this, but from the moment we met, I fell in love with you, and while I tried to cover up my feelings, I made excuses to see you, to touch you, and to kiss you. I love you Adelina Veraso. I love you so much. I meant what I said, you make me lose control, you demand my attention every second of the day, and I wouldn't have it any other way. Not a day goes by that I don't reminisce on your voice, your smile, your actions, your sweet perfume, your kind ways, and just who you are. I love you." He declared, as tears welled up in his eyes.

I opened my mouth to say something but was cut off, as someone else spoke up and said, "well well well, what a fucking cozy picture."

Chapter 34- "Cat Fight! The She-Wolf Way"

Adelina's pnt. Of view

Demitrey quickly stood to his feet, placing an arm in front of me protectively.

But I shook my head and placed my hand on his arm bringing it down, causing his eyes to meet with mine.

Then I placed myself to stand right next to him, and simultaneously, our eyes landed on the two figures standing at the entrance of Demitrey' s cell.

The first person my eyes zeroed in was a smug looking Serena, who seem to have gotten into some trouble with the wrong wolf, since her throat was scarred with canine teeth marks.

She was wearing very tight skinny jeans, with a white shirt and a leather jacket, matched with leather boots.

Almost like my black jeans, grey shirt, leather jacket, and leather boots.

Her eyes were settled on me with what I believe she mustered up as a fierce glare.

Too bad mine outdid hers.

I could feel anger blazing through my veins just at the sight of that female.

I mean, she is not ugly, as far as appearance on the outside.

But we all knew what evil creature lurked on the inside.

With her wavy silver blonde hair, bright blue eyes, and slightly pouty lips, she wasn't all that bad.

Too bad she slept with my man and couldn't seem to keep her paws to herself when it came to me.

She looked as though she wanted to pounce, and my fists were begging for her to do so.

I wanted to throttle that she-wolf.

I was going to end her.

And my wolf was quietly encouraging that I do end her miserable existence in the back of my mind.

Nevertheless, I managed to move my gaze away from her and to the figure next to her, which was a man with his arms crossed behind him, and a mask settled upon his face.

His hair was dark brown, gelled and styled to the side.

His clothes included blue jeans, and a red shirt.

His mask was a white mask, with eye holes and a mouth hole, though he did not speak.

It was hard for me to see his eyes, but I could feel his gaze on me, resulting in alien goosebumps that rose uncomfortably on my skin.

I took a deep breath in and managed to calm my nerves.

This is why I was here, to help save the pack.

Time to own up to my position.

Time to play Luna.

I raised my head defiantly and trained my eyes on the two dark holes of the mask.

"Who are you?" I asked calmly, after taking another deep breath.
"Show your face you coward." Ordered Demitrey, in a deadly quite tone.
"Yeah you sneaky bastard, show yourself." I spoke up once again, standing next to the real Alpha.

Serena scoffed and rolled her eyes as she said, "can I shut her up already?"

My eyes shifted over to her quite calmly as I said "Hoe I wish you would. These walls are begging for a paint job, and I think your blood will do nicely." I smirked as I replied confidently.

She took a step forward, as I mirrored her actions.

She moved her neck from side to side as a cracking sound echoed through the hollow cells.

And I just kept my eyes on her every move, as we circled each other.

She smiled an ugly smile as her eyes gazed over at me.

"Oh, I have been waiting on this day for so long." She sighed excitingly.

"For once you and I are on the same page." I agreed wholeheartedly with a bitchy smile of my own.

Her smile suddenly faded, and she made a run for me, her fist raised.

With just a second to spare, I ducked and saved myself a brutal nose job.

What she wasn't expecting was for my fist to meet with her nose the second she turned around.

The sickly cracking of her nose bounced off the walls of the dungeon as she staggered back, aghast.

She touched her nose and seemed surprised as blood trickled on top of her lips.

She wiped it away, angry, then made a run for me.

I wasn't expecting a blow to the nose, and soon blood was also running from my nose.

My head swung back, but I quickly recovered.

I've had way more violent physical altercations in the past for heaven's sake, her punch was nothing compared to those.

She smiled as though she won the lotto and made the biggest mistake.

She turned her back on me, blinded by her pride.

I ran up to her, grabbed her by the hair, swung her around and pushed her, causing her face and chest to come into harsh contact with the concrete wall.

With her being disoriented, I took the advantage, and tripped her leg, causing her to land on the floor on her back.

The second she was down, I straddled her, held her by the collar of her jacket, and my fist went to work.

It was like a programmed machine.

My fist continuously made contact with her face, as she laid there limp.

At first, she tried to pray me off, scratch my face and neck with her claws, but to no avail.

I didn't relent on my attack, if anything, her feeble attempts to free herself only made me want to hurt her more.

I was going to kill her, and nothing was going to stop me.

When her eyes were closed, and her breathing became ragged, I stood off her, and made my way back to Demitrey.

But the bitch just wouldn't let up.

She laid there for a few seconds, I take it that she was reviving from my vicious attack.

I caught her movement in my peripheral vision as she stood up and ran my way.

I played the waiting game and the oblivious card, but the second she was on to me, I turned around with my hand raised and buried my extended claws into her flesh.

She froze, surprised, and probably confused at the invasive object in her body.

She looked at me, and I looked at her, then I smiled a victorious smile as I saw defeat take over the features of her entire being.

I gave her a second to understand that she just lost to Demitrey's mate.

That she, Serena, the Alpha's mistress, was defeated by me, Adelina, the Alpha's mate.

When I felt as though she finally caught up with the story, I smiled again, then I ripped her throat out.

Blood sputtered from her wound and her mouth as she fell to her knees.

I wiped my hand then smiled again as I said, "that's right bitch, bow to your Luna."

Then, with my foot, I pushed her down, and once again made my way to Demitrey.

He pulled me in his arms and said, "that's my girl."

He leaned in as though to kiss me, but then the masked figure cleared his throat, and we looked over at him.

He clapped slowly and sarcastically, as he said "that was quite the performance, eh? I got to give it to you Aden, you always seem to surprise me."

And my heart stopped.

Chapter 35- "The Expected Unexpected"

Adelina's pnt. Of view

"No, it can't be." I gasped at the masked figure.

Why would he do such cruel things to my pack and to the Alpha?

"Come on, don't act so surprised." He said casually.
"No. I refuse to believe that you would hurt others like this! They've done nothing to you!" I said shaking my head.

Then I looked over at his as I demanded "Tell me! Why did you do it huh? Tell me Peter!" I exclaimed, my fist balled in anger, my heart beat picking up its pace.
"Ha! Peter? Who said anything about Peter?" Said the figure as his body convulsed in laughter.

Then he stood up straight, and his hand moved to the mask.

And slowly, almost teasingly, his fingers clasped over the mask as he removed it.

And for the hundredth time that day, my heart stopped.

Third Person's pnt. Of view

*Flashback to the day Kade escaped the dungeons. *

When Kade managed to rile up a fight between the two guards that stood at the entrance of the dungeon, and made enough distraction for him to escape, what no one else noticed, including Kade, was the other figure that lurked in the shadows.

The figure moved at a very relaxed pace, and even took the time to shake its head at the imbecile rogues.

Especially when it spotted Kade sneaking past them, and into the castle.

When the figure did make it to the castle however, the game changed.

He stealthily snuck around the halls of the castle, trying his best to avoid the rogues that lurked around, until he literally bumped into one of them.

The figure grabbed the rogue by the throat and dragged him to a room.

When the door was closed and secure, he hauled the rogue by its throat and pinned him against the door as he demanded "who's in charge of this place?"

"Th-th-the Alpha!" Stuttered the rogue, his hands up and trembling in surrender, his eyes wide in terror.

"And where can I find this Alpha?" Asked the figure, his fingers tightening around it's prey's throat.

"Second floor, first door facing the staircase, it's the office, he spends most of his time in there." Blurted out the rogue.

The figure smiled in a sinister way and said, "thank you." And just like that, he twisted the rogue's neck, and left his body to fall limp on the ground.

He shoved the corpse aside, then made his way out of the room.

Then he went back to stealth mode, until he found himself standing in front of the office.

With a simple shrug, he opened the door, and invited himself in.

There, behind the desk, sat the masked man, who the second he heard the door close, spoke up in a makeshift authoritarian voice and said, "who dares enter without permis- oh it's you." Said the mask man as he noticed who entered the office.

Then a few seconds later, his body stiffened, and the mask man said, "what are you doing here?"

The figure who stood at the door shook his head, and slowly started approaching the desk, when he reached the guest chair facing the desk, he placed his hands on the back of the chair, and fixed his eyes right on the eye holes of the mask and said "Cut the crap, you know why I'm here. Where is she?"

The masked man visibly swallowed out of fear and said, "she's not here, she's gone."
"Gone where?" Said the figure in a slow, angered tone.
"That is none of your business, if she wanted you to know I'm sure she would've told you," said the masked figure, then he leaned back casually and shrugged as he added "and hey, you never know, maybe she got tired of you breathing down her neck about everything."

The figure shook his head, then stood up straight as he turned his back on the masked man, making his way for the door, while the masked man smirked, as though he won.

Except what he didn't expect was for the figure to use his wolf abilities, jump over the desk and have him pinned to the wall with a knife to his throat.

And it wasn't just any knife, it was a silver knife, bathed in wolfs bane.

The masked figure felt all the blood run from his face as the wolfs bane started to slowly eat away at his skin.

The searing pain made him grunt in agony, and he started struggle against the one holding him captive.

The man shook his head and said, "enough of this shit."

Then in one swift motion, he grabbed the mask off of the man's face, and threw it to the ground.

He looked up into the fearful eyes of his victim as said "there that's better. Now, I'll give you one last chance to tell me, where is she Peter?"

And Peter went rigid.

If he told the truth, he would die, if he didn't tell him, once the truth was discovered, he would die.

So, either way he dies.

So, Peter shrugged and said, "I killed her."

Peter watched as his captor's eyes became as black as the night sky, and just like that he felt it.

The knife ran through his throat, and Peter felt his body drop to the floor.

He felt as his heart went into overdrive, and blood pumped from his throat.

He couldn't breathe, he couldn't heal, and the wolfs bane was eating away his flesh.

He felt heavy, and he was burning up with pain.

Who knew that Karma was such a bitch?

Peter was meeting his end, and he never even had the chance to tell Adelina what he kept on the inside since the day he met his mate.

He never got a chance to explain the reasons for endangering her mate, and her new pack.

But most importantly he never got to defeat Demitrey.

Many won't understand, but even though Peter had a mate, he shared a special bond with Adelina. The problem, however, was that, somehow, he found himself still not over Adelina.

He tried to move on, and he would make little progress, just for him to dive back in deeper than before.

He knew Adelina would never see him as such because she was loyal and knew that he had a mate.

But when he found out what happened with Demitrey, he couldn't bear the thought of her with that beast, so he started taunting Demitrey, knowing that an Alpha will go to desperate measures to protect his mate.

Too bad that he never got to accomplish his plans.

With that last thought, Peter's upper half plummeted to the floor, and just like that, Peter was dead.

The man stepped over Peter's corpse, and grabbed the mask off the floor, as he placed it on his face.

Part one of his revenge plan was complete, now all he had to do was wait for his next victim to arrive.

He ordered some rogues to get rid of Peter's corpse, then he took his place behind the desk.

There was a new Alpha in town, but this time he wasn't looking for a Luna to love.

No, the Luna he was waiting on, was the Luna whose blood he was going to spill.

End of Flashback

Adelina's pnt. Of view

I couldn't believe my eyes.

I mean, was he truly here?

And if he was here, what was he doing here? What did he want?

My mind was buzzing with questions, yet all I could muster to say was one word, more specifically, one name.

"Valinick."

Chapter 36- "The beginning"

Third Person's pnt. Of view

Adelina stood shocked, but mostly confused.

She blinked a few times just to make sure the picture playing in front of her eyes was genuine.

"Val? Wha- I thought you were-"

"Peter? I know." Said Valinick smugly, then with a shrug he added "at first this was him, this was all his doing. Well up to this point."

"What do you mean?" Asked Adelina, still somehow in the dark.

"Wow, you are not very bright, which, at this point still doesn't show me what he saw in you." Said Valinick while he tapped his chin, as though he was thinking out loud.

Then his eyes once again focused on Adelina as he said, "what I mean is, Peter did all of this for you, so he could have you."

"So, what does this have to do with you?" Asked Adelina carefully.

"Well, up to recently, nothing. Absolutely nothing. I could care less what that idiot was up to, but then he crossed the line." Explained Val, as his facial features hardened with anger.

"What did he do?" Asked Adelina softly, trying to avoid arousing Valinick's sudden anger any further.

Valinick looked over at the woman who faced him with hooded eyes.

He lied when he said that he didn't see what Peter saw in her.

Because he did see it.

Anyone could see it.

She has spirit.

There's a fire in her eyes that burns with power and passion, and she was a fighter.

She, herself, is a weapon, a weapon very well disguised by her charm and beauty.

She had a humane side to her, very kind, generous, and absolutely approachable.

But that was it.

She was naive, yet she knew how to play on her innocence, even if it was subconscious.

The night he danced with her, he knew that her mate had marked her, but that's how he noticed her strength.

She was strong enough to withstand the power of the mate bond, and she was willing to leave her mate, but not before making sure her friends would be safe.

She was born and equipped to be a Luna, and that was both a blessing and a curse.

Because of her nature, it was hard for anyone to resist her, even for Val.

He wouldn't mind the picture of having such a woman as her by his side, but such a woman caused him the only family he had left.

"Tell me Aden, has Peter ever told you how he and I were related?" Val asked Aden simply, as he kept his voice neutral, void of emotion.

"Well, no." Answered Adelina, then she added "I didn't know you existed until we met at the wedding."

Valinick quietly chuckled as he nodded and said, "well then you should be able to understand that I only tolerated Peter because of Clarissa."

"Peter's mate." Confirmed Adelina.

"Yep, that's the one." Said Valinick, "I'm surprised you actually remember her." Added Val almost sarcastically.

"What? Of course I remember her. Where is she? Is she okay? Does she know about any of this? Does she-"

"Oh drop the act Adelina. That caring card won't work on

me. Don't even pretend to feign worry for her." Declared Val, cutting Adelina off.

"What? What are you talking about?" Asked Adelina, shocked at Valinick's outburst.

"I said stop it!" Ordered Valinick, his voice and anger rising.

"Stop what? I don't know what you are talking about!" Yelled Adelina, matching Val's tone.

"SHE'S DEAD! OKAY? She's dead. Peter killed her, and it's all because of you." Announced Valinick, pointing an accusing finger at Adelina.

And that was it.

The truth was out there.

Adelina felt as though she was hit with a bucket of cold water.

She felt numb all over.

She couldn't move, nor could she speak.

Her tongue felt as though it weighed tons in her mouth, and all she could muster was a "wha- huh?"
"Oh what now? Don't tell me you're paralyzed by guilt or is it that a cat got your tongue." Teased Valinick, as he felt his anger seeping through every inch of his body.

His wolf was aware of the enemy and was suddenly thirsty for blood and vengeance.

Meanwhile, Adelina found herself stumbling backwards, until her back encountered the wall.

She couldn't wrap her mind around what was said.

It was all happening too fast.

Clarissa was dead.

Peter killed his mate.

And it was all because of her?

Why?

How?

How could Peter manage to kill his own mate? The one he married? The one he swore in a church to love until death did them part.

Who could even be coldhearted enough to pull it off?

Not even Adelina could kill her mate, even though he put her through so much, she would never imagine killing her mate.

"You're probably wondering how Peter did it, and most importantly, what it all has to do with you."
Spoke Valinick, as he took in Adelina's ghost white face. He could tell she was shocked.

"Well, allow me to explain." Continued Val, once he received no reply.

"You see, our dear Peter never got over his feelings for you, in fact he was so taken by you that he was sure you were his mate, until of course Clarissa came in the picture. Now, at first everything was fine. You backed off knowing how the whole mate thing works, and you were happy for them. So happy to the point where Clarissa trusted you, until of course she realized that Peter wasn't exactly over you. How is that possible? Well, it's quite simple. You see, it's very unlikely for people to get over their first love, in fact, hardly anyone, whether human, part wolf, or part bat, has ever gotten over their first love. The only possible way for one to overcome the power of their first love, is through the power of true love, but you see, one must be willing to let go of their first love to be with their true love. But that is where the problem lies. It appears our dear Peter was afraid of losing you in his life, he was too much of a coward to let go of the past and begin anew. And so, the mate bond eventually weakened between him and Clarissa. At first my cousin, Clarissa, didn't make much of a deal out of it, she thought Peter needed to adapt to the thought of having a mate, but once she realized that he only smiled genuinely when you were around, that he would look at you differently than how he looked at her, it wasn't hard for her to piece the puzzle together. My cousin was angry, and she contacted me, and I told her to see if the actions were retaliated on your side, but to no avail. You are naive. Yet surprisingly you've managed to survive in this cruel and dangerous world. It wasn't hard for Clarissa to gain your trust, in fact it was too easy, but alas, she got nothing out of it, except of course her death. I told her how to sneak questions about Peter on you, I taught her how to observe your body language along with his, and how to catch the double meanings in conversations, but it was all for nothing. It's either you were a very good actress, or totally oblivious to the fact that Peter was in love with you." Explained Valinick, who was then cut off by Demitrey, who finally voiced his opinion since Valinick revealed himself.

"Oh trust me Valinick, my dear mate here is very naive, so there is no way she was acting. I can assure you of that." Said Demitrey in Adelina's defense.

Both Val and Adelina looked over at Demitrey, but he said nothing else, so Val continued.

"Eventually, Clarissa caught on to Peter and his attraction for you, and she was taken over by anger. She wanted to hurt you, kill you even. I mean could you blame her? Like every other she-wolf, she dreamt of the day her mate would find and claim her. She trained, kept fit, learned to take care of a home, and she acquired all the skills needed just to be the best mate she could be, yet all she got in return was that her so called "mate" was taken by another she-wolf. But then again, she couldn't blame you either. Yes, you and Peter dated before he found his mate, and once he did, not only did you back off, but you changed your views of him. You no longer saw him as attractive, but instead as a brother. You saw him as a best friend, nothing more, and nothing less. You were so loyal to their relationship that you spent more time with Clarissa than with Peter. She could've killed you, you know. I mean you ate with her, slept over with her, drink from the same cup as her, and even sometimes shared wardrobes with her. There are countless of times where she called me, explained that you were coming over, and that she would hurt you, but you being so oblivious and unaware of the reason why she hated you made it difficult, but then, she found her salvation. You were being shipped away to the most known ruthless Alpha, Alpha Demitrey Jackson, who turned out to be your mate. Now you may have not known that he was your mate when you first met him, but the minute you told Clarissa about him, she already knew he was your mate. Even though that day you were crying, she could tell the attraction you had for him, by the way you described him, spoke about how you felt around him, she already knew, I mean she already had a mate, so she knows the signs, but that was also the problem. Because just like Clarissa noticed, so did Peter, and so, the letters started. Tell me Aden, have you ever stopped to think about what Peter was up to that day when he ran up to his room after you told him about what took place between you, Demitrey, and your father?" Questioned Valinick.

    And Adelina shrugged " I thought he was angry, maybe even shedding a tear or two."

"Ah but that's where you're wrong. Alpha? Mind

enlightening your dear Luna here? Please do tell, when did you receive the first letter?"

And Demitrey paused.

He opened his mouth, but then closed it.

Then he sighed and shook his head, as though it all made sense.

"That afternoon when I got home, the letter was already waiting for me, the day your dad announced that we were going to get married." Revealed Demitrey.

"Exactly, so you see my dear, the minute he realized that you found your mate, and eventually, you would fall in love, true love, and forget about him, the sneaky bastard he was got to work, which brings us to how this, your mate mistreating you, your running away, your pack and mate being captured, and the war, started."

Chapter 37- "Dirty secrets" Part- 1

Third person's pnt. Of view

Adelina took in a deep breather, the action somehow mirroring her brain's reaction to all the new details being given to it.

It was surprising that she was able to breathe at all, because with everything that was just said, it felt as though all this unveiled information was slowly suffocating her.

The words, details, and pictures that flashed in her mind, felt like a cold hand slowly creeping up her chest, while its dainty fingers wrapped themselves around her throat, and slowly, torturing, tightening around her air pipes.

She started seeing stars, and then it really became hard to breathe.

She found herself gasping for air, her lungs greedily grasping and absorbing the sweet oxygen.

Demitrey noticed her discomfort and stood at her side as he held her hand, the tingles of the mate bond instantly coming to life, and calming her nerves, while she leaned against the wall, in order to compose herself.

When she managed to calm her breathing, and regain control, she built up the courage, and thought over what Valinick said about Peter's attraction to her, and she must admit that he hit the spot right on.

She always did feel as though Peter was too close for comfort whenever Clarissa wasn't around but seeing as though he was always protective of her, she never made a big deal out of it.

She shook her head and sighed, maybe she really was naive.

"Anyway, the next day when you left with your mate, our dear Peter got to work. He already planned out various ways he would get you to hate your mate.

He knew how much you longed for a mate, and knew what you've always wanted in a mate, so all he had to do was play the right cards, and your mate would screw over, and I guess in the end, you would come running willingly into his open arms.

And you know what? The irony of it all is the fact that you played right into his game.

Tell me, remember the day you arrived? You had a run in with your mate's mistress, and then later a run in with your mate that left you in tears." Questioned Val.

And I didn't have to think much about it, that day was engraved on my memory, so with a silent nod, I answered.

He chuckled and shook his head as he looked over at Demitrey and said "Alpha, would you mind telling Aden what happened a few minutes after she was escorted to her room? Before you went up to see her?"

And Demitrey pondered over his answer for a few seconds before shaking his head as he looked at Adelina and said "Yeah, after Cilia escorted you up, I made my way to my office, and there on my desk, there was a second letter, but this time it wasn't just a letter, there were pictures of you and I when we were leaving your pack. The letter explained that the pictures were to serve as proof that whoever was threatening me meant business, hence the reason why, when I went up to your room, I was angry. I was never actually mad at you because of Serena, like I said, the minute I knew you were my mate, she was nothing in my eyes, but I had to keep my act up. Especially when the pictures became living proof that we were being watched."

"Exactly." Voiced Valinick, then he addressed me as he said, "and Luna tell me, what exactly did you do, after your mate paid you a visit?"

I thought over that day, and it all clicked into play "I called Peter and told him exactly what happened."
"And that ladies and gentlemen brings me back to my point," exclaimed Valinick as a sudden victorious smile settled on his lips, then he pointed at me and added "you, my dear Aden, played right into his game."

Was it sad to admit that this all, somehow made sense? It was all connected.

"Now you're beginning to see where this is going aren't you." Stated Valinick, as though in a question, but in the form of a fact.

I was about to agree when something snapped in my mind.

"Wait!" I suddenly exclaimed, "So what does Clarissa's death have to do with me?" I questioned.

"Wait, wait, and slow down. You can never be more anxious than the narrator." Claimed Val, then he pointed to himself smugly, "I'm telling the story here."

He then cleared his throat, being the drama king that he was, and once again started to speak.

"So, once you called Peter and spilled out all the dirty secrets, he received his confirmation, and since he was the mastermind behind the entire thing, his game could go however the cards were played. 1- Play with the Alpha's mind, get him to push you away, and eventually into his arms. 2-get the Alpha to do something so rash that you would reject him, and go back home, where he could have you close. 3- If the Alpha did fall for you, he would threaten to kill you, and get the Alpha to do anything to protect his Luna, no matter the cost. So, you see, either way he was going to win. Except of course he underestimated the key fact that your naïve nature was also your biggest strength. See all his plans came to play, Demitrey did push you away but you were so naive and kind at heart that you always came back. He hurt you to the point where you rejected him, but then you formed a bond with individuals in the pack and so you didn't plan to go back home. And well the Alpha did fall for you, I mean he no longer cared for his mistress, and he electrocuted a guy just because he touched you at the club, so the Alpha falling for you was Peter's last resort. And everything would probably have worked out, if Clarissa didn't have a run in with Serena."

"What?" Both Demitrey and I questioned simultaneously.

"Oh yes, didn't you know?" Questioned Val, feigning shock.

"Well this is interesting." He added with a smile.

Adelina found her eyes trailing down to where Serena's deceased body lay, and she wondered "what did she have to do with this?"

"I'll gladly explain. You see Serena started seeing a change in Demitrey the minute you came into the picture, and though it wasn't really up to her, as his mistress, she had to make sure that Demitrey didn't fall for you." Explained Valinick.

"What do you mean it wasn't really up to her?" Questioned Demitrey.

And Val scoffed.

He rolled his eyes and shrugged as he said "come on Demitrey, did you forget who introduced you to Serena?" Demitrey stood for a second then said "no, I remember quite well actually."

"Okay, so now, take a trip down the memory lane, what was the first thing you learned about being an Alpha?"

Urged Valinick.

"That Alphas don't have mates." Replied Demitrey.

"And why don't Alphas have mates?"

"Because mates make you weak."

"Bingo!" Clapped Val, as though he hit the jackpot.

"So, if I say that Serena had to make sure you didn't fall for your mate, although it wasn't entirely up to her, who does all that point to?" Questioned Valinick.

And Demitrey tensed as he said coldly "my father."

Chapter 38- "Dirty Secrets" Part- 2

Third Person's pnt. Of view

"There you go." Supported Valinick.

"So wait? What does his father have to do with this?" Questioned Adelina, her curiosity suddenly peaked.

"My father," started Demitrey, just as Val made a move to answer, "Was the one who introduced me to Serena. See ever since I was little, my dad always taught me that mates were your weakness, that Alphas shouldn't have mates. He taught me that Alphas were ruthless, strong leaders, with no weaknesses. He made sure to drill the idea that mates for Alphas were nonexistent. So, when I turned 18, he introduced me to Serena, saying that she would make an incredible mistress to help me when I need a little distraction. At first, I brushed off the idea, but then he told me the story of what he did to my mother, and he also made sure to leave a warning, that if I did ever find my mate, he would make sure to destroy her. Luckily for us, he met his death before I could meet you, but it seems as though he left his legacy behind." Demitrey concluded, his eyes flashing over to Serena's corpse.

"Yes, well, that was a lovely story, but can we please get back on track? I kind of had this scenario all planned out in my mind, and it doesn't involve you becoming the story teller." Said Valinick, with the most self-centered tone I've ever heard.

When none of us replied, but only stared at him, he shook his head and said oh so gratefully "thank you. Anyway, when Serena got in contact with Clarissa it was because of Peter's letters. She tracked one of the letters all the way back to Peter and your pack, except when she got there, instead of Peter, she met Clarissa, and the two instantly made a connection over one common thing, their hate for you. Clarissa told me how both she and Serena worked out this plan to get rid of you, all she had to do was play the part of being Peter's eyes and ears in the pack. Hence the reason why he knew when you didn't pay attention to Serena Demitrey. Plus, have you ever thought how she found you guys when you travelled back to Adelina's pack? Anyway, as far as Serena and Peter, it was a win-win situation no matter how the game played out, if Demitrey pushed you away, you would be out of the picture, she would get Demitrey, and Peter would get Aden, if Peter got Demitrey to do something drastic enough, she would get Demitrey, and Peter would try to seduce you while comforting you, that would also get you out of the picture, but, as we can all see, that really didn't work out well for neither her or Peter. Especially when you, Demitrey, almost ripped out her throat yourself. Isn't that right?" Questioned Val.

"Wait, you did that to her?" Asked Adelina in pure shock.

And Demitrey's eyes scanned the lifeless vessel that occupied the floor.

"Yeah, she came into my cell talking a lot of shit, and showing off how she was Peter's second in command, meanwhile I was already angry, moody, and absolutely irritated, my wolf was also restless, so I ended up attacking her, almost killed her, which explains the teeth marks that were on her throat when you first saw her earlier. But that also earned me a beat down by Peter." Explained Demitrey, as memories of Peter beating down on him flashed in his eyes.

"I thought I made myself clear!" Boomed Valinick as he pointed to himself, all the while clearing Demitrey's thoughts "*I* am telling the story."

Both Demitrey and I locked gazed simultaneously, then we both looked over at Val and raised our hands up in sign of surrender, "the stage is yours." Declared Demitrey.

And Valinick smiled a tight-lipped sarcastic smile and gave one nod of his head as he said curtly "thank you."

He made a move to speak but paused as he gazed over at us, when he realized that we were quietly waiting on him, he smiled and said "now, if we are done with switching the roles of narrator, I'll continue the story. See, it wasn't hard for Serena to gain Peter's trust, and everything came to pass, the wedding was Peter's excuse to see you, but that backfired, especially when the Alpha placed his mark on you, so now it would become twice as hard to get you to love him. Peter overtaken by anger almost declared his love to you. Not that he didn't try when he was saying his vows, I mean seriously Aden, how could you not notice the way his eyes would shift over to you every time he said, "I Love you"?" Questioned Valinick, almost as though the thought bothered him.

"See? I knew I wasn't the only one who noticed the way he looked at you!" Exclaimed Demitrey, but when he noticed Val's hard gaze, he quickly muttered "my bad." Then he made a show of zipping his lips and throwing the key away.

Valinick kept a hooded gaze on Demitrey as he cleared his throat and said "Well yes. Moving on, Peter caught his mistake right before he could make a fool of himself, but I guess it was a little late, because we all witnessed you running out of the reception hall, into the woods, and eventually away. Never to be seen again. Until six months later of course. Anyway, after you ran away, Peter blamed Demitrey for putting Aden through such hardships, and decided on taking over the pack to serve as punishment.

But then again taking over the pack, and placing you in a horrifically filthy dungeon wouldn't be the right punishment for the man who stole his first love, so how exactly was he going to make you suffer enough? You see, no matter how idiotic I think Peter was, he was still clever enough to know exactly how to punish an Alpha. Tell me Demitrey, why did you wait 6 whole months to get in contact with Adelina?"

"Because I knew she wouldn't want anything to do with me, and I wasn't going to be one to blame her. I did unforgivable things to her, and I'm still so ashamed, so I didn't want to get in contact with her. I was willing to pay the price of my wrongdoings." Admitted Demitrey, as he scratched the back of his head in shame, his cheeks tainted pink.

"Exactly! See, Peter hitting you, beating on you, and hurting you physically did nothing to torture you, I mean

Alphas are strong, but he knew your only weakness would be the solitude of your mind, with your wolf constantly lashing out at you for hurting your mate, your conscious taking a bite at you for pushing Aden away, and your heart hurting because your mind was worrying about your mate's well-being, along with your pack constantly complaining, and you feeling helpless because as the Alpha, you couldn't do anything. But he knew eventually, you would get over that guilt, and reach out to your Luna. Especially with a little push. Tell me, what exactly pushed you to reach out to her?" Asked Valinick.

"My pack, they needed the strength of their leaders to protect them, and get them out of trouble, I had to put them first, and worry about the consequences of my actions later." Replied Demitrey, his eyes never meeting mine.

"And that's where he got what he wanted. See, he knew the minute James escaped that Adelina was coming back, I mean she was their destined Luna, and there was no way she was going to refuse. I must say, I'll give Peter kudos for developing such a masterful plan, but then again, there were way too many flaws and loopholes, and sadly Clarissa was one of those loopholes. You see after James' escape, Clarissa came to confront Peter about everything, she texted me that she was on her way to see him, and I waited patiently for her to give me an update, but nothing came. I felt a sad air take over the atmosphere, but I tried to not let the negative thoughts get the best of me. But alas, it was all in vain. When I confronted Peter, he admitted to killing her, and so, we've concluded our story, and now, " added Valinick as he calmly pulled out a gun from his back and pointed it at me "I'm going to kill you."

Chapter 39- "Winner & Loser"

Third Person's pnt. Of view

"Woah." Said both Demitrey and Adelina.

"Calm down," said Demitrey, as he slowly took a step towards Valinick, "you don't have to do this."

"One more step, and the trigger gets pulled." Threatened Valinick.

"Alright, alright. Relax." Prompted Demitrey.

"Oh I am relaxed, if I wasn't, your mate here would be been dead the second I walked in." Explained Valinick, as Adelina stood frozen, her mind in a frenzy.

Peter was in love with her.

And he's dead.

Clarissa hated her.

And she's dead.

Serena was obligated to be Demitrey's mistress.

And she's dead.

And now, Valinick was going to kill her, because everything happened, because of her.

"Hey Alpha! The war is ove- WOAH!" Exclaimed James as he walked into the cell, and straight at gun point, when Valinick turned on him, causing him to raise his hands up. "Well, isn't that good news, too bad your Luna won't be around to celebrate with you." Said Valinick.

James made eye contact with Demitrey, he had Val's attention, and he already saw the plan playing out in Demitrey's mind.

"Wh-what do you mean?" Said James, his hands still up.

"Well, I'm going to kill her." Said Valinick, as if it was the most obvious thing in the world.

"Why?" Asked James, as Demitrey slowly and silently creeped up to Valinick.

"Well, long story short, I'm avenging a family's death." Explained Valinick.

"Right, and what does the Luna have to do with this?" Asked James, distracting Valinick, as Demitrey edged closer to them.

"Long story, I'm sure it will make a great eulogy at her funeral." Replied Val, then in the blink of an eye, he turned facing his approaching enemy, with the gun barrel pressed against Demitrey' s forehead.

Valinick smirked, then arrogantly asked Demitrey "do you take me for a fool?"

"Actually," smirked Demitrey, "Yes, I do." And before Val could register what happened, James' fist went flying towards his temple.

He ducked last second, but hardly had anyway to escape, being that he was caged in between Demitrey and James.

Demitrey back up just in time before James' fist came in contact with his face, allowing Val enough room to maneuver.

Val knew he wasn't going to make it out in time, so he turned and aimed the gun, two shots rang out, just before he was slammed to the ground, by Demitrey.

With one punch to the head Valinick was out cold, just as Adelina's body plummeted to the ground.

Demitrey heard the noise and turned to find James holding Adelina.

She had two gun wounds.

One on her right shoulder, and the other seem to have penetrated inches below her ribcage, and blood was quickly drenching her shirt.

Demitrey wasn't thinking straight when he ripped James from Adelina and held her to his body.

She was having trouble breathing, and blood was trickling from the side of her mouth.

Her eyes were blinking in a craze, her chest heaving as she tried to catch her breath. The blood was greedily flowing from her failing body, to the dry ground beneath her.

Demitrey's vision suddenly blurred, and it wasn't out of anger.

Tears of fear and worry drowned his vision and he cradled Adelina's body in his arms as he whispered "no, no, no, no, baby, hold on, stay with me. Please, please, I can't lose you."

Adelina, smiled, then coughed as she mustered to whisper "now you want me to stay with you? So, it takes me getting shot for you to be romantic?"

Demitrey chuckled as he caressed his hand against her face, then leaned down to kiss the tip of her nose, even when she was fatally injured, she still smiled.

He truly didn't deserve her as a mate.

"I'm sorry." He said, then he started sobbing, "I am so sorry. Please, forgive me. I thought I was doing the right thing by pushing you away, you are my mate, and you were destined to be mine. I had to protect you. I love you Adelina. I know I had a crazy way of protecting you, and the word love coming from me is probably bizarre. But I didn't know what else to do. I love you baby, please, please forgive me." He sniffled and sobbed, his tears pouring on Adelina.

She looked up in his eyes sincerely and she said with a smile "stop apologizing. If I make it through this alive, you will have a lot of making up to do. Well, that's if I don't leave again."

Then as if something clicked, he gasped as his eyes widened and said "Aden, you have to mark me. The mate bond, it'll be complete, and your healing will be accelerated. I don't care if after this you reject me, but please, I don't want to let you go, at least if anything not now. I want that, if you leave me, I want it to be because you walk away, not because you are fatally wounded. Please." He begged.

Adelina smiled again, the pack was safe, and why would it matter if she died now? She has been good all her life, she became a Luna, and she made the biggest sacrifice anyone could've ever made. She accomplished so much, it wouldn't be a regret if her time was now.

In fact, she was starting to feel very sleepy, and her eyes could hardly stay open.

"Baby please, please don't give up on me now. I'm begging you. If you let go, I will end my life too." And that was enough motivation to wake Adelina's brain up.

She would never be at peace knowing someone else would take their life because of her.

If Demitrey was gone, and she was gone, who would lead the pack?

Over the time spent with the pack, Adelina learned about what Demitrey and his warriors truly do.

So, if he offed himself, the pack would be in danger, with no leader to guide them.

She couldn't allow that to happen, so she weakly lifted her arm, as she faintly whispered, "Come here."

Demitrey leaned down, and Adelina made it seem as though she was going to kiss him, but instead, her canine teeth extended, and she plunged it into his skin on his marking spot, and everything changed.

Adelina felt a surge rush throughout her entire being, and her body went rigid against Demitrey's.

She felt their bond connect and grow, the strength knocking the breath out of her. She then felt her connection reach through Demitrey, and out to every member of the pack.

She could feel them, she could hear them. But most importantly she felt him.

She felt Demitrey, and his wolf.

She felt her wolf spiritually intertwine with Demitrey's, and she felt herself grow stronger.

She was now connected to the pack, and their Alpha.

They were all now one.

Adelina retracted her teeth, and she felt herself spiraling down into darkness.

The last thing she felt was Demitrey's soft lips lingering on hers, then she felt her body being lifted, and by the eruption of tingles, she knew exactly who it was.

Demitrey felt the moment he and Adelina connected.

They clicked together like a puzzle, and when their wolves connected, it all felt so right, like they were meant to be.

He knew the impact would knock her out because she was physically weak, but he also knew that it would save her life.

Now when she woke up, it would be a whole different ball game.

She could always reject him, and move on, but for now, at least she was going to be okay.

James led them out of the dungeons, and into the yard, where everyone, young and old, big and small, stood waiting for their arrival.

The minute the pack spotted their Alpha and Luna, Kade, the beta bowed, followed by every other member of the pack, James included.

They all bowed respectfully in show of respect, then one by one, the crowd split up, and left a central path for their king and queen.

With a proud sigh, Demitrey carried his Luna down that path, all the way to the clinic, followed by Diana.

Their Luna was home, the pack was free, and everything was going to be okay.

Or so they thought.

During the entire ruckus, and the Luna being injured, no one really thought to hunt down Valinick as he escaped out the dungeons and into the woods.

Val ran as fast as his legs could take him. The trees and branches whooshed by his peripheral vision, while some carefree branches took a slice at his face and other exposed skin.

He could hear the thumping of his heart and could feel the blood rush through his body.

He could also feel the ground shake under each pounding footstep.

Valinick didn't relent on his run until he reached the cabin, where when he crashed through the door, coming face to face with an anxious Clarissa.

She rushed to her feet the minute Val appeared.

He took a second to catch his breath then looked up into the hopeful eyes of his cousin, then with a smile he said "It's Done. She's hit, and the wounds appeared fatal."

Clarissa jumped with joy then hugged her cousin, she helped him settle on the couch as she said, "Part 1 is done."
"Part 1?" Questioned Val.
"Yes, see with the death of their Luna, the pack will be devastated, but most importantly, the Alpha will be weak and vulnerable. Adelina stole my mate, now I'm going to seduce hers."

"But wasn't getting rid of her revenge enough?" Asked Val shocked.

"No! She took everything I had."

"She's dead!" Pressed Val, trying to make his cousin see some reason.

"Well, payback's a bitch." Shrugged Clarissa.

"Well, you're on your own for this one. They already know my face, there's no way I can help you." Explained Val, after thinking over Clarissa's words.

"Oh I know, but there is one more thing you can do for me. See you already know way more than you should. So, I have to tie up the loose ends." Said Clarissa as she walked behind the couch.

Val sat patiently, waiting to hear Clarissa's request, when Clarissa placed her hands on his shoulders.

She massaged his tense muscles, and Val found himself closing his eyes as he leaned into the calming rub.

"I always hate loose ends you know," conversed Clarissa, as Val hummed in response, "loose ends always leave a mess, and the mastermind always has to clean up the mess after. Now you know me cousin, I always hated cleaning up." Finished Clarissa, as she removed her right hand off his shoulder, and pulled out the gun cocooned in her back.

"Mmh I know, I remember you fussing at me whenever I left a mess in your room." Chuckled Val.

"Aa I'm glad you remember, so I hope there are no hard feelings… but you're a loose end, and I'd rather clean up now than later."

And just like that, Valinick felt the barrel of a gun press at the back of his head, and before he could even blink, a shot rang out of the secluded cabin and into the forest.

Clarissa made a show of blowing off the smoke from the barrel of the gun, then she got to work.

Demitrey knew her face from the wedding, so she would have to change her appearance.

It was time for a makeover.

She looked over herself in the mirror as she felt a victorious smile take over her features.

Peter, the mate who didn't want her was dead.
Adelina, the bitch who stole her mate was dead.
Serena, one of her loose ends met her end.
And Valinick, her faithful, but too nosey cousin was also dead.

She won.

Chapter 40- "The Alpha"

Third person's pnt. Of view

Adelina laid peacefully on her bed, while the monitor constantly beeped rhythmically, reflecting her sound and alive heart.

Demitrey sat unmoving on the same chair that has become his second bed, while his eyes scanned over Adelina's figure.

His eyes, bloodshot from silent tears and lack of sleep, swept over her facial features, while his mind constantly played lively memories of his mate.

She seemed so serene, and it was as though there was a faint smile just aligning her lips.

This has been the picture for the past few days. Demitrey would settle on the chair after taking a shower and cleaning up in the patient bathroom, and he would spend his hours just admiring her. His eyes never leaving their target.

He has yet to step foot out of the room.

He only leaves the room, to go to the attached bathroom when either Kade or James come in, allotting him just enough time to shower and change his clothes.

He hasn't taken a bite since the incident, and neither did he feel hungry.

His body felt numb and weak. His head was pounding with a constant headache, but he wouldn't allow any relief for the pain he felt.

He knew he deserved every second spent in agony, and more.

He couldn't seem to think of why he went so wrong. He was so set on keeping his love safe, that he didn't realize that he was also pushing her away. Not only so, he was so worried about not messing things up with her, that he did exactly that.

He thought over what Valinick explained patiently in the dungeons.

He couldn't help it when his heart constricted while angered, hateful, and remorseful sobs ransacked his body. He pulled at his hair in frustration, intensifying his headache. Sometimes he covered his mouth as he cried out, his lungs hardly keeping up with air that whooshed from his mouth as he continuously sobbed his misery.

His nose clogged, his throat burned and ached, but he couldn't stop himself.

He was so far gone that he soon found himself punching the walls.

His knuckles started bleeding, but he didn't seem to mind. He wanted to hurt himself. He wanted to feel pain for all the wrongs he did. Especially to the one he was supposed to love.

His knuckles soon became numb, and he was sure that he had broken some bones. But that didn't stop him.

He deserved it.

The pain.

The suffering.

He deserved it all.

He was about to hit the wall again when Kade grabbed his shoulder.

He turned him around as Kade said "pick on someone your own size."

Demitrey wasn't thinking straight when he swung, and Kade captured his arm seconds before his fist could meet his face.

Demitrey didn't even try to fight when he found himself breaking down again.

He fell to his knees and shut his eyes as tears poured out.

He didn't think he had any tears left but looks like he was wrong.

Kade fell next to him, and held his best friend, as the Alpha demonstrated his most vulnerable side.

When Demitrey's tears were now silent, and his voice was gone, Kade quietly stood, and left the room, giving Demitrey space.

He hated himself. He couldn't and wouldn't stop the tears that haunted him. Nor did he want relief for the current knife stabbing at his heart, or the pain shooting up his arms from his knuckles.

He wasn't even allowing himself to heal.

The pain was torture. But he deserved it.

He felt like nothing. He felt below nothing.

What he put his mate through, he didn't deserve to live.

He should've been the one to take the bullets instead of her.

She did nothing wrong.

He was constantly drowning and punishing himself by reminiscing all the heartbreaking moments he put Adelina through.

The image of her tears felt like knives jabbing and cutting away at his heart. The memory of her weak and bleeding vessel sprawled out in his arms burned through his soul, and he once again found his eyes flooded with regretful tears, and what felt like an army marching on his head.

"Alpha? Alpha?" Came Aunty D's voice, but she wasn't heard.

Demitrey was so focused on punishing himself by drowning his mind in the most painful and gruesome memories of all the wrongs he did to Adelina, that he didn't even realize that there was someone else in the room.

Aunty D quietly and carefully padded her feet across the room and softly placed her hand on the Alpha's shoulder.

His tortured, tormented, and remorseful eyes slowly drifted over to a worried looking Diana.

Diana focused on her Alpha's orbs. They were empty of the happy and powerful leader she, and were now just filled with regret, sadness, but most of all, the loss of hope.

Diana, along with the entire pack, were now all aware of what took place in the walls of the castle between the Luna and the Alpha, and they could only imagine what their Alpha was going through.

Diana knew that Demitrey had every reason to feel remorse, but she didn't want him to lose hope.

If it's one thing Diana knew about her currently comatose Luna, was that she was a kind soul.

"Alpha, you have to get some rest, and let me take care of your wounds. I assure you, the second anything happens you will be the first one contacted. And I won't allow any visitors in, and Kade and James will be standing guard at the door. You can't be an Alpha if you are weak and vulnerable." Explained Diana.

Demitrey looked sincerely into Diana's eyes as he said, "I don't deserve to be the Alpha."

Diana shook her head and said "that is nonsense talk. Nobody's perfect. You made a few mistakes. No one ever gets it right the first time."

"I know. But if it wasn't because of me, she wouldn't be here right now." Sulked Demitrey, as his shoulders sagged in defeat and remorse.

"Young man that is enough! Now you may be my Alpha, but I am still in charge of this facility. And unless you want to be dragged to bed by the ear, I suggest you straighten up, and go get some rest!" Declared Diana, as a stern look settled upon her face, and she placed her hands on her hips.

"Okay, okay." Sighed Demitrey, putting his hands up in surrender "I'll leave, but can I at least talk to her for a minute? In private." He looked up at Diana.

Diana's stern stance relaxed, and she cleared her throat as she said, "you have five minutes."

With nod from Demitrey, Diana turned, and left the room, closing the door to give Demitrey some privacy.

Demitrey stood and brought his chair over to Adelina's bed, where he sat.

He opened mouth to begin, but found nothing to say, as his eyes started scanning her face.

She sure was beautiful. Both inside and out.

He took a deep breath and opened his mouth again, this time he began "Aden, I-" then he paused and sighed.

He stood up and started pacing the room, while he rubbed his hands on his face, then grabbed his hair with both hand as he grunted in aggravation.

"Look," he began as he turned to her lying form, "Adelina, you have to come back. Come back to the pack... Come back to me. Kade and I are trying our best to keep everything under control, well mainly Kade, but they want me and you as the Luna to take over, and I can't do that, unless you're here with me. I want you to know that I'm going to be begging and groveling for your forgiveness. But please, for now, just come back. The pack needs you." He sighed as he sat back down next to her and looked at her face as he admitted "I need you."

He could've sworn he saw Adelina's face somehow brighten, while the side of her lips slightly quirked, but he blamed that on his exhaustion, and hope.

He took a deep breath as he said "Look, I'm pretty sure everything I say will probably come off as bullshit to you. But I didn't know what else to do. I'm so sorry baby, for everything. I'm not sure what I was thinking at the time, but I now know that I was wrong. I already told you, I won't blame you, nor will I try to stop you if you leave, but Adelina, please, please, I'm sorry baby. Forgive me."

Pleaded Demitrey, as he broke down in sobs, and at that exact moment, he felt a soft touch that wiped his tears. He knew by the eruption of tingles who it was. But he still couldn't help his surprise, when he looked up into Adelina's soft eyes as she smiled and said softly "shut up I'm trying to sleep." Followed by a chuckle.

Chapter 41- "The Luna"

Third Person's pnt. Of view

Demitrey's face lit up with a smile as he looked at the girl he was ready to kill himself for.

She could barely keep her eyes awake, but the smile on her lips was bright and alive.

"Are you going to keep smiling down at me like a creep or are you going to rest?" Questioned Adelina, as she slightly opened her eyes, then her smile widened as she added "you look like shit."

Demitrey was struck dumb, and he did look like a creep because he had no comment, his mouth seem to have frozen in a bright smile, and he was just so happy to hear her voice.

He didn't know how much he missed it till now.

He shook his head and finally said genuinely "that was the best compliment anyone has ever given me."

"Well I guess saying that you're an ass would second that?" Asked Adelina in an innocent tone, but her smile told she knew exactly what she was doing.

"Anything from you my love is a compliment." Cheesed Demitrey.

Adelina made show of rolling her eyes then she said "Okay sir. Now, please leave. I need to sleep, and you need a century worth of beauty sleep. So, shoo." Adelina tried to move her hands, but then decided against it when she felt the needle of her IV tube slightly shift under her skin.

Demitrey once again shook his head and said "Right. Sorry Princess, I'll leave you to it. I'll come see you later?" He finished in what sounded like a question.

It was silent for a second, until "Are you telling me or you're asking me?" Asked Adelina with one eye open, and a raised eyebrow.

"Um... I don't know." Said Demitrey, as his cheeks suddenly flushed red, and he scratched the back of his neck, his eyes looking anywhere but Adelina.

Was the big bad Alpha blushing?

He stood from his chair and turned his back to her for a moment. When it seems as though he had enough courage to look back at her, Demitrey pocketed his hands, as his cheeks enflamed some more then he asked sheepishly "can I?"

Adelina was struck appalled.

Demitrey. The big bad and ruthless Alpha, was asking her, Adelina, the runaway Luna, for permission?

She must have been dreaming.

"You're joking right?" Asked Adelina, an unbelievable expression plastered on her face.

Be still her heart, because she wasn't believing her eyes, or her ears.

Demitrey drew in a shaky breath as he said "I- well, I-I'm sorry." Then just like that he shook his head and made his way out the room.

What in the world was that? Thought Adelina.

Things were quite hazy since the day she got shot.

She has been in and out of consciousness and couldn't really get a grasp on her physical being.

It was as if she was floating and was in no control of herself.

The last thing she is sure about, was her marking Demitrey, her connecting with his wolf, as well as the pack.

Since then she felt herself wrapped in a cocoon of protection.

She felt warm, and complete, but her body needed time to recuperate. And although she had lots of rest, there was always a nagging in the back of her mind that continuously brought her to consciousness.

Her Alpha, her mate, was in distress.

She could feel his heart wrench. She could feel the regretful turmoil that ransacked his body, his mind, and his soul.

His remorse was quite suffocating, and it was as if she was witnessing first hand all that stabbed at his heart.

She knew he hardly slept. She knew he spent most of his time crying, but most of all she knew the reasons why.

The number one was his regret, because he mistreated her and pushed her away. He caused her unimaginable pain, and he wanted to punish himself for that. He felt as though he failed at being the mate she wanted, no matter what his intentions.

Number two was his fear. His fear that she would never forgive him. He feared that the minute she was healthy enough she would up and leave. He feared that he would never gain redemption for his wrongdoings towards her.

Number three was hatred. Hatred for himself. His stupidity. His arrogance, but mostly, hatred for allowing past experiences to cloud his judgement.

Adelina realized that Demitrey, at times, willingly drowned himself in painful memories of the past because his past is monstrous.

And when he reminisced on the past and his regrets, they felt alive, like a monster out to get him. He would pursue his past, then let his fear of it torture him.

If he made amends with what took place in the past, it would no longer haunt him, nor would his past serve as punishment for his mistake.

While Adelina was comatose, her wolf was contacting Trey, Demitrey's wolf. And her wolf became like two pairs of eyes that studied his past.

She learned that Demitrey grew up without a mother, and he always thought that his mom didn't want him. But once his father felt like he was old enough, his father told him exactly what he did to his mother.

His father ever since was harsh. Made sure that Demitrey despised everything about his mate.

His past was horrendous. His father abused him and used any tactic he could get his hands on just to make sure that Demitrey became just as heartless, and as ruthless. He tortured Demitrey mentally, painfully, and emotionally. It was so rash that Demitrey tried his best to be as perfect as he could. He wouldn't allow himself to fail. He *wasn't* allowed to fail. His father made sure to instill that in Demitrey's morale.

But through it all, Demitrey made it out human.

Demitrey offed his father the second he had the opportunity.

His pack's reputation was tainted because of the father's misleading's, but he did use that to an advantage.

Demitrey no longer used the pack as a weapon, but instead a Calvary, a salvation for those who had no hope.

She found out that when Demitrey found her, he was happy, until the threats started coming.

She felt Demitrey's internal battle with himself when it came to her.

She knows that he had good intentions, but being brought up the way he was, she realized that he didn't like to rely on anyone. Nor did he open up very easily. And, he didn't want to fail.

Demitrey Jackson made a mask for himself when he was under his father's custody, and he has worn that mask ever since.

Trey explained that Demitrey didn't want to let Aden know she was in trouble because just in case he failed at being a good mate, just in case he failed to protect her, he didn't want to fail her entirely.

He wanted to be the mate of her dreams. The one made perfectly for her.

She felt it when he beat himself up about mistreating her. She felt it when he was confused about his feelings for her. She felt it when he reminisced what her father said about mates, and she felt it when he would beat himself up for even considering his father's words.

But most importantly, she felt his defeat.

Demitrey was tired. He was lost, and she felt the constant regret nagging at the back of his head.

Looking back at all the factors that went into the equation of his mistreating her, Adelina had no idea what to think.

He was supposed to love her, but then again based on his background he could've easily rejected her or killed her.

He chose a mistress over her, but then he really did tell the truth about not sleeping with her. Even when she was leaving the hotel.

According to Trey, the second Adelina walked out the door, he pushed Serena away and went to the bathroom. While he was in the shower, he heard some noises coming from the room, when he opened the door, he found Serena standing by the room door and just moaning out loud.

At first Demitrey was confused, but after hearing Val's story, he figured it had to do with her and Adelina, and Serena playing the mistress.

Adelina was beyond shocked.

She wasn't sure what would she do.

She knows of many other individuals who have suffered way worst fate than hers, and by the grace of God, she was still alive, and well he didn't reject her.

He did mark her forcefully, and he hit her, but many others have been raped, beaten to the point where they end up in the hospital or worse, and some even committed suicide.

She couldn't determine how she felt. It was just confusion.

Total confusion.

And even now, as she laid on her hospital bed, her eyes barely open, she could feel his distress, she could feel his regret, his remorse, his exhaustion, and it all felt like an elephant just sitting on her chest, and a hippo resting on her shoulders.

She felt suffocated by all that Demitrey was holding inside, but there below all those layers of regret, shone something remarkable and unique. What felt shining through all those layers of despair, was something she wouldn't have dreamed to think of, or say out loud in the past.

And yet even now, she was afraid to think of it, because if she admitted to what Demitrey felt, it would make everything all too real, and just waking from a coma, that four letter word would be enough to give her a heart attack.

Chapter 42- "The Moon Goddess" -Part 1

Third Person's pnt of view

"Okay, okay everyone, it's time to let the Luna rest, you will have a chance to see her later." Said Diana as she ushered everyone out of the room.

As soon as the last person was out the door, Adelina's smile dropped, because although she felt happy to be alive, and happy to be surrounded by such as supportive pack, she hasn't seen Demitrey since the day she woke up, and that was about 4 days ago.

She didn't know how to feel.

Maybe relieved, because she had time and space to think?

Or was it somber because she missed her mate?

She constantly found herself going over that question in her mind.

How does she feel?

This had been the similar scenario since she woke up.

Diana in her excitement announced that the Luna was awake, and just like that, member after the member, her room would crowd in with visitors, flowers, cards, and teddy bears.

Then after hours of smiling and laughing in genuine joy, Diana would usher the last of the last visitors out, and she would be left alone.

Aden hasn't heard from Trey, and neither has Demitrey come to see her, but based on what Kade and James has told him, the Alpha is not doing so well.

He is constantly beating himself up, he won't eat, he won't sleep, and at times he purposefully tortured himself.

Adelina knows that what Demitrey did cross the lines, however, she's not sure who to blame because all he knows is violence and power.

Ever since he was young, his father abused his power, and continuously tortured Demitrey through violence.

The only time Demitrey got relief was through violence and by fighting back.

The only way Demitrey gained power, was by violence, killing his father, and taking over the pack.

Demitrey was never shown love, and once he found love, he was so afraid to lose it, that he retaliated to the only thing he knew best, violence, and show of power.

He made mistakes.

Nobody is perfect.

If only Adelina could reach out to him and tell him that he needed to stop beating himself up, but he blocked everyone out.

Adelina had so much quiet time, yet her mind's thoughts seem to fill up the room, like that of a roaring crowd at the world cup games.

She wasn't sure if she should stay and be Luna.

She wanted to talk things out with Demitrey, but what was she going to say?

Sorry for seeing you as a monster? And not try to reach out to you?

Adelina also found herself partially blaming this whole ordeal on herself.

Maybe she should've kept an open mind about her mate, and his motives. Maybe she should've seen the front he put on whenever he became too vulnerable. Maybe she should've tried to talk with him, reach out to him, instead of ignoring and avoiding him, hurting him by playing the jealousy game, telling him proudly that she would leave him, and pushing him away.

Maybe she should've noticed the signs, the different emotions that flashed in his eyes, the change in actions, the one second he's hot, the next he's cold.

She should've noticed the pattern.

Maybe she should've tried to tap into the humane side of him, the one that kissed her softly, held her and caressed her.

As his mate, maybe she should've tried to see past the mask.

He hurt her in ways she never imagined her mate would.

Yet couldn't she try and see past his flaws and mistakes? Like she wanted her mate to do?

Adelina realized that neither she nor Demitrey grew up with love. She yearned it as much as he did. And she was also as afraid as he was when she found him.

She didn't want to mess it up. But then again, he never allowed her room to reach out to him.

Or maybe he did.

When he explained that she made him lose control, when he told her that they couldn't keep kissing, when his emotions got the best of him, all of those were signs, she at least should've noticed something.

Her heart was constantly battling with her mind.

Her emotions were going haywire, and her inner thoughts were as loud as a booming amphitheater.

"My, my, the quiet of a room may not be so quiet after all, especially not with the chatter of your thoughts." Came a voice from behind Adelina.

"Who's there?" Exclaimed a startled Adelina, as she tried to see behind her, but then again, that was almost humanly impossible.

"Now, now, sweet child, no need to be startled." said the voice, kindly and tenderly.

Then in her peripheral vision, Adelina caught a short elderly woman with hair as white as snow move next to her bedside.

The lady wore a soft smile, and her eyes wrinkled at the corners, as her cheeks warmed with a rosy blush.

Adelina had never seen this woman around the pack before and she should've been afraid, or at least not feel as calm as she was.

"You... I know you... I think." Said Adelina.
"Yes dear you know me. Everyone knows me." Said the woman, her voice soft and motherly. Her eyes gleaming.

Adelina looked over the kind woman's features.

Although a senior, she was gorgeous. Her surrounding aura felt familiar, yet strange. It was powerful, yet it felt as though they were connected, and the air around her seem as though it was glowing.

Then, as if something clicked, Adelina's eyes widened.

"M-m- moon goddess." Breathed Adelina as she felt her heart quicken.

The woman softly laughed as she waived her hand and said, "oh sweet child, please, moon goddess makes me sound old, please call me Selene."

"Selene." Nodded Adelina after a while of staring in wonder

Then, her eyebrows furrowed.

"What are you doing here?" Blurted out Adelina.

And Selene rose a curt eyebrow.

Adelina looked down in shame, her cheeks reddening as she muttered "sorry. I mean it's not every day the moon goddess comes to see you." Rambled Adelina.

And Selene smiled.

"You're quite right. Well the answer is quite simple. You summoned me." Replied Selene.

"I did what now?" Questioned Adelina, raising a curious eyebrow.

"Well, both you and the Alpha. To be more specific, your wolves reached out to me, and it's funny because I destined you and the Alpha to be mates for a reason, and you guys are so alike, tell me child, what is troubling you?"

"I- well, I don't know what to do. There's this internal battle within me. My mind won't shut up, my heart won't relent. My instincts are going haywire, and my gut is in total chaos." Sighed Adelina, as tears suddenly flooded her eyes.

Before she knew it, she was full on crying.

What was she going to do?

"Now now girl, will you stop that. You're making this way harder than it is Adelina. Just follow your heart. Do what you know feels right. Stop trying to fight with yourself. Breathe, work it out, and go with what feels right." And just like that, Adelina leaned down to wipe her eyes, but when she looked up, Selene was gone without a trace.

Meanwhile, Demitrey found himself standing on top of the cliff that outlined the tip of the forest and marked his pack boundaries.

He found the view peaceful, somehow bringing calm to his turmoiled and battered heart, soul and mind.

He hasn't seen his mate since that day that he walked out, and he wasn't sure if she hated him or not.

He wasn't sure she even wanted to see him.

And he wouldn't blame her.

He marked her.

Out of fear, anger, and jealousy, he tied her to him, and now, she hates him.

She had to.

And that stung. Like a knife plunging repeatedly in his heart.

But he brought it on himself.

He deserved the pain, and so much more.

And maybe, just maybe, throwing himself down this cliff, this very rocky and jagged cliff, could be just the amount of pain he needs.

He would break his bones and tear his skin in agony as his body plummets down the side of the cliff.

Demitrey peeped over and saw a broken tree that left a sharp edge rooted in the rocks.

He imagined himself perched upon that tree. The speared edge piercing straight through his heart, and slowly, painfully, in a torturing manner, he would feel himself fade away from the world, away from existence, and away from Adelina, then maybe she would feel safe and happy.

He would no longer be around, the mate bond would be broken, and she would be free to choose whomever she wanted to love.

The thought of Adelina made him smile.

So maybe, just maybe, all it took was a single step.

Demitrey closed his eyes, tears welling up under his eyelids.

A pain bubbled hot in his throat, and his heart was hurting.

He felt a calming wind suddenly blow towards him, and he breathed it in and allowed the tears to fall.

One last time he whispered "Adelina, I'm sorry baby. I'm so sorry. I love you." Then he raised his leg.

All it would take was a simple step, and a simple breath.

"Now, we both know that this is not the best way to go." Said a voice, startling Demitrey, causing him to stumble backwards, and safe away from the cliff's edge.

He looked up with a startling gaze and found an elderly woman looking down at him with a kind smile, and her hands clasped calmly in front of her.

"Who are you?" Questioned Demitrey, "What are you doing here?" He added.

And Selene rolled her eyes as she turned and looked over the cliff, "of course you and Adelina are mates. You have so much more in common thank you think." She chuckled and shook her head, then she said "my name is Selene. I was summoned by Trey and Aden." Explained Selene.

Then she heard Demitrey gasp.

She shook her head and chuckled. They always had that reaction.

"M-m- moon goddess." Breathed Demitrey.
"Yes, yes, but I prefer Selene. Anyway, I don't have much time. You need to go to your mate. She needs you." Said Selene.

Demitrey stood, and sighed defeated as he said "she hates me. What she needs is to be surrounded by her friends and her pack. The ones that support her. Not the one that caused her so much pain."
Selene found herself rolling her eyes again, of course they were made perfect for each other.

"Now you listen to me young man, go to your mate, talk to her, and open up. Stop wearing that mask. Reveal yourself. Be yourself." Urged Selene.

Demitrey shook his head, his eyes cast down "She will never forgive me." Said Demitrey as he turned his back on the kind elderly woman.

She had a familiar aura to her, but with her being the moon goddess and all, it made sense.

With his back turned to her, as Demitrey contemplated his errors, he felt an otherworldly warmth and presence envelope his body, and he heard a young, rejuvenated, soft, yet mystical voice say "Go to her Demitrey, talk to her, I know how you feel, and what you are going through. I destined Adelina to be your mate for a reason you know." And just like that Demitrey turned to face the elderly woman, except she was no longer there, it's as though she vanished in thin air.

He breathed and shook his head.

What was he to do now?

It was late in the evening when Adelina heard a knock on her door.

She was sleepy, but when she felt her heart skip a beat, with a quiet "come in", she eagerly waited for the person to reveal themselves.

The first thing that came through the door was a bouquet of flowers, followed by a familiar scent that wafted through the doors.

She didn't have to see his face to know who it was.

When Demitrey closed the door, he turned to face an expectant yet surprised looking Adelina, with a shy smile, and rosy cheeks, he scratched the back if his neck as he said "hi."

Chapter 43- "Talk of the past" Part- 1

Third person's pnt. Of view

"Hi." Replied Adelina almost shyly.

Demitrey's blush deepened as he carefully walked towards her and handed her the flowers as he said "um, these are for you."

Adelina gladly accepted the flowers and replied "thank you. They're lovely." And Demitrey smiled.

He pulled up a chair then sat a few feet away from Adelina as he asked "how have you been? How do you feel?"

"I've been okay, getting numerous visits from pack members, and Diana says I'm healing pretty well, especially the bullet that pierced inches below my heart." Replied Adelina.

"Oh that's good." Was all Demitrey could muster.

"What about you, how have you been?" Asked Adelina.

"Oh you know, I'm alright." Replied Demitrey, avoiding Adelina's eyes.

Adelina noticed his actions and she raised an eyebrow as she said "when was the last time you slept? And don't even think to lie, the bags under your eyes will serve as evidence."

"Uh, I'm not sure." Replied Demitrey honestly.

"Well you need to sleep." Stated Adelina.

"I'll sleep." Agreed Demitrey, but Adelina chuckled as she said "sorry bud, but I don't believe you. Now, when Martha came over with her triplets for a visit, they were able to turn that," pointed Adelina to the couch in her room "into a bed. So that's exactly what you are going to do." Declared Adelina.

Demitrey gazed over at the couch, then turned to Adelina as he asked with a raised eyebrow "seriously?"

"I'm not laughing." Simply stated Adelina.

"But-"

"No buts. You and I have a lot of talking to do, along with many things to smooth out, so I suggest you get some rest while the offer still stands." Voiced Adelina.

"But I-"

"Uh uh."

"Aden-"

"Nope, not a word. Go get some rest, I mean you really do need it. You look a mess anyway." Added Adelina, then she turned off the lights.

Demitrey's eyes glowed in the darkness, but then he sighed defeated when he realized that she wasn't going to change her mind, and he made his way to the couch.

He opened the bottom half and took some blankets and extra pillow from the closet, and the minute his head hit the pillow, he was out like a light.

Adelina's pnt. Of view

The next morning, the sun shining through the window woke me, and a few minutes later, so did Demitrey.

He seemed confused for a second, but then looked over at me, and smiled.

He looked as though he was going to say something, but the door opened, and Diana made her way into my room, with my breakfast tray.

"Good morning Luna. Here is your- oh my! Alpha? What are you doing here?" Exclaimed Diana, after having a mini heart attack.

"He came to see me last night, and it was too late for him to go back to the castle, so I told him to stay here." I explained.

"You "told" the Alpha to stay here?" Asked Diana, as she emphasized the word "told" to show her surprise, "yes, I did." I replied with as proud smile.

"Okay, well, I'll get you some breakfast Alpha. Excuse me." Said Diana, then she was out the door, and soon came back with a tray for Demitrey, then afterwards she checked my vitals, and left Demitrey and I alone.

I didn't even eat half of my plate, and Demitrey was already done devouring his food.

After we finished breakfast, for a while, Demitrey and I just sat in silence.

Each of us dazed, trapped in our minds.

None of us willing to speak.

Then, I finally mustered the courage to ask him again.

"Why didn't you tell me? And don't lie to me this time. I want the truth." I said with a tone of finality.

Demitrey sighed, and closed his eyes, then be said "well, I did do it for your protection, and well I didn't know what else to do."

"You could've just told me, we would've worked it out. Together." I said exasperated.

"Well, me telling last time didn't actually help now did it?!" He suddenly snapped. Then he closed his eyes in remorse as he added "Sorry. I didn't mean to startle you."

I took a second to breathe before I spoke again, and carefully, I asked "last time? You've lost someone in this situation before?"

He didn't answer right away, but when his eyes opened, they were guarded, as though he was preparing himself for something painful, then he drew in a breath, and quickly released it, as he rubbed his hands together.

After another silent second, he started "her name was Leia," and my ears perked up to hear the story.

"She used to work as a maid at the castle when my dad was in charge. One day, when I was about 15, she overheard me asking my father about my mom, again, which he usually answered with *she gave you up the minute she pushed you out. She didn't even want to look at you. She didn't want you.*" Then followed by a serious beating, because he hated when I mentioned my mom."

"Anyway, that day Leia was the one to tend to my wounds, and as she worked on cleaning and bandaging them, she said *"he's lying you know. Your mother was the sweetest, and she cared for all, young and old. She was kind, a great Luna, and a great teacher. When she found out that she was pregnant, she was jubilant. But not your father. He threatened that if the child was a daughter, he would kill them both, but your mother was blessed, and she had you. She fell in love with you the minute she held you, and nothing could ever replace the happiness that washed over her, and we could all feel it. Your birth was a milestone in our pack's history. But that happiness didn't last. When you were about 6 months old, your father rejected your mother, and he kept you away from her. The Luna became overwhelmed with sadness and grief, and one* day, we felt it, when she headed down to the cliff, and threw herself over. That, your mother's death, was another milestone in our pack's history. The pack became shady, dark, and sad. No one could really smile the way they used to, and your father became ruthless and cruel. Until little toddler you started running all over. Your joyous and effective smile made us all feel as though your mother was still here, like she was living through you. And your eyes, identical to hers. I watched you grow around these halls, you used to always smile, you were always helpful, and nothing could dampen your mood. But then one day, you went to school, and if I remember correctly, I believe that your teacher assigned the family tree project, and you came home, and started asking questions about your mom, but alas, you asked the wrong person. That day, when your father told you that your mom didn't want you, it was the first time we saw you cry. But then you got past that, and as *a four-year-old you jumped back to being your joyful self, until you became of age to really understand, and you asked your father again, and just like he snuffed out the light in her spirit, and ended her existence, he snuffed out your happiness. You no longer helped, you no longer smiled, nor did you go running around the pack grounds making people smile."* Ended Leia, and we stayed silent for a while."

"When she was finished tending to my wounds, she cleaned up and got ready to leave, and that's when I grabbed her arm, and asked her if she could tell me more about my mom, and she agreed. It became like a ritual for us, we would meet up at her little cottage near the forest, and she would offer me tea, cookies, milk, or anything she had available, then we would sit on her patio and gaze out into the forest, and she would tell me tons and tons of stories about my mom. I started to smile again, I started to help out the pack, and started to spread smiles like old times, just because it was what my mom did."

"I felt closer to her that way. Leia and I formed a bond, and she became like my second mom. I truly cared for her as though she was my own mother, and over that year, our bond only grew stronger. But my father noticed the change, and soon, I noticed, he had some people watching me. Leia and I hardly met, but that didn't change anything, I kept on smiling. One day, she didn't show up to the castle for her usual shift, but I brushed it off, however, after a week I became worried, and I went to visit her. I made sure to double check and assure that I wasn't being followed, and to my surprise the usual guards that worked for my father weren't following me."

"So, I went by the store, got her some cookies, and made my way to see her. She explained to me that she quit at the castle because she supposedly wasn't "*as young as when she started*" so that day, we took a while to catch up, and she even treated me to another story about my mom. When it was about late in the evening, I kissed her goodnight on the forehead, then made my way back to the castle. Once I reached there, it was quiet, and I guessed that everyone went to sleep. Mind you by that time I was 16, so while on my way to my room, I was passing by my dad's office, and that's when I heard my father's second in command say *"I took the boys off your son today, and instead followed him myself. He went to visit one of the ladies that recently retired from here, her name is Leia, and she's the one that has been telling him about Merila."*

"Merila is my mom's name, anyway, I then heard the words that would haunt me forever, my father simply said, *"find her, and kill her."* Without thinking twice, I ran to Leia's cottage, and told her about the threat. I told her to run, and find a place to hide, but no, instead she said she would stay and fight, that she wasn't afraid of my father. I admired her courage, but I knew the danger she was in, and being the stubborn woman that she was, she already made up her mind, so I made her a promise."

"I promised that I would fight to the death to protect her. I remember she cupped my cheek, then kissed me on the forehead as she simply said, *"it'll be okay."* Just as she finished, the door of her cottage crashed open, and guards trampled in. I placed her behind my back between me, and the wall, and I declared *"if you want her, you're going to have to go through me first."*

"The guards laughed, and Saul, my dad's beta said, *"move aside kid, we only came for the lady."* And I didn't think twice when I said, *"fuck off."* Then it all happened in a blur. The first few guards came, and I fended them off. Being that my father put me in strict training since ten. But then that's when the game switched up. I trained with Saul and the guards, most of them knew the tactics that I used, and just like that they got the upper hand. They all attacked at once, and I was soon just a bleeding body on the floor. My vision became hazy, until it was fully gone. There, in my own pool of blood I laid for days. In pain, in agony, but most of all grieving. I failed to protect her and keep my promise. I lost someone important, someone that I cared for, someone that helped me feel connected to my mother, and I also lost a mother."

Demitrey sighed, and I noticed tears slowly streaming down his face.

He cleared his throat then continued "anyway, when I was finally able to get on my feet. Leia was already gone. But I didn't let her sacrifice go to waste. Instead, I smiled ten times more and harder. I helped the pack as much as I could, and at night, I went to the clearing by the cliff, and I trained on my own. I made my own practice dummies, and

I taught myself new skills and tricks, and that's when I met Kade."

Chapter 44- "Talk of the past" Part- 2

Demitrey' s pnt. Of view

My eyes scanned over Adelina as she sat quietly with her eyes cast down. She seemed so enhanced in her thoughts that I was afraid to know what she was thinking.

I am such an idiot. Drowning in my own stupid thoughts, closing myself from others, and hurting the one person I should've care for.

I placed my hands on her. I crossed the line.

Maybe this was a bad idea. I shouldn't have come here.

She hates me. She had to.

Maybe I should tell her to reject me, if she makes up her mind to do so, the bond would be automatically broken. I would accept her rejection and pass the pack on to Kade.

He is a loyal beta, and he would be an honorable Alpha.

Yeah, maybe I should tell her to reject me, she wouldn't have to bear with me, and she would be able to love. She would be happy. She would be able to forget about me, and all the shit I put her through. She would be an amazing wife and mother to a family that deserves her.

And me, well, I believe everything would be better off if I was gone.

"There you go with that look again." She finally spoke up breaking her silence.

My eyebrows rose quizzically, and she frowned as she said "you're beating yourself up again. I can tell because I notice how troubled your eyes became, but you're still holding back. What are you feeling?" She questioned in the end.

But I remained silent. What if she despises me? Especially if she heard my turmoil thoughts.

"Demitrey what are you thinking?" She asked me again, a bit more urgent.

But I couldn't bring myself to say it.

She will hate me.

She just had to.

"Demitrey talk to me!" She demanded curious and worried.

"Do you hate me?" The words fluently left my lips, my eyes finally connecting with her own.

"I-" she started but then closed her mouth.

She opened her lips as if to say something, but they soon became sealed.

Adelina's pnt. Of you

Did I hate him?

Well, did I?

Should I?

But most importantly shouldn't I?

Demitrey' s pnt. Of view

I looked over at her.

My eyes observed her facial features as she contemplated her response.

I'm pretty sure I know what the response would be.

And I would learn to accept it.

She had to hate me, because I hate myself.

And I know, hate is a strong word.

But how could I be so blind? Hurting the one person I should've loved, thinking I was protecting her, just so she could end up on a hospital bed and all because me.

I bet she was happy in Italy.

I shook my head, and tears welled up in my eyes, but I wouldn't allow them out. I was taught to never allow them out.

I wanted to run, transform into Trey and just run my fury out. I wanted growl and howl. I wanted to roar until my voice was gone, and I wanted to free myself of all this regret bubbling inside until I had no strength left.

But no.

I wasn't going to allow it. I was taught to never make my emotions known, I was taught to leave it all inside.

And plus, I want these emotions to build up, and slowly suffocate me.

The pain, I deserve it.

The aching heart, I deserve it.

The regret, I deserve it.

I deserve for my monstrous past to rise, take control, and torture me endlessly.

I deserve to suffer.

I deserve it all.

I shook my head once again, and finally spoke up, "you don't have to answer the question until you're ready, but until then, I will continue on with the story. As mentioned before, at the age of 16 I started training on my own, and at 17, on the eve of my birthday, I met Kade. He was found at our pack's boundary line. He was beat up bad. His pack had been attacked by rogues, and he was the only one to survive. He was taken to the clinic, and after his recovery, my father wasn't sure what to do with him. So, I volunteered to take him under my wings, I even remember telling my dad that "*every Alpha needs a beta, right? Well, let Kade train with me, and if he earns my trust, the spot would be filled.*" That day, the entire room, my father's beta, the head pack warriors, and the other elites of the pack all laughed their heads off. But my father didn't seem too amused, instead with a sarcastic yet strict reply he said "*fine, he stays, but he is your responsibility. He messes up, I end his life.*"

"And His warning didn't go unheard. By day, Kade and I were under strict surveillance, but by night we trained. We bonded, and we became each other's keeper. I learned that he was just a few days younger than me, and that during the war, he lost his father, mother, and older brother.

Rogues ravaged his pack, and his parents urged him to run and not look back."

"He taught me some strategies and skills when it came to combat, and together we learned, and trained. We gained each other's trust, and we became best friends. We had each other's backs no matter what, to the point that one day Saul accused Kade of stealing from the pack's treasury, and my father was quick to issue an execution. I remember they had him tied to a post, and they had one of the archers ready to aim straight for his heart, with a silver arrow and a tip bathed in wolfs bane. Instant kill. But I wasn't going to have it. I stood in front of him, the arrow aimed for my own heart."

"My father and I debated for hours, until finally he decided "*fine, I will let your pathetic excuse of a friend go. However, you will be tied to this post, and Saul will give you 50 lashes of the torture whip, if you plead to stop, your friend dies, if you let out even a peep, your friend dies, if you fall to the ground, your legs no longer holding you up, your friend dies. And if you pass out during the fifty lashes, when you wake up, you will find his body perched on the branch under the cliff."* And just like that, I was stripped of my shirt and pants, left only in my boxers."

"I was tied to the post by my hands angled up, and everyone, I mean everyone young and old was to witness it. To be honest, the first few lashes were the worst. The first one came unexpectedly, I'm not sure if I was even mentally, physically, or emotionally prepared for it. The whip fell on my back, and it felt as though it just ripped through my skin. It burned as though a fire was frying my every cell, and the blood, the sweat, and the heat of the sun only made it worse. I lost count at some point, but somewhere in the middle, I started seeing stars. My back arched upon reflex after every strike, and blood oozed and bathed the floor."

"I had to close my eyes once I saw the pain in my pack's eyes. They were all so afraid, the women, and the children were tearing up, and even the strongest of the pack's warriors would flinch, cringe and look away. I couldn't dare to look at Kade because if I did, the strength in me would leave. I closed my eyes, and gritted my teeth, and I tried to breathe. My back was scorching, my lungs heaving and all I wanted to do was disappear. The last few hits from Saul started feeling weak, and I could tell he was tired. When I heard him breathe out the word fifty, a whoosh of air escaped my lips, and I withheld the last strike. I made it through. I didn't peep a word, I didn't fall, nor did I plead to stop. I made it through."

"Saul backed away from me and breathed. Two warriors started to make their way to take off my restraints, and the crowd started to cheer, until a loud "*ENOUGH!*" Boomed from my father and silenced the crowd."

"In my peripheral vision, I noticed he grabbed the whip from an unexpected Saul, and he let out his fury. While Saul only aimed for my back, my dad aimed everywhere, my head, my neck, my sides, my back, and my legs. The whip cruelly licked and bit at my skin, and my body trembled in protest. I started going numb, but I held on. My knees started to give way, but I held on to the post with my arms dear life. At a point I wanted to scream, cry and beg to stop, but no, instead I gritted my teeth. I wouldn't give in."

"My skin ripped and shredded, blood mixing with sweat and the heat of the sun just added salt to wound. Around me, women were screaming helpless, and warriors at times even grunted, but I couldn't. When my knees buckled, my face and chest rubbed against the hard-wooden post. I fell to my knees once my father ripped at them with his whip, at that moment I felt defeated, and even if I wanted to grunt, hiss, or scream, my strength was gone. I started dazing out on my knees, my vision disoriented. And then, I felt it."

"Kade ran and wrapped his arms around, causing my father's blinding anger to land on his own back. He held me tight, and breathed with each assault, but he whispered to me *"hold on brother, we will make out."* With every lash, he just kept on whispering *"hold on brother."* I breathed defeated. And finally, a peaceful wind washed over me, and for a second, I thought it was over. That my life was over, and you know, I actually felt at peace. It became dark, my father's angry whips, and Kade's painful grunts just faded, and soon, I was finally at peace. But then weeks later I woke up with sore legs and back, a very annoying beeping, and a smiling woman, who later I learned to be Aunty

Diana. She nursed me back to life, helped me back on my feet with some therapy, and took care of my wounds. My first visitor was of course Kade. I learned that seconds after I passed out, Saul finally stopped my father, some of the warriors carried me to the clinic, and I was there for a while. Kade's wounds were not as bad as mine, and so he healed faster, but day by day, I regained my strength. The pack, group by group came for visits, and then one day my father showed up with a young lady, who later, I would come to know as Serena."

Chapter 45- "Heat" Part- 1

Adelina's pnt. Of view

I was struck dumb, and quiet.

How could a father be so cruel?

I mean my father is a complete asshole and a pervert and he was also cruel, but his father took cruel to a whole other level.

Shoot, although he's already dead, I wish I could've killed him myself.

"Say something." Demitrey sighed, almost pleading.

I thought about his story, and I asked the one thing that came to mind "can I see them?" I said looking up at him, and it's as though he read my mind.

For a moment he said nothing, but then he stood up, and his fingers went to work on unbuttoning his shirt, one by one.

As his fingers worked the buttons skillfully, his eyes never left mine.

I felt a heat suddenly rise to my cheeks, and I bit my lip shyly and looked away.

In my peripheral vision, once he was beautifully shirtless, he made his way to me, his stance almost teasing, then he turned his back on me, and crouched to my level.

My eyes slowly peeled from the floor, and unto his back.

There, scars webbed and ran all across his back. Some paler then the other, some longer than the other, and some looked as though they went deeper.

Subconsciously, I found my fingers reaching out and slowly, almost carefully, I touched one of the scars.

The minute our skin met one another, he slightly jumped, and gasped, but he didn't move away, and the mate bond tingles came alive.

I traced his scars, and I just felt the urge, so I leaned down and kissed one, then I whispered, "I'm sorry."

He was frozen for a minute, then with a blush, I moved away from him.

He was still crouching by my bed when I shook my head and said "but wait, that day when you were in my room, shirtless, when you were walking out the door, I didn't see your scars. Why?"
"Because, look." He said, and I looked down at his back, and his skin was completely clear.
"At times, I am ashamed of them, and I double my skin,

and so the scars are near invisible. When I train with my men, I don't show my scars, but," he said, then the scars once again appeared on his back "the minute we go into battle, I take off my shirt, and proudly show them my scars. I hid my from you because I already gave you thousands of reasons to hate me, so I hid my true self from you, and I didn't want you to be afraid of me, but now," he breathed and turned to face, as he looked me straight in the eye "I no longer want to hide from you. I don't want to hide anything from you. I mean it when I say I love you."

I didn't reply.

I had no words to reply.

He stood up, and with an almost relieved smiled, he leaned down and kissed me on my forehead. I closed my eyes and savored this moment.

Then he removed his lips and placed his own forehead on my own, and his eyes connected with mine.

There in that moment was a connection.

Did I forgive him? I don't know.

Do I hate him? Not sure.

Will I forget what we have been through? Definitely not.

Can I learn to like him and maybe even love him? Only time will tell.

After a few shared silent seconds, he moved away, but as he turned, there on his right side, I noticed a jagged scar, not straight and clean like that of the whip, but it was distinctly shaped.

I was about to ask him what the scar was when a quick knock came from the door.

Before I could say wait, the door open and in came Diana with a tray of lunch, but she froze with eyes wide as saucers, as her eyes landed on a shirtless Demitrey.

Demitrey also frozen stared wide eyed at the intruder, and in all honesty, it was quite the comical picture.

"Eh hem." I cleared my throat and Diana's eyes travelled between me and Demitrey in quick motions, and a blush was slowly taking over her cheeks.

"Uh- um... I'm sorry." She quickly blurted out, placed the tray on the table next to my door, and she scurried out a deep blush on her face.

Demitrey finally awake from his trance shook his head and chuckled, his eyes travelling to me.

I shook my head and blushed as I said "why do you always put me in these awkward situations? First with

Cilia, and now Aunty D."

He shrugged and said with a sly smirk "well, I'm sorry if our chemistry always attracts attention. I mean it's not like she caught me on top of you or anything. Maybe next time." He winked with a full-on smile and I gasped and said, "you jerk!" Then I threw a pillow at his head.

He caught it in instant reflex and said almost scolding "no, no more assaulting of mates. And thanks for the pillow."

"Give it back so I can whack you some more!" I demanded.

"No." He simply said.

"I said Give it back!" I once again said.

"And I said no." He said childish.

"Fight me then." I pouted.

"Are you sure we will be fighting, or will we be doing something else?" He said, his eyes darkened, and his voice lowered teasingly, and just like that, I felt another wave of heat travel over me. My cheeks flushed, and I felt a bit of friction between my legs. I tightened them shyly, and I found my eyes travelling down his sculpted, very well-built chest. Before I realized it, I licked my bottom lip, and his eyes caught the movement, causing his own tongue to dart out and wet his own.

I felt a jolt in my stomach, and my legs tightened even more as a tingle travelled to my treasured place, and I felt my nipples harden against my hospital gown.

I felt a pull towards him, and his body swayed as if he wanted to come to me.

I wanted to say, "come here." But instead I shook my head, cleared my thoughts and sighed as I said, "please put on your shirt."

And with a "gladly." He slipped his shirt back on.

I almost whimpered as the beautiful image was covered from my eyes, but instead I sighed a breath of relief.

What was that?

Chapter 46 "Heat" Part- 2

Adelina's pnt. Of view

Later on that day, Aunty D came back with rosy cheeks, eyes cast down, and explained that it would be better if I was discharged back to the castle.

She said that I would have a nurse in the castle, to check up on me, and if I needed anything, the nurse would be just a few feet away.

She also warned that I don't get too involve in strenuous activities, that I take it slow, and that I am careful.

The funny thing was, when she said "strenuous activities" her eyes quickly darted between Demitrey and I, and I wanted to tell her that nothing happened, but then that would make everything even more awkward.

The minute I stepped out of the clinic doors, I came face to face with way made by a body of people.

On each side pack members stood with smiles on their faces, and they waved, some gave me flowers and teddy bear to add to my collection in the cart being pushed out by none other than the big bad Alpha himself.

The pack warriors bowed their heads in respect, and I even spotted Katharina and James together.

By the time we made it to the castle, the cart was overflowing with gifts, but as soon as we stepped through the doors, followed by Katharina and Cilia, James and Kade bolted the doors to stop anyone from coming in.

I was escorted to my room by both Cilia and Katharina, and we spent some time talking and catching up.

I've learned that Katharina has been given access to stay with us as long as she wants, and she has even given James consent to mark her.

Cilia and Kade moved in together, and from a little birdie, I learned that they are expecting!

I was super excited for them, but I was also sleepy.

Once the girls noticed that I started to dose off, they quietly left my room, and I was taken over by sleep.

Third Person's pnt. Of view

Adelina found herself waking up in the middle of the night with only one thing in mind.

Or better yet, one person in mind.

The thought of him caused waves of heat to wash over her, and no matter what she did, she couldn't overcome the want and the craving she currently had for him.

Adelina's pnt. Of view

"*You're going into heat. Demitrey is the only one that can help you, go to him.*" Said Aden in my head.

"**No, I'm fine. A cold shower is all I need.**" I resisted, and then, an image of a shirtless Demitrey flashed in my eyes, and the want for him only grew and I felt a jolt in my abdomen.

"*You can't possibly be serious right now! For once stop being stubborn.*" Insisted Aden, as another image of my mate licking his lip with dark eyes flashed in front of my eyes.

Aden was manipulating my mind, and I found myself biting my lip in response.

"**No! I won't give in to lust. I'm not ready for that!**" I tried to fight, but it was all in vain, even I wanted him, without Aden manipulating me.

But I wasn't ready for that commitment. I saved myself for my mate, and he is just a few doors down from me.

But when I open myself up to him, I want it to be one hundred percent my decision, not because of my carnal want or nature.

Not because it is my heat season!

"Ugh! Fine! Guess I'll do this myself! You'll thank me for this!" Declared Aden.

"Wha-" before I could finish my question, I felt paralyzed.

My body was moving towards the door, but I wasn't mind conscious of my actions.

Aden had taken control. And all I could do was watch.

My eyes and mind were the only thing I was conscious of, but with physically, I wasn't in control.

I felt in a prison of some sort, I could breathe, I could see, I could hear, but I wasn't in conscious control.

I'm not even sure how she took full control of me, she's never done that before.

I saw her exit our room, and I knew exactly where she was headed.

I fought and tried to regain control, but Aden wasn't allowing it.

Third person's pnt. Of view

Demitrey was slowly starting to be seduced by sleep when Adelina barged into his room, then closed the door, eyes ablaze with Lust.

She crossed the room in seconds, and instantly straddled Demitrey to the bed.

Demitrey froze as he said "Aden? Babe what are you doing?"

Adelina placed her index fingers on his lips and said "shh."
Then she slowly, teasingly caressed her hands on Demitrey's bare chest, causing him to be fully aware, and fully aroused.

Her hands dragged lower and lower, as she bit her bottom lip, while Demitrey could feel himself harden beneath her core.

He shook his head, and grabbed unto Adelina's hands, he wasn't going to let her do this, not when she wasn't in her right mind.

He could tell she was going into heat, but he knew Adelina wouldn't act in such a way.

She pouted, and leaned down as if to kiss him, instead she went straight to his mark, and kissed it, just enough for Demitrey to loosen his hold on her, and she went back to teasing him.

It was hard to withstand the pull of the mate bond, especially when she was in heat, but he wouldn't take advantage of her, so once again her cleared his head, and held her hands captive, and in one swift motion, he flipped them over.

Adelina gasped aroused, then once again bit her lip, as she gazed at Demitrey through her eyelashes.

Their position wasn't fully conscious to Demitrey until Adelina wrapped her legs around his waist, and pulled him to her body, causing a friction to form between them as their bodies collided.

Demitrey drew in a deep breath and looked down at the temptress laying under him.

He was tempted alright.

He wanted to take her, adore her body, worship her beauty, and make her feel like the queen that she was, and although she was fully aroused, and her actions were quite suggestive, he could tell that her wolf was mostly in control.

"We are not doing this tonight." Warned Demitrey, and Aden pouted.

She teased her fingers across his skin, igniting a fire of lust and need.

She felt herself heat up from head to toe, and all she wanted was what Demitrey could provide.

In the blink of an eye, she wrapped her arms around his neck, and caused their lips to crash and mold perfectly with each other.

Their lips connected like a puzzle, their tongues fighting for dominance.

Demitrey subconsciously found himself sensually grinding his hips into her own, and she wrapped her legs around him to increase the tension.

His fingers suggestively travelled over her skin, as her fingers tangled in his hair keeping him as close as humanly possible.

Demitrey broke the kiss and started kissing her mark.

Adelina hissed and gasped, her body on a frenzy.

Their connection was sexy, raw, naughty, and absolutely stimulating.

When Adelina felt ready to land on cloud nine Demitrey pulled back, and straddled her, with both his legs on each side of her.

He smirked when he noticed her surprise, then as if scolding me he said, "I said not tonight."

She gave him the soft puppy eyes and tried to caress her hands on his chest again, but he captured him with his own as he said in a serious tone "keep touching me, and I will tie your hands to the headboard."

Adelina smiled suggestively and said "Oooh, yes daddy, tie me up."

And Demitrey had to restrain himself.

She was torturing him, and she didn't even realize it.

"What would you do to me afterwards?" she whispered seductively.

Demitrey couldn't hold himself back as he said "I would tie

your legs as well, spread apart from each other. I would start kissing your lips, then your mark, and slowly make my way down. I would caress your sides with my hands, and your breasts with my tongue, I would look you in the eyes, and slowly, teasingly make my way to where your eyes would beg me to touch. But I wouldn't just yet. I would kiss your lips again, and then make my way down. I would start with your outer thigh and make my way to your inner thighs where I would most definitely leave my mark, then I would hold my eye contact with you, and when you least expect it, my tongue would dart out slowly, lick your essence from the bottom to the top. I would take my time between each lick, and no matter how much you beg, I wouldn't speed up. I would take my time to lavish in your sweet essence, my eyes never leaving yours. Only when I was satisfied, would I speed up for your pleasure, and just as payback for your teasing, my fingers would join in too, but on my own pace."

Aden was struck silent.

His eyes were so dark, so possessive, so powerful, and so sexy.

She could see him battling his lust, and she wanted him to give in.

So, with an alluring gaze, a provocative smile, and a sultry tone, Aden said "so do it. I promise I'll behave." She smiled innocently as she placed her hands above her head in surrender.

"ENOUGH!" Boomed Demitrey with his Alpha tone, and Adelina whimpered.

Demitrey's eyes cleared up, and he said "No."

Just like that Aden shoved him off her body and got off the bed as she said, "you're no fun."

"I know babe." Agreed Demitrey.

"I don't like you." Added Aden, her face contorted in anger.

"I understand babe." He agreed again.

"You're annoying." She said, her anger rising.

And Demitrey shrugged.

"You're so ugggh!" Argued Aden, then she receded back, giving Adelina full control once again.

Demitrey shook his head and noticed that Adelina was back to normal.

He took on a deep breath, and called Adelina over as he said, "come here baby."

Adelina looked as his inviting arms but stood her grounds as she shook her head no.

"Come on baby, you can't stay mad at me forever." He said with a teasing smile, and Adelina sighed.

She made her way over to him, and he invited her in the bed.

Aden once again took control and tried to seduce Demitrey once again, but he shook his head and said, "not tonight babe, you're not in your right mind, and I won't take advantage of you."

"Help me." Adelina whispered, Aden truly giving up.

And he cradled her in his arms, and spooned her, allowing his warmth to calm her and sedate her arousal.

And just like that, they fell into a deep peaceful sleep.

Chapter 47- "Good Morning!"

Third Person's pnt. Of view

Adelina found herself waking up with her arm and leg draped over Demitrey, with his back to her.

At first, she was shocked frozen. She was literally clinging on to him.

She took a slow deep breath, and quietly, almost carefully, she removed her limbs off Demitrey and back to her own body, with a blush on her cheeks.

She contemplated on getting out the bed and making a run for it when her eyes landed on Demitrey's back.

There, once again, scars ran all over his back.

She couldn't even imagine how much pain he must have been in, and the fact that he wasn't allowed to sound out his pain must have made it even worse.

She slowly lifted her fingers, and once again she started tracing his scars, one right after the other.

The pad of her fingers caressed over the lengthy scars.

She couldn't count how many there were, some crisscrossed, while others were cut short by fellow scars.

Adelina once again leaned close to Demitrey, and she softly placed her lips on one of the scars.

She wasn't even sure why she was doing this, but she just felt the need to.

So once again, she leaned down and kissed another scar.

Her lips lingered there enough for her to feel the tingles of the mate bond to come alive, so she kissed his scar again.

She pulled back and started to touch his scars again, when out of nowhere she heard a very deep, and very gruff voice say, "you know babe, the worst time to tease a man is when they first wake up in the morning, with a boner."

Adelina gasped and tried to pull her hands away, but Demitrey caught it, and turned to face her, then he kissed her thumb, followed by her index finger, and followed through until he reached her pinky, his eyes never leaving hers, causing a permanent blush to settle on her face.

"Good morning." He said, his voice still laced with sleep.

"You sound sexy in the morning!" Adelina blurted, then her free hand slapped over her lips, her eyes wide in shock.

Demitrey took a second before he started laughing, and Adelina's surprise turned into anger.

"What are you laughing at?" She asked, with a raised eyebrow.

"You." He said, the he pinched her nose and added "you're so cute, yet so sexy."

"Shut up." Adelina muttered, her cheeks once again flaming, causing yet another laugh to erupt from Demitrey.

Adelina was embarrassed and irritated, and he was making her mad by laughing, so she took a pillow and straddled Demitrey, unaware of how suggestive her actions were.

Adelina rose the pillow over her head, causing the singlet she wore to bed to rise and expose a bit of her stomach, as well as her shorts which rose higher showing Demitrey a full view of her outer and inner thighs.

Demitrey' slaughter seized, and his eyes widened.

She was sitting a few inches above his pelvis, hence the reason why she was unaware of how aroused he truly was.

"Babe what are you-"

Pluff came the sound of the pillow colliding with Demitrey's head.

"Not so funny now is it?" Asked Adelina, her turn to smile.

"No, babe, you have to get off m-"

Pluff she hit him on again.

"Nope, you're going to suffer the wrath of the pillow." Said Adelina, and she relentlessly started hitting him with the pillow.

Adelina found herself giggling, while Demitrey tried to cover his face with his arms, but the smile on his face was very evident.

After a few more hits, Adelina stopped to look down at him.

His dark, hypnotic eyes looked up at the beauty currently straddling him.

She had a beautiful smile on her lips, and she looked happy, how could he have ever hurt her?

"What? Tired already?" Asked a smirking Demitrey, and Adelina frowned.

She raised the pillow over her head ready to bring it down, and Demitrey sat up and said, "oh no you don't."

They were playfully struggling for the pillow, when Adelina froze.

She felt him.

She felt *him*, under her, and a blush once again ran to her cheeks.

Demitrey noticed her blush and quickly wrapped his arm around her waist to keep her from running away.

Adelina's eyes were cast down, and she seemed embarrass.

"Adelina look at me." Demitrey spoke softly, but Adelina didn't comply.

"Babe, hey," he said, placing two fingers under her chin, slowly bringing her head up, "look at me." And Adelina's eyes flashed over to his.

"Don't be embarrassed, not with me. You're my girl, and I want you to be comfortable with me. I'll take care of you." He spoke, his voice a comforting soft tone.

Adelina looked at him for a second, then placed her hands on his bare chest, and Demitrey gasped.

His eyes stayed glued on hers, and he noticed her bite her bottom lip shyly.

She pushed Demitrey back down into the bed, until he was lying down with her on top of him.

She now straddled him directly in his pelvis, and she could feel his arousal.

She stared into his eyes and just looked at him.

He sure was a beautiful creature. As well as a strong one too, and not just physically.

She felt herself longing to take a daring step with Demitrey, so she didn't think, she just acted.

She leaned down and slowly kissed him.

Her lips landed on his, and at first Demitrey didn't react.

He didn't want to scare her.

Her hands pressed softly against his chest, and she pushed herself further on him.

She opened her mouth and licked Demitrey's bottom lip, asking for permission, and he gladly allowed it.

Demitrey softly placed one of his hands on her cheek to deepen the kiss, and he wrapped the other around her waist to pull her even closer.

But Adelina removed his hands, interlocked her fingers with his own and placed them on each side of his head.

Her chest was completely aligned with his own, and she felt her nipples rub against his bare chest.

It was a new feeling, but she wanted to feel even more, so she took her lips away from his and leaned down further to kiss his mark, in the process, she felt his arousal grind against her core, sending a jolt of ecstasy to travel throughout her body.

Slowly, she nipped and kissed his spot, and Demitrey drew in a harsh breath.

He wanted to free his hands, and wrap his arms around her, but he was trying to restrain himself.

This was her show, he would let her take the lead.

Adelina bit Demitrey's mark, and she felt a heat wash over them.

The mate bond became alive around them, and she felt driven to go farther.

Adelina found that she enjoyed the jolt that traveled through her when she grinded against Demitrey's member, so that's what she did.

Her hips moved sensually against his own, and Demitrey grunted.

Demitrey was really trying to hold himself back, but she was making it difficult.

Nowadays, she seems to endlessly torture him.

She kissed the mark she gave him, and once again went to kiss his lips, but as she did so, his member rubbed perfectly against her clit, and just like that a soft moan escaped her lips, right next to Demitrey' sear, and he lost the restraint he had.

He shook his hand away from hers and grabbed on to her hips.

He sat up and intensified the friction between their bodies.

Their hips met one another in a constant motion, and Demitrey wrapped one of his arms around her back and buried his lips in her neck.

He took his onslaught on her mark, where he kissed and bit, and Adelina found it harder and harder to keep her sounds of pleasure in.

Once Demitrey was satisfied with his work, his lips went to their next target.

With his teeth, he dragged the straps of Adelina's singlet off her shoulders and down her arms one by one, then he kissed his way from her neck, down to her right breast.

At first, he just left pecks here and there, but then, he took her nipple in his mouth, and Adelina drew in a sharp breath.

He sucked and licked at her erect bud, and Adelina grabbed his head and pushed his head further against him.

She felt a shock of pleasure to straight to her core, and she had the sudden urge to be touched there.

It's as though Demitrey read her mind, because Adelina felt his other hand travel down between their bodies, and right into her shorts.

She felt it when his fingers met her bundle, and she felt it when his finger slowly stroked her, his lips still teasing her nipple.

She felt his middle finger once again land on her clit, and slowly, it started rotating in a circular motion.

His finger played her clit, and Adelina couldn't help it.

"Aah, Demitrey! Aah." She moaned.

And then, Demitrey bit her nipple, he nipped it in a quick motion, and Adelina yelped, then he licked it, and blew a cold air on her erect bud, and she drew in yet another sharp breath.

Demitrey once again kissed her lips, and he looked at her as he said, "I'm going to touch you baby, if it hurts. Just tell me to stop. Okay?" And Adelina just nodded, she didn't trust her voice.

He kissed her again, and then she felt it.

One of his fingers slowly stroked her lips, and she could feel as though water was trickling out of her treasured place.

Then, he slowly inserted his finger into her, and at first it felt alien, but then he started to take it in and out, slowly, and constantly, and she found her hips slowly moving against his finger.

She winced a little, once she felt him hit a spot that slightly burned, but after the burned died down, it felt good, and it left her wanting more.

She started moving her hips against him, and he looked into her eyes and said softly "are you okay?"

"Uh huh." Her voiced sounded breathy.

"I'm going to add another finger baby, if you don't feel okay, just tell me when, and I'll stop." Demitrey said then kissed her nose.

And then he added another.

Adelina hissed, but she relent as her hips moved atop his hand.

She leaned down and kissed him, and she pulled his bottom lip into her mouth and bit him.

He growled animalistic ally, and curled his fingers inside her tight lubricated walls, and Adelina moaned out loud.

She pulled his head back to her chest, and he heeded her command as he once again took her nipple in his mouth.

Adelina suddenly started feeling a motion building up in her uterus.

It felt strange, yet good, and she was curious to see what would happen.

Her actions started becoming wild, and the situation only became more arousing once Demitrey started nipping her mark again.

She felt the buildup reaching its peak.

Demitrey felt her walls tighten around his fingers and he grunted with need.

He wanted her so bad, but he would wait, he would take it slow, and when the time was right, he would make love to his queen and his goddess, slowly, and carefully, and when she wanted, he would give it to her hard, fast, and deep.

Adelina felt herself getting up there, she felt hot, she felt sexy, and she felt bold.

Almost there, she thought, and that's when a knock came from the door.

It was two quick knocks and Kade walked in saying "Hey Demitrey let's go for a ru- OH SHIT! Dude! I am so sorry. Alpha, Luna, excuse me!" He said and practically ran out closing the door behind him.

Adelina sat frozen on top of Demitrey, her mind clear of the lust that once surrounded them.

Her cheeks instantly flushed, she pushed herself from Demitrey and the bed, she fixed her night clothes, and literally ran out of Demitrey's room without looking at him, and straight to hers.

Once she was safe and sound in her room, behind the locked door, it was then she was finally able to breathe.

Chapter 48- "Date ? -Demitrey"

Demitrey's pnt. Of view

What in the heavens just happened?

I questioned myself, my eyes glued to the closed door that Adelina just ran out of.

A part of me wanted to go after her, and reassure her that it was okay, but another part of me told myself to give her some space.

I sighed and slid my hands over my face in aggravation, then I laid back in bed.

I was going to kill Kade.

But then again, maybe him interrupting us was a sign, I mean, had he not come through that door, we probably would've taken things way farther.

And I wouldn't be the one to argue that decision.

I want her so bad, but the wiser part of me wants to take things slow with her, I really do, and she is so beautiful, so innocent, yet a tease with absolutely no idea what she does to me.

She plays around not really thinking of the effect, and once she sees where her teasing leads to, she becomes afraid, self-conscious even, that's why I wanted to take things slow with her.

I don't want to rush things, I don't want to scare her, and I don't want to hurt her the way I did before.

I'm pretty sure she still has many questions, and there's so much more I want to tell her and talk to her about. That's why I have been trying to keep my lust at bay, because I don't want to damage what we have any further.

I'm trying to be a gentleman, and I'm trying to not disappoint her. At least not again.

The last months, weeks and days have been a crazy, scary, a mind-boggling rollercoaster ride, and I've changed so much.

Changed for the better.

From a feared Alpha, to the worst mate in the world, who caused the one woman he was supposed to love to run away. Then I became a captive, causing my mate to come back just so she could take bullets for me. Then I became a sad case who was also suicidal. I became vulnerable, and I was afraid of losing her again, if not completely this time.

Yet through all that, I am shocked that I pulled through.

After Adelina left, I found myself in a dark hole. It was cold, lonely and suffocating. I didn't think I'd make it out. For once I imagined what it would be like to take the easy way out, instead of facing the darkness head on.

I closed my eyes, as the feeling that I felt at the top of the cliff washed over me.

I was so close, one heartbeat away from being wiped out of existence. At that moment, the wind kissing my face, the sun setting, and the birds chirping almost seduced me into giving into that darkness.

Key Word: Almost.

I remember breathing in, my mind made up, and even when my heart felt heavy, my mind was working hard to convince me that this was the way to go.

I wasn't at peace. Standing at the top of that "legendary" cliff, I was afraid, I was alone, I was over everything.

I couldn't help but wonder if that's how my mom felt that day she decided to let go.

My mom… I shook my head, would she had been proud of me for becoming a coward that ran from his problems? Or would she embrace me, telling me that I did my best?

I suddenly found a smile creeping onto my face just thinking what it would be like to meet my mom, even if it meant dying. My heart skipped, and my smile grew as I imagined just how soft her kisses could be, and I couldn't help but fantasize what her warmth would feel like, and what her scent could compare to. Had I gone through with it, at least the moment would've been poetic. I could see it now... "The Big Bad and Feared Alpha, taking his own life out of guilt and fear."

I found myself chuckling at the thought.

Who knows? If I went through with it, maybe I'd see Leia again.

At my thoughts, a bitter tasted pooled in my mouth, my heart dropped, my chest constricting out of discomfort… I would've also joined my father, and I bet he would've loved to have all of eternity to gloat about the failure that I was in his eyes.

After a moment, I sighed and dismissed my absurd thoughts. Death was not something to play with, there's a reason even the strongest man, in his last moments become afraid, because death is the unknown…and the unknown is feared.

At the moment, I didn't fear death, but I did fear the unknown future of Adelina and me.

I didn't know what to do.

There were so many blurred lines when it came to her and I.

I wanted to be there for her, like I should've been from the beginning.

I wanted her to see me. The real Demitrey. The one Leia knew, the one that would've made my mother proud. I wanted to also be that Alpha that took a whipping for his fellow pack member and best friend, the Alpha that cares of each of his pack members, and the Alpha that freed those oppressed by cruel Alphas.

But most importantly, I wanted to be the mate Adelina dreamed of.

I love her, and I'm not ashamed of it.

I just wish I turned to this chapter way earlier in our story.

My mind was constantly wandering over Adelina. She was so beautiful, a temptress, but as much as she knows what happens between mates, she's also very oblivious of how quickly the tables could turn from a simple kiss, to a full-on heated session.

But the way she took control this morning, guiding me, teasing me into doing what she wanted me to do, that was amazing, but Kade, he had to come in, and ruin it all.

I was really debating on whether on not I would kill him.

My mind started working on how to hurt my best friend when a knock came from the door, at first, I wanted to turn whoever it was away, but then I decided to open the door, and see who it was.

I got off the bed, and made my way casually to the door, opened it, and my eyes met Kade, so I slammed the door in his face, and walked back to my bed.

He instantly opened the door, then slipped in and closed it as he said "come on dude, how was I supposed to know that she was going to be with you this morning. She's never with you."
"Doesn't matter. I'm still going to kill you." I said, laying back down on my back.
"I mean, it would've been easier to detect if you guys were getting your freak on if I could've heard you, but since

people started finding their mates in the castle, and you insisted on having the walls soundproofed, there's nothing I could've done." He explained, his hands up.

"You could've waited for me to say something like, oh I don't know, COME IN!"

"You NEVER say come in!" Retorted Kade.

"What are you guys arguing about?" Walked in James, as he added "I thought you were getting Demitrey so we could go run Kade?"

"Well, when I arrived, Demitrey was already getting a warm up." Replied Kade, rolling his eyes.

"Kade, do me a favor, shut up." I said, then I flung a pillow at Kade's head, who causally caught it.

"What do you mean?" Asked James.

Kade looked over at me, as I looked over at him. His face slowly brightened with a Grinch like smile, and it's almost in his eyes he was saying "payback time."

Before I could say anything Kade closed and locked the door using his speed and then declared to James "I walked in on Demitrey and Adelina getting freaky during a make out session. His mouth was on one of her you know what's, and his fingers from my point of view were in her you know... yeah."

Third Person's pnt. Of view

James stood still for a second, then his head slowly turned towards Demitrey, his eyes dark.

He didn't look very happy.

"You did what?!" Boomed James, then he added "that's like my little sister man! Couldn't you have like taken her on a date first?"

"Dude, you're talking like I was the one who seduced her." Groaned Demitrey.

"You didn't?" Asked both James and Kade simultaneously.

"Nope. This was her show" Said Demitrey, smiling affectionately, his mind drifting over to his little seductress.

"Oh," said Kade, then he looked over at James who said, "my baby sister is growing up!"

Then James averted his eyes to Demitrey and said, "don't you ever touch her again, until you ask her out on a date."

"Fine." Said Demitrey.

"I think I'm going to get Cilia to talk to Adelina about her behavior." Added James, this time sounding more like a father.

"Oh come on, you're acting like she's a child." Said Demitrey, then he added "Adelina might be a little innocent and oblivious, but she's also a seductress. There's a fire in her eyes, and she's curious too."

"Hey! Don't talk about her like that." Said James, his face comically contorted in anger.

"Whatever." Replied Demitrey, as he stared back at James, with his own makeshift of an angry face, as Kade's eyes travelled between the two.

Then just like that, they burst into fits of laughter.

Demitrey, Kade, and James absentmindedly found themselves creating a bond, and the person that brought them together, and was their main connection was Adelina.

"Okay, but seriously though, when I ask her out on this date, where am I going to take her?" Asked Demitrey, and both of his friends looked at him and shrugged.

Chapter 49- "Date? -Adelina"

Adelina's pnt. Of view

I found myself lying in bed, covered from head to toe, my mind in a frenzy.

Questions flew all over my brain, questions I wouldn't even dare to answer. I continuously found myself asking: what in the world just happened? And what would've happened if Kade didn't interrupt?

The fact that I provoked everything to happen made my heart skip a beat.

What was happening to me?

I was so confused, flustered, yet curious. I wasn't even sure if I'd ever get the courage to face him again.

In fact, I don't think I have the courage to get out of this room.

This was such an embarrassing turn of events, I couldn't even clear my mind of the steamy images for a second.

The way he held me, the way he caressed me, made me feel wanted, that's all I ever wanted from him, but maybe we went there too fast.

Yeah, it's my fault, I really shouldn't be rushing things, and in fact I need to be harsher on him for everything he's done to me.

I should make him pay.

But how? Before I could think up that answer, a few knocks came from the door, distracting me from my puzzled mind.

I held my breath as the knocks once again resonated from the door.

On the third set of knocks, my idiotic mouth opened itself and said, "nobody's home." And then I heard the familiar voice "Adelina open the door. We need to talk."

"But I don't want to talk." I whined back.

"You're talking right now." Said the voice, and I could imagine the owner of that voice rolling their eyes.

"That's because you're making me talk." I retorted.

"Well, can you at least open up, I got your favorite rum raisin flavored ice cream." And that's all the motivation I needed.

I jumped out of bed, and speed walked to the door, opening it to an expectant looking Cilia.

I grabbed the ice cream tub from her hands, along with the spoon, and grinned widely as I said "come on in."

I went straight to my bed and sat in a crisscross position, opening the ice cream bucket in a haste.

I dug the spoon in and moaned in pleasure once the cool, creamy, and delicious treat met my tongue.

I felt better already.

Halfway through the tub, and the ice cream started melting, that's when I finally looked up at Cilia, who was watching me attentively.

"So, you want to tell me what you were doing in Demitrey's room this morning?" She asked in a very serious, almost motherly tone.

"Um... no." I simply said, then occupied myself with the

tub, which until now, I never noticed how well drawn the label was.

Cilia chuckled and shook her head and made her way to me.

She sat next to me, and opened her arms, where I leaned into her comforting hug.

"It's okay you know. Things like that happen between mates." Comforted Cilia.

"I know. I just, this time I was the one who started it. I'm not even sure why." I replied, my confusion slowly rising.

"Hun, you're sexually frustrated. Your mind and body want his, but your heart is holding you back. Now I know that you and the Alpha have a long way to go, and I know that Demitrey has a lot of making up to do, but that doesn't mean you have to punish each other. Life is about testing the waters, taking risks, and having fun. How do you guys expect to move on if you guys refuse to allow yourselves to become fully vulnerable to one another? Like take me and Kade for example. From the moment I met him, I knew he was my mate. But I was afraid. I've had terrible relationship experiences, and I knew he was battling his own demons as well. I tried my best to avoid him, and so did he, based on my request, but then when you came everything changed."

I found myself moving from the hug, and I turned to look closely at Cilia.

She looked thoughtful as she continued "you know, you and Demitrey share a great bond, stronger than you think. Before you came, the pack was doing okay, but it felt like we were still missing a piece of ourselves and you know why? Because the Alpha was missing a piece of himself.

Once you came in, we felt like things were starting to knock into balance, but not everybody knew that you were the reason why. Before you came, Kade used to pursue me. But I would always tell him no because I was afraid of being vulnerable to him. My vulnerability was once taken advantage of, and it left a scar that for years never healed. So, I held myself back from him, not realizing that I was hurting us both."

Cilia chuckled a bit, then she wiped s a few tears that escaped her eyes.

"He brought me flowers, chocolate, always gave me compliments. In my eyes he was the perfect gentleman, but I still held back. I was afraid. I didn't want to be hurt again. I spent so long licking my wounds, mending my heart, and building a wall to protect myself, that I didn't even want to open up to my own mate. But when you arrived, something just changed. I looked at you and the Alpha, I noticed your eternal struggles, and after that day I walked in on you guys, something just clicked. I wanted to run to Kade and tell him I accept him as a mate, but then held myself back. I was being a coward. I told myself that I was bring careful, but deep down, I knew that that was just an excuse." She paused for a moment looking down at her hands.

When she looked up, she looked pensive, and a small smile started forming in her lips.

"It wasn't until the night at the club that we finally accepted each other. Matter of fact, I was actually surprised since I've turned him down all those times. But we were meant to be together, and that's all that matters. So, you see Aden, I know that you and Demitrey have lots to work out. But don't lock him out, I know it's a risk to open your heart up again to the same man that hurt you, but don't you think it's worth it? Think about it." And just like that, she got up, kissed me on the forehead, then grabbed the half empty ice cream tub, and she left.

Wow.

What was I to do now?

Would it be fair to my battered heart to leave it vulnerable again? Maximizing its chances of getting hurt even more?

No, of course not.

But would it also be fair to close my heart to someone as battered and vulnerable as Demitrey? To rid him of his chances of finally having true love? Especially when he has revealed some of the most sensitive parts of him to me.

No, of course not.

So what do I do?

Take a risk?

Or be selfish and protect myself? Look out for number one?

Ugggh!

My mind was going haywire, I found myself massaging my temples, thinking giving me a headache.

I sighed and laid back on my bed.

What was I supposed to do?

Is there any right answer to my questions?

I wish I could have a sign.

What should I do?

Someone give me a sign!

I grunted frustrated. I tossed and turned.

At some point I laughed as I debated on whether to summon Selene in order for her to give me a sign.

Then to my utter surprise, there came a knock from the door.

I looked over at the door, and my heart skipped a beat.

No way.

Another set of knocks resonated from the door, and I found myself reluctantly making my way out of the bed, and to the door. My heart beating harshly against my chest.

Once I reached the door, with a clammy palm, I turned the knob, and opened the door, and I came eye to eye with Demitrey.

For some reason, I had an intuition that he would be at the door.

But that didn't help when I instantly slammed the door shut in his face before he could even say a word.

"Ow!" Said Demitrey, his voice sounding nasal.

"You hit my nose." He protested.

"Oh my God!" I exclaimed and opened the door, looking at Demitrey as he nursed his nose.

"I am so sorry. Are you okay?" I asked, landing my hands

against his cheek as I looked over his nose.

But then he chuckled and said" Gotcha!"

It took me a second before I caught on to what he did, so once I did, I stepped back, with an angry face, and slammed the door shut again.

I was about to step away from the door when he pleaded "Adelina wait! I'm sorry, can you please open the door? Please baby."

"No." Was my stubborn reply.

"Come on please? It was just a joke. I'll never do it again if you don't want me to." He sighed.

Then I shrugged.

Here goes nothing.

I opened the door, and my eyes, on instinct met with his own.

I noticed when his breath hitched, as we held each other's gaze.

There were so many emotions playing in his eyes, as well as there were various emotions playing on my mind.

Dear God, what was happening?

"Um, I was wondering, Adelina, if um, you would like to um, you know, g-go, on a d-date with me." Demitrey stuttered, his eyes never leaving my own, but his cheeks blushed.

Demitrey... stuttered, and blushed all at once?

The big, bad, and feared Alpha, Stuttered, and blushed.

Had anyone tell me that a year ago, I probably would've laughed my butt off, then tell the person to find themselves a hobby because they truly had nothing better to do than to toy with me.

But here Demitrey was, stuttering and blushing, and he asked me on a date!

I need to answer him.

But what should I say? I mean it's just a date, it's not like he's asking me to marry him or anything.

But it's a date!

Am I ready to date him?

Should I date him?

Cilia just told me to take a chance.

Take risks!

So what should it be?

"I, um..."

Chapter 50- "Plan: DESTROY ADELINA!"

Clarissa's pnt. Of view

"... *Well, from what I've heard from my mate, Alpha Demitrey is planning on taking Adelina on a date, so I think that's when you should start executing your plan.*" Said the voice of my source on the phone.

"Perfect. Keep up the good work and find out exactly where he's taking her." I ordered, a smile on my face.

"*You got it.*" My source confirmed, and then the line went dead.

I smiled like the Grinch, while I tucked my phone away, my mind already going over my plan.

If everything went well, my plan would go out smoothly.

And this time Adelina would be out of the picture for good. I remember that day when I found out that Adelina lived. I almost wished I hadn't killed Val, just so that I could kill him that day.

Flashback

I had readied myself to meet the Alpha. I remember walking into the pack boundaries, but there were no guards to stop me. I made my way in to the large clearing from the forest, I passed the dungeons where Adelina met her end, and I smiled. I made my way towards the castle, when a group of people caught my eye.

"Grandma come on! The Luna is going to come out soon." Cheered a little boy as he dragged his elderly Gran behind him.

I gulped, my throat suddenly running dry. I blinked as I began to follow the small crowd. My heart was thumping, my breathing no longer calm and collected. I bended into the crowd, everyone too preoccupied to see that there was a stranger amongst them.

The little boy and his grandmother absentmindedly led me to the clinic doors where the entire pack was standing. Everyone carried some type of gift, their expectant smiles making me sick to my stomach.

"What is happening" I questioned a young woman that came and stood next to me.

She smiled brightly as she clutched a rose in her hand "the Luna! She pulled through after the rogue shot her. She's being discharged today! I didn't have much to give so I brought her this rose. I hope she likes it!" she smiled at me, then moved closer to the closed doors.

I felt my fingers clutch into a fist. How many tries was it going to take to finally rid this world of Adelina?

At my thoughts, a nurse made her way out of the clinic doors. She was an elderly woman, kind enough smile, and she declared "I present to you our Luna.!" And the doors opened.

It was her. I found my breath catching in my throat. There she was, that sickly bright smile on her lips. Her eyes looked over everyone that was here to worship her, her smile growing, and that made me gag. The shocked ransacked my body, and I found myself running form the crowd, as I hid behind a tree, throwing up every content in my stomach.

When I was able to catch my breath, I managed to look back at the crowd just as a little boy handed Adelina a rose. She smiled and pet his hair, then gave him a kiss on the forehead, and that alone sent another wave of bile up my throat, and I soon found myself retching, as I hunched over.

By the tome my stomach began to hurt from the violent emesis, Adelina had already made it to the castle, and the guards were making their way back to their posts. I was trapped.

I found myself sneaking around the castle, until late when the guards where changing posts, then I made my way out of the pack bounds.

End of Flashback

After the Luna had settled back into the pack, I found myself constantly looking for a weak link in the pack, and one day my patience paid off, and I found the perfect spy.

This time I would make sure Adelina was dead, and with the Alpha vulnerable and grieving, I would swoop in, mend his heart, make him fall in love with me, and I would take Adelina's place once and for all.

I found myself parked in front of Adelina's old house, or should I say, her parent's mansion.

After I offed Val, I realized that I was going to need a new team that hated Adelina enough to wipe her off the face of the earth.

Peter was too stuck on her, so he would never hurt her.

Val wasn't actually able to kill her, because being the talkative idiot that he was, and being the conceited jerk that he was, he had to waste his time telling a story, being in the spotlight, and based on my inside source, he lost track of time, got cornered by Demitrey and James, and while he got his butt whooped, he missed his shots, and so, I found out how that vermin Adelina was still alive.

Hence the reason why, I had to make new plans, and with Adelina offing Serena, I had to get a new inside man, as well as a new team.

I figured, for my plan to work, all my members had to be fully on-board. All of us would need the same amount of craving and the same amount of motivation to want to kill Adelina.

And the only correct motivation I knew we could all use would be the hate.

The hate for Adelina Veraso.

And I knew just the individuals that match such a criterion.

The thought of that vile creature made me tighten my fist.

I despised that female.

I couldn't wait to make her suffer and watch her die slowly and painfully.

When the people I came to visit finally arrived home, I gave them a few minutes before I drove up to the gate.

The guard saw me, and already knew that I was Peter's grieving mate.

I decided on returning to my original appearance, because when I offed Adelina, I wanted her to know that I was the one who ripped her away from her mate, like she ripped mine away from me.

The guard let me through, and I parked my car and made my way to the mansion.

Once I reached the door, of course it was unlocked.

I made my way straight to the kitchen, and as usual, on my way there, the Luna was passed out drunk on the couch, and the Alpha was nowhere to be found.

At first, I wondered why Peter stayed in such a pathetic pack, and when I asked, he admitted to staying for Adelina, that she was like a "sister" to him, and that he wouldn't leave her alone or in danger.

Of course, soon I realized that he saw her more than just a "sister", and I think she saw him as more as well, because she was always around him.

If she's crying Peter loses his head, and when she was leaving, he wasted money to get her a phone.

Like hello, I'm your mate, spend money on me!

Oooh, Adelina Veraso, you will pay!

I shook off my anger and continued my way to the kitchen where both Wilma and Wanda where sitting down having a smoke.

When they saw me, Wilma, the oldest raised an eyebrow and said, "let me guess, Adelina is still alive huh."

"Yep." I said, grabbing myself a cigarette, and lighting it.

I dragged in a long puff, held it in for a second, and then slowly released the soothing smoke, my eyes closed, as I imagine my anger slowly leaving my body with the smoke.

We sat there for a few hours, just drowning our minds in thoughts, and drowning our lungs in harmful chemicals.

After a while of silence, Wanda, second to oldest, asked "so what's the new plan?"

"Oh the plan is still the same. We will destroy Adelina, all we're doing is changing the strategy, and adding some replacement players." I said.

"So I'm guessing these new players are me and Wanda?" Asked Wilma.

"Plus, our inside man, or should I say woman." I winked then smirked.

"How did you even get that Italian chick, what's her name again?" Asked Wanda.

"Katharina." Confirmed Wilma.

"Katharina to even go along with this plan?" Continued Wanda.

"Well, the mate bond between a wolf and a human is not as strong as it is between two wolves, so once you told me where she goes every weekend, all I did was pay her a visit. It took a little convincing though, I think my gun and the liquor did the job. And after I got her drunk enough to spill everything inside of her, especially when she admitted to not really liking Adelina, all I had to do was when she became sober the next morning, I told her that I would go to Adelina and tell her what she said, she begged and said that she would do anything, and she did. So now I have my inside woman."

"But how can you be sure she won't tell James?"

"Because, I threatened her, I told her if she spilled anything to anyone, I would hunt down her parents, and kill them, then I'd bring their heads back as proof." I said.

"And she believed you?" Asked Wilma.

"Oh yeah."

"Huh, she's not as bright as she looks then, and you're insane." Said Wanda.

"Tell me something I don't know." I said smugly, dragging in another puff of smoke.

I smiled proudly, and we once again fell into a deep quiet.

While our minds were all in their separate thoughts, the Alpha made his way in the kitchen, and the atmosphere instantly changed.

His bloodshot eyes scanned over us but lingered mostly on Wanda.

He made his way over to her and placed his hand on her cheek and slurred "you look just like her. Adelina. My Adelina. The one that got away."

Wanda turned her face away in disgust, and that angered the Alpha, because in the blink of an eye, he backhanded her, causing her to fall off the chair.

Wilma stood up abruptly and pushed her father away as she yelled "seriously?! Get a life you bastard!"
And the Alpha grabbed her by the hair forcing her to her knees.

I smoothly exhaled out another puff of smoke, then swiftly pulled out my gun and placed it on the Alpha's temple.

"Alright, easy does it now. You let me and the girls walk out of here, and I won't have to waste a bullet on your pathetic self. Now." I said very calmly, my finger leisurely sitting on the trigger.

The Alpha's eyes scanned mine, and he knew that I wasn't playing, because after a few seconds, and I didn't budge, or blink, he pushed Wilma away, and she quickly went to her sister's aid.

They both got on their feet, and I pushed them behind me.

We slowly exited the kitchen, me walking backwards, my gun still aimed for the Alpha, once we were sure we had enough space between us, the sisters and I bolted for the door.

I unlocked my car, and in haste we sped out of the mansion.

"Were you really going to shoot him? "Asked Wanda after a moment of silence.

"Nah, the cartridge is empty." I said, and just like that we started laughing.

But then Wanda winced, and touched her bruised cheek, and I looked at her through the rearview mirror and I said "now, let's go get that bitch who's the reason behind all this bullshit."

And they both agreed.

You better watch your back Adelina, because we are coming for you.

Chapter 51- "The Moon Goddess" -Part 2

Adelina's pnt. Of view

"I um... no. I just need some space right now Demitrey." I said, and I noticed a falter in his merry expression.

"Oh, okay, I understand, well if you change your mind, you know where to find me." He said, then he kissed my cheek, and turned and left.

I closed the door with a sigh and placed my back on the door.

I looked over at my bed, and it was too many steps away, so I slowly slid down the door, until I was fully sitting down.

I brought my knees up to my stomach, wrapped my arms around my legs, and placed my head on knees.

I felt like crying.

I'm not even sure which reason to blame.

"*So, you want to tell me why you turned down a date from our mate?*" Snarled Aden.

"**Ugh, God, not right now Aden, I'm not in the mood to hear your ranting right now.**" I sighed again.

My heart. It felt as though was tearing apart.

What is wrong with me?!

"*Why are you punishing us Adelina? Seriously, I can feel that you want him, so why are you being stubborn! Why are you torturing and punishing yourself? And me?! Can you just talk to me?!*"

"**ENOUGH! Just shut up!**" I declared then blocked her from my mind.

I needed to clear my head.

This was too much.

I looked over at the window, and the bright and warm weather looked so inviting, so I decided to go for a run.

Anything to help clear my head.

I changed into my workout shorts and top after brushing my teeth, I grabbed my bag with extra clothes and blankets, then I made my way out of the castle and into the woods.

The minute I was engulfed by the forest, I transformed into Aden, and we were off.

At first, we were just running.

We went zooming by trees, dodging low branches, and jumping over dead logs on the ground.

I wasn't even sure where we were heading until the clearing started coming into view.

Once I did look over, and made sure the coast was clear, I transformed back to my human form, quickly dressed myself, and walked into the clearing.

I opened the blanket under the shade of a tree, and sat down, just looking out into the vast horizon.

The cliff ended about a few hundred feet from where I was sitting, and from then on it was a beautiful canvas of nature.

Different shades of green, brown, and multicolored spots here and there, along with a soft breeze that added to the soothing embrace of Mother Nature.

It helped clear my mind for a little. Something about the picture made me feel at ease, at peace.

"Need a companion?" Said a voice which startled me and caused me to gasp.

My head turned sharply, and there stood Selene with that calming smile on her face.

"Oh, do not be afraid darling, stop being so startled." She said, then gracefully sat next to me.

"So, want to tell me why you made that decision today?" She asked in a motherly voice.

"He asked me on a date." I stated, my gaze still settled on the calming horizon.

"Yes, he did." Agreed Selene.

"And I wanted to say yes, I really did." I admitted.

"But?" Said Selene.

"But I thought about everything that's happened. I mean it took me getting shot for him to finally open up to me about a part of him. And I know that there's a lot more he's not telling me." I explained.

"So why don't you ask him? He's changed, he's actually willing to open up." Asked Selene.

"Because, it's not actually easy to go up to the guys who abused and say "hey, want to tell me more about why now you're such an abusive jerk?" I questioned sarcastically.

"Well, if that's how you want to word it, sure." Approved Selene.

"I don't know, there's just too much going on in my head. Too many questions, too many ifs, too many doubts."

"Then talk to him. You're making this too complicated for yourself. You're hurting yourself, and him at the same time. He's reaching out to you, but you turned him down." Brushed Selene.

"Well at least for once I'm thinking about me. Maybe I want to be selfish this time. You know, all I ever wanted was to be loved. And turns out, my best friend, Peter, who was actually in love with me, is dead, the person who was closest to being an actual sister to me, Clarissa, is dead. The kind of person that I thought you could've blessed me with as the perfect mate, Val, turned out to be a psycho bent on revenge. My parents got rid of me. My father tried to rape me multiple times, my mother is a drunk, and somehow, the only time my mate thought it'd be romantic to say "I love you" is when I was practically bleeding near death! Throughout my entire life, it's either I'm fighting off my dad, helping Pete and Clarissa, dodging my sister's attacks, and just trying to get by day by day. Then BAM! My mate shows up, and guess what he does? Instead of showering me with love, he chokes me! Instead of holding me close, reassuring me, being there for me, he throws me against walls! Instead of whispering sweet nothings, while being corny but cute and romantic, he slaps me! He plays me for a fool, goes on and off with me, not to mention that he constantly chose a hoe over me, yet I could hardly fight off the temptations because of the stupid mate bond! No matter what he did, I couldn't help my attraction, and my wolf would sabotage and manipulate me, and, and it's all tiring! All I wanted was a break! For heaven's sake give me a break!" I sobbed and held my head as I heaved and broke down.

My tears poured out and blurred my vision, my head was pounding, and I couldn't help it that I just broke down and cried.

Everything hurt.

The realization of it all just hurts. So much.

Speaking these words made the realization of everything that I went through all too real. How? How did I survive such a turmoiled life?

My heart felt like it was being stabbed, ripped and shredded by a jagged knife.

My lungs burned from the abuse of my unsteady breaths, and my exhausting sobs.

My mind felt as though it was having a total meltdown.

My entire body shook as I let out the defeated sobs.

All I wanted was a break.

I dragged in a deep breath and turned to Selene and said "and you know what the worst thing was? I kept on fighting! I kept trying, kept on hoping, but I think little by little, every blow that life threw at me, every time I fell and got up, I think my hope broke off piece by piece, eventually just a living broken shell of a human, turned into a murderer. I think hope killed me. Hope willed me and pushed me to fight, and eventually, once hope left, I was nothing. So, excuse me if now I want to be selfish. Excuse me if now I want to take time and build myself back up. To be honest Selene, I'm broken, and even when or if I get back on my feet and be independent, I don't think I'll be the Adelina you destined to be a Luna. For once moon Goddess, I think you've made a mistake. I'm a broken heart and soul who needs to be repaired. And unless you planned to have a broken Luna, for once you made a mistake."

I looked away, back at the horizon, wiped away my tears and sat quietly next to Selene. A lot was said, and you know what? It felt damn good to say those things.

I breathed in the fresh air, yet my tears wouldn't stop.

They silently streamed from my eyes.

I released all I held inside, and I guess the tears I've been holding back are escaping as well.

It felt good to let it all go, let it all out.

I somehow, once again, felt at peace.

"It's rather interesting…" started Selene as she smiled and stated "because through everything I've heard, you still fight. You're still fighting right now. You're a fighter Adelina. You don't give up. You never do. And that's who I chose to be Luna. But a Luna can't ever truly rule without her Alpha. I won't tell you what to do from now on, the game is in your hands, but just make sure that whatever decision you make, it is not for personal gain, because that will come back and bite you where the sun doesn't shine. Anyway, I'll leave you to your thoughts. I'll be seeing you soon Luna." She declared.

"But I-" I turned to reply to her, but she was gone, disappeared into thin air.

I sighed. She was one stubborn woman.

"*Mmh, I wonder who she reminds me of.*" Said Aden in my head, and I could hear the sarcasm dripping from every one of those syllables.

"**Shush.**" I scolded.

"*Look Adelina, I'm sorry. I shouldn't have been pestering you like I was, and I shouldn't have manipulated you when you were in heat, nor should have I sabotaged you. But don't forget, we are both one person. You hurt, I hurt. But you're hardheaded, so sometimes I feel like you need to be pushed into the water for you to see that it's there. I'm sorry, and you know I love you. I would never do anything that would place us in harm's way. But I heard what you said to Selene, and I never knew you held all that inside. So, girl this is your show, I'm here for you, whatever you say goes.*"

"**Thank you.**" I replied with a kind smile, even though she couldn't see it.

I took in a deep breath, and sighed in relief, it felt as though a weight was taken off my shoulders. It felt great to breathe without feeling as though an elephant was sitting on my chest. My head was clear, my mind calm, my heart light and at ease.

I stayed at cliff for a few hours, but after a while I became hungry, so I packed up, placed my bag on my back, then transformed into Aden, and then we made our way home.

Chapter 52- "The Moon Goddess" -Part 3

Demitrey's pnt. Of view

"Well?" Asked Kade as soon as I made my way inside my room.

"She said no." I simply said.

"Aww man, sorry to hear that." Replied James.

"No, it's okay. She asked for space. She deserves space. She deserves happiness. So, whatever makes her happy." I said sighing, but meaning my words.

"Yeah, well, do you want to go for a run?" Ask Kade.

"Nah, I think I'll stay here for a while."

"Okay man. See you later."

I waved, and they both exit the room, with Kade closing the door behind him.

Once the guys left, I went and laid on my back, with one arm over my head.

"*Hey.*" Said Trey casually.

"**Hey.**" I replied.

"*So, she turned us down huh.*" He stated.

"**Yep.**" I replied.

"*And you're okay with that?*" Asked Trey.

"**Yes, I am. I don't want to rush things, and if she needs time and space, then that's what I'll give her.**" I replied in hopes of trying to convince myself that I'm doing the right thing instead of persisting.

"*But what if that time never comes, but instead she decides to leave for good?*" questioned Trey, and I could hear the lack of confidence in his voice.

"**Then I'll leave her be. I've already hurt her in so many unforgivable ways, so if she decides to go, it'll tear me apart, but I'll let her go. Adelina is a strong headed woman who knows her self-worth. She's so strong and a fighter. I can't believe I've ever reverted to becoming** like my father, trying to snuff out the light that made her who she is. I was so blind. I made mistakes, and if she looks back at it all, she has no reason to stay, at least not for me." I admitted.

"And you're sure you're okay?" Asked Trey.

"No. I'm not Trey. I was never shown love growing up. My father nearly killed me multiple times. I was forced to become this cold asshole with a mask, who hurt the one person meant to show me love. I pushed her away. It took me too damn long to finally come to terms with myself and break that mask, but its years and months too late. You know some people are just not meant to be loved. So, if she leaves, just knowing that she's happy will make me satisfied. Doesn't mean I'll ever be okay. I'm a broken heart and a tortured soul Trey." I concluded.

"Ugh, both you and Adelina sound exactly the same." Said a voice by the door.

I looked over by the door startled, and there stood Selene.

"What the actual fu-"
"Finish that sentence, and I'll pull your ear young man." scolded Selene.
"Sorry." I said looking down in shame.
"Oh it's quite alright child. Now, tell me what's on your mind." She said, then sat gracefully in a chair.
"Well, I asked Adelina on a date." I started explaining.
"Yes, you did." Confirmed Selene.
"And she turned me down." I concluded.
"And so you're just going to give up?" Questioned Selene.
"Well, I'm not giving up, I'm abiding to her wishes. She asked for time and space, so I'm giving her what she wants. It's right thing." I said, nodding my head, knowing that I

was doubting my own words.

"Are you telling me, or you're trying to convince yourself that it's the right thing?" Asked Selene.

"Well, it is the right thing. Right?" I asked her, now completely confused.

"Well, in this situation, does it feel right? I mean if your heart feels as though it's tearing apart, and your mind is confused, should those be the effects or symptoms of doing the right thing?" Questioned Selene with a raised eyebrow.

I looked away and shook my head. This was too much.

Too much confusion. Too much turmoil.

My emotions were burning in my throat, my heart hurting, my mind lost.

"Stop over thinking and overanalyzing. You're both confused, but that's why everyone has that special someone, to help clear the confusion and the obstacles."

Explained Selene.

"But what if you're the reason those obstacles are there in the first place?" I asked looking up at Selene.

"Oh for heaven's sake! The past is the past Demitrey. You're a changed man, let what happened go, that's why it's called the past. What does your instinct say? What is the gut feeling you're getting in this situation?" Urged Selene.

"That I should walk right up to Adelina and show her that I love her, and that I'll stop at nothing until I earn her love and forgiveness." I declared, my gaze determined.

"Then do it!" Encouraged Selene.

I look down in contemplation, I should do it. I would do it.

I smiled ready to tell Selene my decision, but when I looked back up, Selene was gone.

I smiled, and closed my eyes, I felt better. I knew what I had to do, but first, a nap seemed to be calling my name, then just like that sleep took me over.

I woke up a few hours later, when I got the sudden urge to see Adelina.

So, I got up, brushed my teeth, and headed straight for her room.

I knocked on the door, and when she opened it, I didn't even give her a second to talk.

I wrapped one arm around her waist, and pulled her into me, then I captured her lips with mine.

I pulled her closer and caressed her cheek as I deepened the kiss.

She shyly wrapped her arms around my neck and pulled me into her room, and with my leg, I closed the door.

There was a dresser next to her door, which I hoisted her up, and placed her sitting on it, while I stood in between her legs.

I glided my tongue across her bottom lip, asking for permission, and to my surprise she allowed it.

I thrusted my tongue in her mouth, and she pulled me closer.

I placed my hands on her thigh and caressed her, and she moaned into my lips.

My hands teasingly touched her inner thighs, but I didn't go there.

At some point she got tired of my teasing, and she took one of my hands, and guided it to in between her legs.

I knew what she wanted, so who was I to refuse her demands.

I felt her bundle of nerves under my middle finger, and in a slow and sensual manner, I started rubbing it in a circular motion while adding pressure.

She pulled away from my lips and hissed then moaned out in the sexiest way I've ever heard.

My queen.

I placed my lips on her mark, and she started moving her hips against my finger.

And I could tell she was enjoying it, because every now and then, she would either hiss, moan, or bite her lip.

Once she bit her lip again, I pulled her head down and kissed them.

Her hands moved from my neck to the hem of my shirt, and swiftly, she took it off.

Then she pushed me away, and took off her own shirt, and her bra, then she pulled me back.

I already knew what she wanted to do the minute she took my head and pressed it to her chest.

I took her right bud in my mouth, while I massaged her left breast with my right hand, and skillfully, my left middle finger, kept its taunting routine on her clit.

When she moaned out louder, I knew she was close, just a few more strokes and she would come undone.

"Hey Adelina, want to go shop- OH God! I'm so sorry. I swear I didn't see anything!" Said Katharina's panicked voice as she slammed the door shut.

I groaned but pulled away from her anyway.

I noticed her flushed face, and I smirked.

I picked up her shirt off the floor and handed it to her, then with my eyes still connected to hers, I slowly put my own shirt back on, and I could tell she was affected because, she bit her lip and her blush got deeper.

I winked at her, then made my way out of the room, and I saw Katharina standing by the door with red cheeks, and eyes cast down.

I walked down the hall proud, with a wide grin on my face.

Oh, I'll give her space alright, but doesn't me that time from time I won't do a little tease and please with her.

Chapter 53- "Tease and please challenge"

Adelina's pnt. Of view

After Demitrey left my room, it took a second for me clear my head.

I sighed, closed my eyes, and dragged my hands down my face.

What the heck was that?

He came out of nowhere, and his actions were so unexpected.

So much for needing to clear my head.

I was just getting off the dresser when Katharina knocked and said, "is it safe to come in now?"

"Yes, it is." I sighed, then made my way to the bed.

Just as I was sitting down, Kat came in instantly apologizing.

"Adelina I am so sorry. I didn't know that Demitrey was here. I promise, I didn't see anything." She said, sitting next to me.

"It's okay don't worry about it. Anyways, what brings you to see little old me?" I asked bumping my shoulder with hers.

"I heard the news, Demitrey asked you on a date!" She said excited.

"Yeah he did." I said.

"Omg this is so cute, where is he taking you?" She asked, a little too eager to know.

"What do you mean?" I asked slightly confused.

"He did tell you where he was taking you right?" She asked, her voice a bit suspicious.

"No, he didn't." I replied carefully. Something wasn't right.

"Aww, it must be a surprise then." She said, almost disappointed.

"No, it's nothing. I said no to him." I cleared out.

"You did what?!" She boomed, then she cleared her throat and said, "why did you say no?"

"Because I wanted to say no dammit. And don't you dare tell me that I shouldn't have done that!" I warned, pointing at her as I sent her a warning glare.

"No, of course not, I'm just surprised is all." She said raising her hands up in surrender, she then briefly got up and said "well, I have to go, I'll talk to you later." And just like that she was out the door.

Well okay then.

I shook my head in effort to get rid of all the thoughts and voices in my head, but it was all too much.

My run helped cleared my head a little as far as my situation with Demitrey, however, now there's a new suspicion that just arose. Kat was acting very strange, and I just have this feeling that something is not right.

No, not the time to think of things like that.

I need to relax, think of something else... Oh! Given that I just came from a run, I decided on taking a shower.

Yeah, a hot shower is all I need.

With a made-up mind, I picked up my towel, and made my way to the shower.

Demitrey's pnt. Of view

I made it to my room with that victorious grin still plastered on my face.

I walked into my room and went straight to my bed.

The guys went running, but I really wasn't feeling up to the physical challenge, and I know, as an Alpha I should be on top of my physical game, but hey, a break or two is not that big of a deal.

I spent a good amount of time just laying around, my mind focusing on random things, when Kade knocked on the door.

With a bored come in, he peeped his head in and said "Hey, the group and I are going to our spot, want to join?"
"Yeah sure, when are you leaving?" I asked, a smile on my face.
"Thirty minutes." He said, then closed the door.

I smiled a devilish smile, then made my way to the shower.

It took me about 15 minutes in total to get ready, then I made my way to Adelina's room.

With a calm composure, I knocked on the door.

"Who is it?" I heard her ask, but I just smiled without answering.

Adelina's pnt. Of view

"Who is it?" I asked a second time, yet there came no reply, instead, all I received was another set of knocks.

Just coming out of the shower, after my last encounter with the Alpha and my towel, I got into the routine of wearing bathrobes, so after tightening the bands around my waist, I opened the door, to a smiling Demitrey.

"What are you doing here?" I questioned, as his eyes started to travel down my figure.
"Hey! Eyes are up here buddy." I snapped my fingers, and his eyes met mine, except, they were already dark with lust.

He took a step towards me, and I took one back, he took another few steps until he was in my room, he closed the door, and locked it, his eyes never leaving mine.

"What are you doing here? What do you want?" I questioned again, however, my voice wavered.
"Oh, you know exactly what I want." He said, his voice low, causing a strange yet pleasing shiver to travel across my skin.
"Um..." I said then bit my lip, not even sure how to continue.

His tongue darted out, licking his bottom lip, his eyes focused on my own, making me feel very hot.

My chest heaved with much needed air, but it didn't help the want that travelled through me.

My hands suddenly felt moist, along with other places in my body, places that I'd rather not mention.

I swiped my hands over the robe, in effort to dry my palms, but in the process, the band on the robe loosened, and my stomach, and a bit of my breast became exposed.

I heard Demitrey hiss in a deep breath, his eyes focused on the exposed skin, and suddenly, I got the most devious idea.

It was time for revenge.

I fully untied the bands, and slowly, more of my skin became visible.

I noticed Demitrey gulp in my peripheral vision, as his Adam Apple bobbed.

I slowly peeled the fabric off my shoulders, down until I was showing a decent amount of cleavage, but before I revealed anymore, I turned my back on him, and smirked in victory when I heard him groan.

I heard his movements as he made his way towards me, I felt his warmth on my back, and slowly, his right hand snaked around my waist and pulled me firmly against his chest, causing a whoosh of air to exit my lungs.

I felt his soothing breath on the exposed skin of my neck and right shoulder, and the minute his soft lips met my warm flesh, a jolt of excitement rode through my body, and straight to my already sensitive and soaking core.

He kissed my skin, and I tightened my legs.

My breathing started coming out short, yet urgent, then when I thought it couldn't get any better, his left hand came around, and slowly, teasingly, rode up my left thigh.

His fingers searched for the opening of my robe, followed by his palm, and slowly, he dragged it up my outer thigh, and into my inner thigh.

His simple touch and kisses caused a moan to erupt from me, and my eyes widened, wait a second, I'm supposed to be the one doing the teasing here.

I suddenly pulled away from him, turned around and pushed him against the door.

My actions caught him by surprise, and while he was still dazed, I found the exposed skin above his collar bone, where I started to nip and kiss.

His hands started to wrap around my waist and pull me closer, but I removed them, and held them against the door on his side of his head, then I got my fingers to work on the button of his shirt.

Once successful, I opened his shirt and my greedy hands got to work on touching and memorizing every muscle, every inch of skin, and occasionally I'd tease his V-line.

I bit his skin, and a low growl erupted from his chest causing me to feel another jolt to my core.

His hands suddenly grabbed on to my legs, and I jumped and wrapped my lags around his waist.

He turned us around and pinned my back against the door.

I went to touch him, but he captured my hands and whispered in my ear "I know what you're trying to do, and you're not going to win babe." Then he thrust his hips against mine causing a pleasing yet torturing friction to erupt between my legs.

I moaned, but quickly cleared my head and asked in a voice coated with lust "is that a challenge?" Then I pulled his hip even closer with mine using my legs.

"Well that's up to you, just know that I'll win." He said, then took my bottom lip in his teeth, and tugged it.

"We'll see about that." I declared the minute he released my lip.

At my declaration, his lips connected with mine, and we dived into a kiss, both of us fighting for dominance, but then Demitrey stopped and pulled away as he said "Oh yeah, I forgot, um the group and I are going to our spot tonight. Want to come?" He questioned oh so casually, as if he didn't have me pinned against the door, with my legs around his waist.

"Demitrey, I already told you that I-"

"I know, this is not a date, just a few friends hanging out, that's all." He stated.

"Okay, when do we leave?" I questioned, the position suddenly quite comfortable.

"Well, when I first came you had 15 minutes, but now because of your little tease and please, you only have 5 minutes." He said shrugging with a smirk.

"What?! Demitrey are you serious? Let me down!" I said struggling against him.

"See now, struggling will definitely not get you down from there." Then he moved in and whispered, "especially since I'm still in the mood." Then just like that he kissed my mark, and picked me off him, and placed me on the ground on jelly legs.

He picked up his shirt off the floor and said, "I'll be waiting for you outside." And with that he left.

Uuugh, that jerk! That tease! That jerk!

I hate him!

"*Do you really? Because from this side, that wasn't the vibe that I was getting.*" Muttered Aden in my head.

"**Shut up.**" I said, but then she started singing the chorus for "It won't stop" in my head, and I couldn't help the blush that settled on my cheeks.

"Well, if I must say," she added after her little solo, *"this time around, you were the tease, until of course Demitrey took over, so if I were to keep score I'd say: Adelina 1, Demitrey 2."*

"Well good thing I didn't ask for your opinion." I shot back.

She was about to reply, but Demitrey said "babe, hurry up!"

"I'm coming!" I replied, then hurried to find an outfit, and get ready, in less than 5 minutes.

However, even while I was running around my room, getting ready, I couldn't help but feel a little uneasy, as if there was something coming.

Something negative, evil even.

But what could it be?

Chapter 54- "Buffet Surprise"

Adelina's pnt. Of view

We were all currently in the car, heading towards "The Spot".

After Demitrey's little stunt, I had to rush and place a random outfit on, which consisted of my grey jeans, and black top, with my black sneakers.

Demitrey was driving the GMC Yukon XL, I was in the passenger seat. In the second row, Kade and Cilia sat comfortably, and in the third row, James and Kat were cuddling with each other.

I kept asking what "The Spot" was, but all Cilia, Kade, James, and Demitrey would do is laugh and say to wait.

By the time we got there, curiosity had won me over.

Once we found a parking spot, we all exit and the car and headed straight for "The Spot".

And you wouldn't believe my surprise.

It was a buffet!

I couldn't help the grin that settled on my face, Cilia chuckled and said "see, told you it would be worth your while."

The smile didn't fade when we walked in, and of course, having the Alpha with us, we instantly got a table.

We ordered our drinks, and then decided on how we would leave the table.

"I say we go in pairs." Said James.
"I'm down." Replied Kade.

They looked over at each other and smirked, then they said, "let's go."

They hurried to get up, and Demitrey spoke up and said, "I'm coming too."

They were pushing their chairs back, when cilia rolled her eyes and said "gees, what happened to ladies first?" "Well Cilia, the ladies are going first." I said and then smirked.

It took a second for the guys to catch on, and Kade said "heyy, don't do that. See I would argue, but, I'm hungry, so I'll take that insult, and still go first." Then, childishly, he stuck his tongue out at me, and being the big kid that I am, I stuck my tongue out also.

We all erupted into laughter, then the guys left to get their food.

Few minutes later, give or take, our girl talk was disrupted by the clatter of various plates being set on the table.

Kade had two, James had two, and Demitrey also had two.

Kat looked over at James in shock and said "James, seriously? Two plates?"

"No babe, the first two plates, I'm eating for two here. Me and Jay my wolf." Explained James.

"But how can you eat all that?" She asked, almost disgusted.

"Well, it is called an all you can eat buffet for a reason." Replied James

"Ugh, you really are a dog." She said rolling her eyes.

"No babe, I'm a wolf, there's a difference." Smirked James as he dug into his food.

"Whatever." Was Kat's final reply.

And a tension settled into the air.

Cilia and I made eye contact, and I could tell she was thinking exactly what I was thinking.

Kat was acting very strange, and I could feel it in my gut that something was up.

"Okay, well, we're going to go get some food now. Kat you're coming?" I asked, breaking the awkward silence.
"Yeah, sure, I just have to go use the restroom." She said in a hurry, then left the table in a haste.
"Okay." Said Cilia.

Then Cilia and I made our way to the buffet tables.

I grabbed one plate, and decided to pace myself, I was going to enjoy this.

I caught up with one of the waiters, and asked for their special hot tea, that once you drink it, allows you more room to eat, then I caught up with Cilia who had two plates.

I went to ask, but she beat me to it as she said, "I am a pregnant woman, and I am eating for two."

"But you're not even showing a bump yet." I exclaimed.

"So?" She challenged, her eyes daring me to make a further comment.

"No comment." I smiled, then we went back to the table.

Kat still wasn't back.

When we reached the table, we walked in on Kade asking James "hey, so is everything alright with you and Kat, I mean, she never acts like this."

"I know, it's weird, she just flipped pages. When we first came, she was fine but one day, after we picked her up from the mall, she was acting a bit strange, but then I assumed that it was because she was still getting used to being surrounded by werewolves and that she was nervous, but then she started acting weird again." Explained James.

"But weren't you going to mark her? She did give you

consent right?" Asked Demitrey.

"Yeah she did, and I was, but then she said the time wasn't right, and that she wasn't ready. I don't know. Plus, a lot of weird stuff's been happening, she's constantly running off, and she's always on the phone." Sighed James.

He looked sort of depressed.

"Do you think she could be cheating on you?" Blurted out Cilia.

"Babe." Scolded Kade.

"Nah it's cool. You know I've had my doubts, I mean the bond between two werewolves is powerful, a human and a werewolf can be as powerful, if both parties are fully committed, and since I didn't mark my claim on her, the bond is not as strong." Replied James.

"So you think she could resist the bond enough to cheat among other things?" I questioned out of curiosity.

"I think so," answered Kade, then he continued, "in my old

pack, we did have a case where one of the males had a human mate, but she never committed to him, and she ended up fooling around and even betrayed her mate."

"Wow." Was all I could muster.

We sat in an awkward silence, and I found my eyes looking over at James.

It was alien to see him in such a down mood, the light in his eyes wasn't as bright, and he just seemed so forlorn and downcast.

I felt sympathetic towards him, he was like a brother to me.

I suddenly felt a warm hand slip in mime, and I didn't have to guess who it was.

His thumb softly caressed the back of my hand, and it was somehow comforting.

He held my hand under the table, and with his other hand continued to eat, as if everything was normal.

James finally shrugged and looked up, then smiled as he said "alright guys, enough of the pitiful silence, your sympathy is killing me. Let's dig in!"

We all chuckled, and started eating, the sad air slowly dissipating.

At some point, I really began to worry because Kat still wasn't back.

I was done with my plate, and as much as I wanted to get up to go on another trip, I just had this gut feeling that something wasn't right, so I spoke up and said "guys, something's not right, I'm going to go check in the bathroom to see if Kat is okay."

"I'm coming with you." Agreed Cilia, and we got up.

I reluctantly slipped my hand out of Demitrey's, instantly missing his warmth.

No, not the time to think about that.

I shook of my silly thoughts, and Cilia and I made our way to the bathroom.

Once we opened the door, there was no one in sight, and the lights were very dim.

"Kat?" I called out, my voice echoing in the dark stalls of the bathroom.

"Are you there? Are you okay?" I questioned, but I received no reply.

"Kat?" I said, bending over to see under the stalls, but there was nothing, not a soul.

I started opening every stall, checking to make sure that they were all empty.

I was nearing the last stall when, I heard Cilia call behind me, "Adelina."

"Yeah?" I said, preoccupied with checking out the stalls.

"Adelina!" Said Cilia a bit more urgent.

"What?" I said turning around, and instantly froze.

I couldn't believe my eyes.

I couldn't breathe, nor could I move.

"No." I finally mustered to breathe out, paralyzed by the sight in front of me.

"Hello Adelina." Said Clarissa with a smile, as she stood behind Cilia, holding a knife on her throat.

No.

To be continued…

Author's note

Hello everyone!

I'd just like to take this moment to thank everyone who decided to give this story a chance and read it!

It is my pleasure to announce that the sequel of this story, "His Mate and his Mistress: The rise of a Luna" is now available on Amazon Kindle!

The story continues for our destined lovers, as the adventures, twists and turns hide at every corner!

Once more, I would like to thank you all for your unending support, and those who have reached out to me, I thank you.

Lots of XOXOXO

Irtania.

.

Printed in Great Britain
by Amazon